MURDER AT THE ICE BALL

LADY KATHERINE REGENCY MYSTERIES BOOK 3

LEIGHANN DOBBS
HARMONY WILLIAMS

SUMMARY

When a tragic accident turns out to be murder, Lady Katherine finds herself embroiled in an investigation tainted by lies and deception.

With conflicting witness testimony, mysterious neighbors who saw the impossible, and a secret someone would kill for, Katherine must dig into the dark side of polite London society to uncover the truth.

Naturally, she has help. Maybe too much help. Along with her loyal maid, Harriet, her pilfering pug, Emma, and her Bow Street Runner friend Lyle, Katherine is joined by budding investigator Pru Burwick and her eccentric Scottish fiancé, Lord Annandale. Katherine *wouldn't mind their help so much if Annandale didn't keep bringing the insufferable Captain Wayland along.*

When the investigation takes a disturbing turn, Katherine gets a lead that indicates someone close to her may not be telling the truth, and she must make a tough decision. Protecting her loved one means keeping a secret from her closest allies. Hopefully it does not also mean letting a killer go free.

CHAPTER ONE

Tuesday, November 5, 1816
Dalhousie Manor, Mayfair, London

"You could have worn something a touch more appealing," whispered Prudence Burwick, Lady Katherine Irvine's dear friend and confidante.

Katherine most certainly could *not* have worn something more appealing. After her stay in the holiday town of Bath a couple months ago, the Marquess of Bath's elderly grandmother had for some unfathomable reason fixated upon her as the marquess's future bride. Katherine would sooner marry her pug than she would marry Lord Bath. Not because he was so very much older than her—her father and stepmother were of a similar age gap and blissfully happy—but because Katherine Irvine did *not* wish to marry.

Anyone.

No, her aspirations resided not in happily wedded bliss but in following in her father's footsteps and becoming a detective of some renown. After the fiasco in Bath, she felt the need to redeem herself acutely. Yes, the Burglar of Bath had been uncovered in the end, but she cringed every time she had to admit she'd had her hand in the cessation of the thefts. Fortunately, the investigative arts were not seen as appropriate to her gender, so the majority of her acquaintances had no notion of her pursuit of criminals. For once, she was glad of that fact.

Pru, a woman every bit as tall as Katherine, with a solid frame and a sharp cast to her nose and chin when she frowned, gave Katherine an assessing look as she toyed with a lock of her brown hair. "Pink might bring out your complexion."

"I don't need to bring out my complexion."

"Green makes you look sallow. Honestly, you should burn that dress."

All the better, for as long as Grandma Bath was in London and her grandson unwed, Katherine intended to look as unappealing as possible. "Perhaps if I added a few flower-shaped buttons to the bodice," she quipped.

Pru grimaced. Pru's mother had gone wild for the ugliest floral buttons in existence and was even trying to convince Pru to add some to her wedding dress as decoration. For all that Pru's groom, the Marquess of Annandale, had seen these notorious buttons and opted to propose anyway, Pru bristled every time her mother's fashion tastes were mentioned.

Katherine pointedly raised her eyebrow at her friend. "Or perhaps we ought to try to enjoy the festivities without worrying about how we look. It isn't every day someone holds an ice ball."

Tucking her hair behind her ear, Pru narrowed her eyes slyly. "Are you not concerned with your appearance because a certain someone is not in attendance?"

Snapping her eyes from surveilling the gathering, Katherine glanced at Pru. Did she know something Katherine didn't? Feigning a smile, she quipped, "You mean Lord Annandale? I assure you, I haven't set my cap for him."

Pru raised her eyebrows. "Neither he nor I are concerned that you have. You know of whom I speak."

Captain Dorian Wayland. Katherine fought the urge to search the gathering again. She hadn't seen him since their escapade in Bath, and she didn't look forward to seeing him tonight. In fact, it was best if they crossed paths only in the Royal Society for Investigative Techniques. Even then, their contact ought to be minimal. Even if Katherine wanted to extend their association, which she didn't, her father would never approve. The Earl of Dorchester *hated* Wayland to such an extent that Katherine had once loathed the very sight of him as well.

However, after the help he'd provided on the last two cases she'd investigated, she'd had to admit her father's explanation seemed a bit thin. From what she had observed of Wayland, he had an even stricter moral guideline than she when it came to investigating suspects. What could he possibly have done to make her father think otherwise?

Desperate to change the subject, Katherine said, "Yes, where is Lord Bath?"

Pru made a face but no longer nettled her friend about Wayland's absence, at the very least.

"I believe I saw him near the doors to the garden."

"What would possess him to stand there?"

Lady Dalhousie, whom Katherine knew to have a penchant for exaggeration and dramatics, had turned the ballroom of her London manor into an ice fortress. The fact that her servants had been unable to wedge the glass garden doors open any farther than a hand span hadn't deterred her in the least. Now, a ghastly ice swan perched in front of the doors, so thin that ice had encroached on the inside and sealed them to the floor. The door had been propped open so the ice didn't melt from the heat of the hearth on the far side of the room, where Katherine stood. Anyone who opted to stand near the swan risked frostbite.

Despite the fact that access to the garden had been detoured down the narrow servants' corridor that ran the length of the manor to an innocuous exit, Lady Dalhousie's extravagance had continued into the garden. The early, bitter winter hadn't deterred her one bit. She'd sensationalized the cold by commissioning ice sculptures in various shapes, not only that of feathered pests. A footman stood post by the exit to the garden, ready to offer cloaks and muffs to anyone who wished to tour the exhibit. Katherine was not among that number.

Indoors, Lady Dalhousie had strewn strings of cheap crystals to reflect the light of the chandelier. They were reminiscent of icicles, very like the prized diamond-and-aquamarine necklace the hostess wore constantly. The result was a room that sparkled like the falling snow in the gaslight of the streetlamps on Pall Mall Street.

Pru shrugged. "How should I know Lord Bath's inclinations? Isn't that your task?"

When Lord Bath and his grandmother had come to London once more, Katherine's father had invited them both to dinner. Frankly, Katherine had been astonished to find Grandma Bath in London given how difficult she must find traveling at her advanced age. As it turned out, she had accompanied her grandson to London because she had an agenda—to marry him off. In order to keep herself off the top of the list of marriageable candidates, Katherine had agreed at once to become his matchmaker even though that did not seem to deter Grandma Bath from trying to persuade her to marry Lord Bath.

The bigger problem was that Grandma Bath did not want him to know she was trying to find him a match. And trying to discover what sort of woman would suit Lord Bath without his guessing at the aim of her questions had been a puzzle in itself. A frustrating puzzle. If the marquess was to be believed, he hadn't the faintest idea of what sort of woman attracted him. *I'll know the right woman when I see her* was not a helpful answer.

Neither was suggesting that Katherine's curiosity would be better applied to finding herself a husband. At least he, unlike his grandmother, didn't consider her a candidate. Katherine would accept her small blessings where they came.

"I don't see him." The only men near the swan were a pair of young bucks who appeared thoroughly soused. One gestured to the swan as if flirting with it while the second pressed his hand to his mouth to stifle his laughter.

Slyly, Pru asked, "Lord Bath or Captain Wayland?"

Katherine glared at her friend. "Lord Bath."

"So you say." Pru lengthened her words. "But I never saw you so concerned with his whereabouts while in Bath."

"I wasn't attempting to find him a match in Bath, now was I? That honor was reserved for a different woman." Katherine raised her eyebrows, rewarded by Pru's blush. "Why are you so concerned all of a sudden?"

The question chased the color from Pru's cheeks. She looked down, playing with a lock of her hair once more. "You haven't seemed the least bit troubled since we returned from Bath."

Katherine stiffened. "Should I be?" They'd found the Burglar of Bath, and the thefts would stop, so what was there to be troubled about?

With a shrug, Pru pretended to pay more mind to

the mingling crowd and enthusiastic dancers. "I have to wonder why you don't seem to find London so dreadfully dull. In Bath, we had excitement every night. Since coming home, the only thrilling thing that's happened has been the early return of our peers to town. And not even all of them." She lowered her eyes, her eyelashes tickling her cheeks.

"You miss Annandale."

"Not only!" Pru exclaimed, raising her head as she colored up again.

She was in love. Katherine had seen it blossom in Bath, and to be honest, she encouraged it. She *was* a matchmaker, if a reluctant one at times, since she primarily used the role to veil her investigations so she didn't raise suspicions by asking questions. She had no objections to falling in love—for other people. Katherine had a name to make for herself yet, and she had no intention of hiding in a man's shadow, her husband's or her father's.

Pru added, "The investigation in Bath was rather heady as well. It's dull having nothing to do."

Pru was right, but Katherine had occupied herself by searching for a reasonably priced townhouse in a respectable neighborhood so she could slip away from the other sickeningly in love couple in her life: her parents. Papa and Susanna, her stepmother, were again trying to produce an heir, cooing and sneaking kisses in every corner. As heartwarming as it was to see them happy, Katherine also found it nauseating.

"If you enjoy investigating so well, why don't you come with me and Lyle to the next Society meeting?" Lyle Murphy, Katherine's closest friend, worked on Bow Street as one of Sir John's Men. He hated the term Bow Street Runner, even if it was accurate. He was forever chasing criminals throughout the streets of London and producing inventions and establishing never-before-used forensic techniques to help the search at the same time. They had met when she'd accompanied her father to a monthly meeting of the Royal Society for Investigative Techniques.

"Can I?" Pru brightened for a moment before she dimmed. "But I don't have the blunt for a membership. Mama would never approve the expense."

"I'll sponsor you this time, and we'll start on the application. The paperwork takes ages to finalize. By then, you'll be Lady Annandale, and I'm certain you'll have the funds for the annual membership." She winked, coaxing a coy smile from Pru.

"Very well, but if I'm to accompany you to the meeting, then you must accompany me to the dressmaker."

"That hardly seems like a fair exchange."

"I need you," Pru insisted, her voice carrying above the swell of music.

"You just finished mocking my attire."

"I don't need your fashion advice."

Katherine stifled a sigh. She didn't have bad taste in fashion. She dressed unappealingly on purpose to avoid the gaze of any men who thought her an interesting target. Since her sisters had married off, the tactic had worked swimmingly.

Pru caught Katherine's hand and gave it a squeeze. "I need your companionship."

How could Katherine say no to that?

"And to keep my mother from choosing the style of my wedding gown."

Katherine laughed. "There's the true reason."

"Please," Pru begged, her eyes wide. Her hand tightened almost painfully on Katherine's.

The main reason Katherine had convinced Pru to keep her company while she accompanied Lord Bath and his grandmother to the ice ball was so that Pru could escape her mother's clutches. Despite the fact that Pru and Annandale had agreed to a long engagement, if Mrs. Burwick had her way, her daughter would be married by Christmas in a wedding to rival the Prince Regent's.

"Very well, I'll go."

After another quick squeeze, Pru released Katherine's hand. "Thank you."

Katherine nodded in acknowledgment and changed the subject. "Now, will you help me search for Lord Bath? I can't find him a match if he doesn't socialize with anyone."

"I know I saw him by the doors."

"Well, he isn't there now."

"Perhaps he went out to view the sculptures?"

If Grandma Bath had wanted to go outdoors to view the sculptures, Katherine had no doubt that Lord Bath would have been hovering at her elbow. He doted on his grandmother, one of his many admirable qualities. He had a good heart and did things for the right reasons, even if he could be a bit misguided at times.

"I am not going outside," Katherine answered. "Even Emma has a difficult time convincing me, and you know how the little pug has a tiny bladder."

"Very well. We'll stay in here and weather Mrs. Fairchild's glare for the rest of the evening."

Katherine stifled a groan and the urge to search the grounds. She didn't want her rival matchmaker to find any reason to come over and nettle her. That vicious woman had accused Katherine twice of crimes she hadn't committed. In public! Katherine wished her matchmaking clients a lifetime of happiness, whereas

Mrs. Fairchild only saw status and didn't understand the power of the heart.

After skillfully arranging for Mrs. Fairchild to make the better match in Bath, at least in terms of status, Katherine had hoped to appease the cantankerous woman. Unfortunately, she must have fallen short of the mark.

To Pru, Katherine said, "Perhaps we'll just peek out the garden doors and see if we glimpse anyone of import."

Pru only smiled, which made Katherine wonder if she'd seen Mrs. Fairchild at all. Nevertheless, if Lord Bath was idling in the garden, it would behoove her to make some effort to find him.

As they reached the intoxicated young men, Katherine quipped, "I'm afraid you'll have to do better than that, friend. She's a notorious ice queen."

"Oh?" The one with the blond hair falling into his eyes seemed thoroughly foxed, so much so that he appeared to have trouble deciphering Katherine's words.

His companion, on the other hand, didn't seem nearly so far into his cups. Tall, lean, and dressed like a dandy, the man smiled. "And do you have firsthand knowledge, Miss..."

"Lady," Katherine corrected, her voice crisp. "Katherine."

"Lord," he answered, raising an eyebrow in challenge. "Lord Conyers. A pleasure to make your acquaintance."

Katherine stifled a sigh. "We've met." The number of lords and ladies was a small one. At one point or another, Katherine had met them all.

Though Lord Conyers didn't warrant remembering. The last time she'd encountered him, he'd been intoxicated. It appeared to be a pattern. She'd pegged him as a rake and a hedonist, and it seemed that time hadn't changed him much.

His smile grew, though it didn't warm his gaze at all. "Ah, yes. Dorchester's daughter, aren't you? You have more fire than your sisters."

"And you have a better chance with the swan. If you'll excuse me, gentlemen."

Katherine used her wide hips to her advantage to shove the statue between herself and the men before she turned to the glass door, which stood slightly ajar. "Help me push," she said with a grunt. "The heat in here must have loosened the ice by now."

They managed to widen the door enough to peer out. Katherine shivered from the chill.

"Do you see him?"

"I don't see any—"

A scream and a horrendous crunch ended Pru's answer as she yelped. Katherine moved close enough to peer over her shoulder. Her blood turned as icy as the outdoor air. In the snow just beyond the shadow of the balcony was the body of a woman, facedown and unmoving.

It looked as though Pru had gotten an evening of excitement and investigation after all.

CHAPTER TWO

H er heart in her throat, Katherine wedged her hip into the gap between the glass doors, throwing her weight into the movement. The doors grated against the packed snow and ice on the ground as they opened farther. Katherine stumbled, slipping on the slick winter coating as she approached the body. She stopped out of arm's reach.

"Oh my word," Pru gasped. "Is she..."

"Out of the way!" An unfamiliar woman's harsh words were loud in the sudden hush of the room behind them. Katherine could all but hear the guests crane their necks to see the commotion.

The slight woman, who was of neat appearance and had hair that appeared at once dark and golden in the mix of shadow and light sifting from the ballroom, elbowed between Katherine and Pru. Fear crossed her face for a moment, her eyes widening as she beheld the woman's dead body. She glanced upward. "She must have slipped on the balcony."

Katherine followed her gaze. A balcony hung ominously above them. If it was covered with snow and ice, it could be very slippery, but...

A gasp rent the air behind Katherine, and she turned to see another woman had joined them in the outdoor air. It was Lady Dalhousie, the hostess of the ice ball and the most notorious gossip that Katherine knew. If ever there was someone who would exaggerate an accident into a malicious tragedy, it was her.

"Oh my." The back of Lady Dalhousie's hand flew to her forehead dramatically, and Katherine waited for her to start wailing.

The stranger remained undaunted in the face of the old woman's dramatics. She turned, her eyes hard in an expression schooled into indifference. "She must have slipped," she said, stressing the word. "What a dreadful accident."

She tapped Katherine on the arm as she passed. Seemingly calm in the face of calamity, she said, "Hurry. She might have survived the fall. We must help her."

Of course. Katherine had to stop seeing murder

around every corner. There were more innocent explanations, especially during such a frigid winter. But why would someone seek refuge on an upstairs balcony to begin with? Aside from the danger, it was abominably cold. The balcony, unlike the garden, didn't hold the lure of viewing the magnificent ice sculptures, either.

The woman in the snow lay still, facedown, with her blond hair spilling in an ominous halo from the coiffure on the back of her head. Where the strands ended, tendrils and splatters of sickly bright-red blood radiated. *She's dead. She must be.*

Her legs were splayed at odd angles, along with her arms to either side as if she'd tried to stop her fall.

The stranger knelt next to the victim's far side. Despite the cold, she removed her gloves and stuffed them into the reticule hanging from her wrist, which she set out of the way behind her in the snow. Katherine followed her lead and knelt on the victim's near side, close to her shoulder but far from the blood drenching the snow. The cold permeated her thin gown, and her knees felt the chill.

Head wounds bled profusely; that didn't mean that the woman was dead. Jolted to the present, Katherine tried to dredge up what meager knowledge she held of medicine and anatomy. "Should we turn her over to assess her wounds?"

Frowning, the stranger answered, "There is a frightening amount of blood. We might do more harm than good if we tried. We should check her pulse and breathing first."

Katherine was astonished by how calm and authoritative this young woman acted. "Are you a physician?" She looked much too young, not to mention an unusual gender for the role—although Katherine, as a female detective, knew how unnecessarily restrictive gender roles could be.

"Me?" Surprised, the woman brushed an errant strand of hair out of her eyes. On the whole, she was a bit forgettable. Not pretty or plain enough to be remarked upon, hair not brown or gold but somewhere in between, wearing a long-sleeved dress similar to Katherine's in cut and color. She was the sort of person apt to be overlooked but for her brazen attitude in a moment of chaos. "No, though my father is a physician. I'm Elizabeth. Elizabeth Verne."

"Katherine Irvine." Given that the woman dispensed with formality to offer her given name, Katherine saw no need to announce her title. She'd rather be judged by her actions than by her pedigree.

Nodding once in affirmation, the woman reached to press her fingers to the victim's wrist. Katherine noticed the victim wore no gloves. Odd... if she'd planned to be out on the balcony, wouldn't she have brought her gloves? And another thing—one of her fingers was scraped, a smidgen of fresh blood on the knuckle. Had that happened on impact or during a struggle?

"I can't feel a pulse," Elizabeth announced. She looked grim but no closer to hysterics than when she'd urged Katherine to help. "Can you?"

Katherine, impressed by Elizabeth's pragmatism and her unflappable demeanor, sought to follow her lead, but the victim had landed on her other arm. Instead, she held her finger to the woman's neck. Still warm, but for how long? "I can't find a pulse. She doesn't look to be breathing, either." Gingerly, Katherine inserted her fingers beneath the woman's chin and tilted her head to see her face.

Her expression was slack with death, her eyes wide. The front of her head was concave from the impact. She pulled her hand away with alacrity. Her stomach threatened to overturn itself. She breathed in shallowly through her nose, trying to ignore the coppery scent of blood mixing with the crisp air. Her hands shook as she fished a handkerchief out of her bodice and wiped away any residue that might have lingered.

"She's dead." Of that, Katherine held no doubt.

"Dead," Lady Dalhousie wailed.

Elizabeth launched to her feet immediately, her expression set as though she meant to take the hostess in hand next. She would have made an admirable schoolteacher, undaunted by any calamity or dramatics.

More people spilled out of the ballroom, among them Grandma Bath. She wore only a thin dress, like everyone else gathered, and looked as pale as the snow. Where was her grandson? Usually, when she was out, no one could pry him away. He was constantly assuring himself of her good health.

At the moment, the elderly woman looked ready to faint dead away. "God help her... Lady Rochford!"

The name *Rochford* rippled through the crowd.

Could it be? Katherine's ears rang as she stared at the back of the corpse's head, the memory of the front altogether too prominent. Lady Rochford was a dear friend of Katherine's stepmother.

"Katherine. Katherine!"

She returned to the present, to the bone-deep chill numbing her cheeks, nose, ears, and fingertips. Pru jostled her again.

"Are you all right? You look as though you might swoon."

Katherine drew herself up, trying to hide the way her knees trembled. "I will not swoon."

"Did you know her? Lady Rochford."

After a moment's hesitation, Katherine murmured, "I didn't. Not well. Susanna... She was a friend of my stepmother's."

"Celia?" A man's voice cracked on the name. "No, it can't be. Celia!"

The gray-haired man shoved aside the women in his path, Katherine included, as he fell to his knees next to the deceased. She recognized Baron Rochford the moment she saw him. Nearing sixty, he seemed to age by twenty years the moment he beheld his wife. He reached for her hand, wailing over it, before he extended his arm toward her face.

"No!" Katherine pulled herself away from Pru, catching hold of him before he turned the woman over. She squeezed between him and his wife, forcing him to look at her. "You don't want to see. I'm sorry."

She'd never seen a man fall to pieces so completely in front of her eyes. For a moment, it seemed to her as though he might simply fade away.

Grandma Bath took him in hand, urging him away from his wife's body and encouraging him to return inside. Elizabeth, having calmed Lady Dalhousie well enough that she wouldn't devolve into hysterics, even if she didn't seem capable of marshaling her common sense and ending the evening's festivities, accompanied the grieving man. Katherine stared after them, half wondering if she should go as well.

When a wife was murdered, the culprit was almost always her husband. Could Lord Rochford have done this? He seemed unraveled in his grief. So much so that even if Katherine attempted to question him, she doubted she would receive a coherent answer.

It might be remorse. Perhaps he pushed his wife in a heated moment and...

Then again, she wasn't sure the woman had been murdered. She could have simply slipped. Katherine shouldn't let her investigative inclinations carry her away. But what was she doing out on the balcony in the first place? And the railing was waist high, so how could she have fallen over?

Stepping up next to her, Pru seemed to read her thoughts. She craned her neck back to look at the balcony overhead. "Do you think she fell or was pushed?"

Katherine let out a long breath, one that fogged in front of her face in a stream. "*That* is something we need to discover."

She strode briskly toward the glass doors, which were still ajar, her slippers crunching in the snow. When she reached it, she turned to see Pru looking at her, confused.

"Whatever are you doing?" Pru asked.

"I'm measuring Lady Rochford's position from the house. For Lyle." Katherine carefully lifted her foot again and placed it heel to toe in front of the last, counting in her head. "He was working on a mathematical technique to ascertain the odds of whether someone was pushed, jumped, or fell from a certain height based on how far they are from the edge of the place they fell from. I don't know if he's used the formula in an investigation yet, but we might need it."

She walked four steps before the colder shadow of the balcony washed over her. Could that be right? She glanced back, but she hadn't miscalculated. She continued on until she reached the doors, just in case Lyle needed that number as well.

"I have a letter you can use to write down the figures if you have a pencil."

Katherine paused and glanced up. "A letter?"

Pru colored up. "From Annandale. I was reading it as you pulled up in the carriage."

"I have a pencil in my reticule. Give me a moment."

By the time Katherine reached the wall, ten more steps away, Pru had fished out the letter. Katherine scribbled down the numbers in the margin, but unfortunately the letter was written on both sides of the page. Although she tried her best to lightly sketch the position of the body in case it was needed, she doubted she did the best rendition, as she tried to leave the words largely untouched.

When she finished, she offered the letter back to Pru. "Keep this safe until I'm able to copy it onto a clean page."

Still blushing, Pru nodded and tucked the letter out of sight. "Shall we hurry to the balcony? There's no telling when someone will have the presence of mind to send everyone home."

Katherine nodded. Fearing that there was still a footman stationed on the other door to the garden, she and Pru entered by means of the glass doors. The majority of the guests were clustered around the hostess, who seemed to be recounting something. Could she have regained her senses so soon? She did love to be the center of attention. Katherine urged Pru down the nearest corridor.

Although the manor was unfamiliar to them, it was painfully easy to find the balcony over the ballroom. The nearest staircase led to the third floor, and the first door on the right opened into a small sitting room facing more glass doors. These were ajar, gaining Katherine and Pru entrance to the balcony.

"There's nothing here," Pru announced. She sounded disappointed.

Indeed, there was nothing on the balcony. No clue that might point to who had pushed Lady Rochford. But there was also no ice or snow. It must have been cleared in preparation for the party. Katherine strode to the railing. It was sturdy, nothing broken. Given the height and the fact there was no ice present, Katherine had no doubt.

"You're right, Pru. There's no reason why Lady Rochford might have slipped. It looks as though we'll have a murder to investigate after all."

CHAPTER THREE

K atherine inwardly cringed as she crept inside the townhouse she currently shared with her father, stepmother, and two younger sisters. Her stepmother, ten years older than Katherine, was often occupied in keeping her sisters, more than ten years younger, in line. Although the oldest, Connie, was nearing fourteen and developing an interest in investigation, Katherine still very much felt like she should be out on her own.

She had felt that way ever since her two older sisters had married and left the stately house in order to start families of their own. It was one of many reasons why she sought out independent living arrangements. The married adults left in Dorchester

House hadn't diminished their eagerness to continue their family, either. Since it was past midnight, Katherine couldn't predict what she might find her parents doing.

And she had to seek them out. Lady Rochford was a friend of Susanna's. Katherine didn't want her step-mother to learn of the death of her friend from the morning news rag. She had to deliver the terrible news herself.

She mustered her courage and stepped into the dark house. A footman had remained awake to accept her outerwear and store it away for the night. She thanked him and asked after her parents and learned they were in the upstairs parlor.

She wiped her clammy palms on her cold skirt as she neared the open door. Papa's voice spilled into the corridor, content. "What do you think of Arthur? There's some strong mythology behind the name."

"I don't want to consider it just—"

When Katherine knocked on the door, pushing it farther open, Susanna abruptly stopped and turned to look at her. A wide smile overtook her face. "Katherine, you're home! How was the ice ball?" It was that smile, betrayed by her twinkling brown eyes, that had swayed Katherine into trusting her when she was young and grieving the loss of her mother. Susanna had a way of making the people around her feel welcome and loved. It was no mystery why the marriage, which had started as one of convenience, had deepened to love. Susanna was impossible not to fall in love with.

~~Which was w~~hat made the news Katherine had to deliver all the more devastating.

Papa, seated next to his wife on the loveseat with his arm around her shoulders and an open book on his lap, studied Katherine with the ease of an expert investigator. He noticed the gravity in her expression immediately and shut the book.

"Katherine, is something amiss?"

Susanna's lips parted, and she unfolded her lithe legs to place both feet firmly on the floor. She fiddled with a strand of her black hair, a nervous habit.

Papa squeezed her shoulders, looking suddenly older than his sixty-one years. His blue-gray eyes narrowed as he waited.

Katherine swallowed hard. Her knees trembled, but she forced herself to remain standing. "I'm terribly sorry," she confessed, her voice hoarse. "Lady Rochford... I'm afraid Lady Rochford fell from a balcony this evening. She didn't survive."

Susanna gasped, and her hands flew to her mouth,

her face turning white. "No. No, you must be mistaken. At the ice ball?"

Katherine opened her mouth, but her stepmother didn't appear to be paying her any mind. Katherine hadn't realized they were such close friends, but given the way her stepmother was reacting, this was hitting her very hard.

"I saw her earlier today. It cannot be. William?" She turned her gaze toward her husband, beseeching.

Papa's expression was hard. He held his wife closer as he looked at Katherine. "Are you certain it was her?"

"Yes."

Susanna wailed. She buried her face in Papa's collar, her shoulders shaking with her sobs. "It can't be. Not Celia, not now..." Fisting her hand in his waistcoat, she raised her head. "William, you must investigate this. Find out who did this to her!"

"My dear, this may not be a murder..." He looked at Katherine as if for confirmation.

She swallowed hard before she admitted, "The family is accepting it as a terrible accident. There were no witnesses." *But I think it was murder.*

"Simply because no one admitted to seeing anything doesn't mean it didn't happen! Celia wouldn't jump to her death—"

Papa rubbed his hand along his wife's slim shoulders. "No one is suggesting she has, my dear. But I wasn't there. I cannot tell you the truth. Perhaps Katherine..."

Susanna sobbed again as Papa held her tight. His eyes hard, he said, "Perhaps you'd best leave us."

Katherine nodded and backed out of the room in turmoil. Should she have said nothing? Should she not investigate? What if she did a bad job? Perhaps this one was best left to her father. She'd never investigated anything that affected a member of her family before.

Shakily, she sought out her own room. Because she had told her maid not to wait for her, the only creature to greet her when she opened the door was her pug, Emma. Katherine dropped to her knees and hugged her tight as the weight of the responsibility of discovering what had really happened to Lady Rochford settled on her shoulders.

"I've never seen a woman killed in front of me before," Katherine confessed to her maid and confidante, Harriet.

The maid's dark, curly hair fell into her face as she wrestled to tie a new ribbon around Emma's collar.

The pug wiggled happily, wagging her tightly coiled tail.

Katherine continued, "I've seen corpses before, but never one so...fresh. It was—"

"Horrifying?" Harriet suggested, looking up. Her eyebrows pulled together in sympathy.

Katherine sighed, leaning back against the pillows on her bed. Although morning had dawned, she wasn't the earliest of risers by choice and had yet to muster the desire to leave the warm bed. The reheated bed warmer, stuffed with hot coal from the kitchen and tucked beneath the mattress at Katherine's feet, provided little incentive to rise when the floorboards would still be cold. In half an hour, perhaps the warmth of the kitchen below would chase away the chill.

"Confound it, hold still a moment more. I almost had it."

Smiling to herself, Katherine sat up again and held out her arms. "Give her here. I'll hold her steady."

Scowling, Harriet was more than willing to comply. As she deposited the dog into Katherine's arms, she asked, "Are you certain it was murder? This is the season when only fools venture out onto the balcony."

"Pru and I checked the balcony straight away.

There was no ice or snow, nothing that indicated Lady Rochford had slipped and fallen."

"There."

The moment Harriet stepped back and Katherine loosened her hold, Emma jumped up to happily lick the underside of Katherine's chin. She bounded out the door to roam the house. Harriet and Katherine let her be. The servants in the Dorchester household knew to watch for Emma before opening any doors leading outside—or to their personal belongings. Emma had a penchant for taking things that weren't hers.

"Now you," Harriet said, shooing Katherine out of bed. "Let's get you dressed and ready for the day."

With a sigh, Katherine slid her legs from beneath the coverlet as Harriet crossed the room to shut the door. The dressing screen was on the far side of the room, near the wardrobe. A writing desk, scattered with Katherine's notes on various investigations, stood on the other side of the room. The room itself was painfully neat, a product of Harriet's attentions.

As the door clicked shut, Harriet asked in a soft voice, "Have you told Lady Dorchester?"

Wearily, Katherine nodded. She rubbed her face, her fingers tangling in the loose brown hair that fell forward as she rested her elbows on her knees. "I did last night. Susanna was inconsolable."

Her stomach shrank as she realized that she would have to find and speak with her stepmother this morning. Susanna might have insight into Lady Rochford's life, and if Katherine still meant to investigate the death, she would need that insight.

Harriet patted Katherine's knee. "That's to be expected. She was a good friend of Lady Rochford's. It isn't your fault."

If her maid was remarking upon it, Katherine wasn't making a valiant effort to hide her feelings. "I know. It's a terrible situation." She stood, her knees a little weak but better than they'd felt the night before. "I'd best dress to face the cold this morning. I'll be going out, no doubt."

Harriet led the way to the wardrobe, where she extracted the day's garments while Katherine washed from a now-lukewarm basin of water.

The maid said, "If you're looking to gain entry to Dalhousie Manor, I might be able to help. I'm friends with the housekeeper. I'm certain I could persuade her to let you question her staff in case someone saw something."

Katherine glanced up as she dried her face with a

hand towel. "How did you know that was exactly what I was thinking?"

Harriet smirked. "You always want to speak with everyone. Now, come. Let's get you dressed so you can go down to breakfast."

———

As KATHERINE tentatively stepped out of her bedchamber, afraid to disturb the household, Emma trotted up to her. Her jaunty yellow ribbon bounced with every step. Pleased with herself, she spat something onto the floor at Katherine's feet and sat on her rump.

Katherine groaned. "You didn't." With a sigh, she bent to retrieve the item. Upon closer inspection, it proved to be a pearl stud earring, the white center encircled by braided gold, a distinctive piece. It belonged to Katherine's stepmother. One way or another, Katherine had to face Susanna.

The back of the earring bit into her palm as she closed her hand around it. First, she needed to fortify herself with breakfast.

She paused in the doorway to the breakfast room. The sideboard was laden with covered dishes overseen by a footman in the Dorchester livery. He added more tea to the cup in front of Katherine's stepmother. Susanna's hair was tucked into a neat bun at the back of her head, and her appearance was tidy, but she appeared haggard all the same. Her fingers trembled as she raised the replenished teacup to her lips. Her eyes were red rimmed and bloodshot as she glanced toward the door.

"Katherine." Tea sloshed over the rim of the cup as Susanna carelessly replaced it on its saucer. "Please, come in."

As she sat, Katherine held out her hand, palm up. "Emma brought this to me."

"My earring." Susanna raised her hands to caress her bare earlobes. "The fasteners on these are always loose. I was afraid I'd lost it. Thank you."

"My pleasure." Katherine held still as the footman placed a plate in front of her. Eggs, kippers, bacon, toast. She wasn't hungry for any of it. "I'm terribly sorry to have to break the news about your friend. I didn't want you to learn of it from someone else."

"I still can't fathom it." Susanna's voice broke. When Katherine raised her gaze, she found tears in her stepmother's eyes. "She's been my closest friend ever since I was pregnant with Maggie."

Katherine's youngest sister was now seven years old.

Susanna swallowed audibly. "We were of an age, you know. Both young, both married to older men and trying to conceive an heir. She had as much trouble as I did, and I was terrified that I would suffer another miscarriage." She dipped her hand beneath the table as though queasy at the thought.

"Celia finally conceived."

For a moment, Katherine couldn't breathe as she pondered the implications. "Lady Rochford was with child when she...?"

Susanna nodded. "She confided in me last week. And I..." She fought for breath as she pressed her palm against her mouth. "We were going to announce this later this week, when your sisters come over for dinner, but... I'm with child too. That is, if I don't..."

Miscarry. The dreaded word hung in the air between them. Great shocks were known to cause miscarriages, and Katherine and her father had been trying for so long...

She reached out to squeeze her stepmother's hand. "You won't. You and the baby both will survive this. I'm terribly sorry. If I'd known—"

With a weak smile, Susanna shook her head. "No, I had to find out sometime, didn't I?" With a sigh, she stared down at her full plate. "I don't know if I can eat after all this."

Katherine's father darkened the doorway. Although years had given him a bit of a paunch, he still stood tall and proud, his shoulders not yet bowed from the weight of time. This morning, he seemed to have more white than gray in his receding hairline.

"You must," he said firmly, stepping into the room. "Darling, you must keep up your strength."

His wife mustered a trembling smile and speared a kipper with her fork. "You're right, of course." She nibbled at the tail end.

When she set it down again, only half eaten, he paused next to her to press a kiss to the top of her head, then her forehead, the tip of her nose, her mouth. Katherine made a face and set her fork down again. If her parents were expecting a child, why were they acting as if they still hoped to conceive? She needed to find a house of her own, the sooner, the better.

The affection had a clear effect on Susanna. The moment Papa lifted his head, the color washed through his wife's cheeks again and her eyes softened. She seemed in better spirits.

Papa confessed, "I'm happy I was home from my consultation early last night. And even more relieved that you decided not to join Katherine at the ball. The very last thing you need is to see something like that." He looked over at Katherine.

A haunted look overcame Susanna again as she looked down. Papa took her hand and kissed her fingers. "Katherine? Can I speak with you a moment?"

Since she had no appetite anyway, Katherine nodded. She followed her father into the corridor, where they could speak privately. His gaze was serious as he met hers.

"Be honest with me, kitten. Do you think Lady Rochford was murdered?"

"I do." She braced herself, expecting to be relieved of the investigation at any moment. Papa was, after all, the one who had taught her everything she knew. He was a better investigator, and finding out what really happened was important.

Papa softly swore. "Tarnation. I'd hoped it was only an accident."

"I could be mistaken. I won't know for certain until I'm able to speak with Lyle and get his opinion..."

"I trust your instincts," Papa said, his voice firm. "I have a case I'm working with Sir John, a consultation. Do you think you'll have trouble solving Lady Rochford's murder?"

Katherine frowned. "You want me to—"

"Yes. Susanna does too. We both have every confidence in your abilities. After all, you did solve the Pink

Ribbon Murders where I could not." He raised his eyebrows.

Yes. She had. Firming her chin, Katherine squared her shoulders and announced, "You don't have to worry, Papa. I'll discover who killed Lady Rochford. I promise."

CHAPTER FOUR

Having helped her older sisters choose the fabric and styles of their wedding gowns, Katherine knew to expect some measure of chaos when she stepped into the seamstress's shop on Bond Street. The shop front consisted of a modest display of no more than three dresses—a walking dress, a ball gown, and a delicate nightdress—positioned between peculiar wardrobes with thin tiered shelves. Some of those shelves were pulled out to display the rich, colorful bolts of fabric or lavish scraps of lace contained within.

Mrs. Burwick strode into the shop with her shoulders thrust back, the hem of her woolen gown wet with the slush on the well-travelled street. Her heels clicked against the slick wood, echoing in the small shop's interior. The curtain to the back of the shop, where women were fitted for their dresses, rustled, and a middle-aged woman's salt-and-pepper hair peeked out. She released a gusty sigh as she spotted her customers.

"Oh, my heart. For a moment, I thought... What a calamity!"

Katherine exchanged a look of trepidation with Pru. Usually, the brides were far more overbearing than their seamstresses.

The woman, with bowed shoulders that approached five feet tall at best, laid a hand on her brow as if fighting a fever. "Can you believe? I only received word a moment ago." She fanned herself with a news rag.

Katherine couldn't believe that a woman whose face turned that pronounced a shade of purple hadn't yet fallen to the floor in a dead faint. Perhaps she ought to have brought Emma to the occasion. The touch of a dog's cold nose worked better than smelling salts to revive a swooning woman.

A young girl who stood an inch or two taller than the seamstress and who shared many of her features scurried out of the back room to latch onto her arm. "Auntie, you must sit down." The girl tucked stray black strands escaping her bun behind her ear as she spared a glance for the shop's customers. "She's had a terrible shock this morning. Please forgive her. How may I help?"

A frown entered Mrs. Burwick's voice as she hazarded a question. "A terrible shock? Oh dear. My daughter is set to be married within the month."

Pru groaned under her breath. "Wishful thinking, Mama," she muttered.

Katherine was likely the only woman who heard. She glanced at her friend, noting the high color in Pru's cheeks. Although Pru had accepted Lord Annandale's proposal, she had done so with the understanding that they had a long engagement. Pru loved Annandale, but she wasn't in as much of a hurry as her mother for the wedding to take place.

"Do I need to seek the arrangements to have a wedding trousseau made elsewhere? I'm certain we passed a shop along the way that seemed reputable…"

The seamstress's niece leaped to reassure Mrs. Burwick before the shop lost a customer. "Certainly not, madam. We are perfectly capable of outfitting your daughter to advantage. My aunt has only recently received news that a longtime customer has died, and it's shocked her greatly."

"Lady Rochford was so young," the seamstress murmured. The crumple of the news rag in her clenched fists was louder than her voice, but Katherine's hearing sharpened at the name. The seamstress leaned against the wall, shaking her head. "She was set to come in this morning with her stepdaughter to have her gowns let out. When they missed their appointment, I never thought..." Her voice wavered, and she pressed her fist against her mouth.

As the woman's niece herded her behind the curtain once more, promising to attend to the customers herself, Katherine frowned. At the very least, Susanna hadn't been mistaken about Lady Rochford's pregnancy. If she was letting out her gowns, she anticipated that she would be getting thicker.

When the young woman returned, bearing a smile, she turned her attention to Mrs. Burwick. "Now, which of these beautiful young ladies is the bride?"

"I am," Pru said, taking a small step forward. Katherine had never seen her so timid. Usually she wasn't afraid to have an opinion.

The seamstress's assistant eyed Pru then turned her gaze to Mrs. Burwick once more. "You'll make a lovely bride, just you wait and see. I'll fix you right up. Are we hoping for a wedding gown or the entire trousseau?"

"The entire trousseau. And I've some ideas on the cut," Mrs. Burwick answered firmly.

Her eyes wide, Pru gave Katherine a pointed glance.

Right. She had a job to do. Thrusting her shoulders back, Katherine stepped forward to take charge of the situation and save Pru from the misery of her mother's fashion choices.

By the time they exited the shop, Katherine was emotionally wrung out. Even her sisters had not been as stubborn and difficult to deal with as Mrs. Burwick. From the way the woman had carried on, she might have been arranging her own wedding, not that of her daughter, whose tastes differed greatly.

With measurements taken and fabrics and patterns chosen, they left Mrs. Burwick to instruct as to the delivery. Katherine took Pru by the arm and towed her from the shop for a breath of fresh air.

Pru looked as worn as Katherine felt. "Are you unwell?"

Although she rubbed the crease in her forehead, it did little to ease her pinched expression. "This entire affair promotes being unwell."

"You love Lord Annandale, don't you?" Katherine was certain that she did.

In fact, she became more certain as color flushed Pru's cheeks. "You know I do. But with the way Mama talks, everyone will think I'm marrying him for his title."

"Have you told him that you love him?" Katherine asked.

Pru nodded. "Of course."

"And he loves you."

Her color deepened to scarlet, and she ducked her head, coy. "I wouldn't be marrying him if he didn't."

"Then who cares what everyone thinks? He knows you don't care a whit for his title."

Her words teased a smile out of her friend. Pru mumbled something that sounded near to *You're right*, but a passing carriage drowned out the sound as snow sloshed away from the tall wheels. Katherine took a step closer to the shop to preserve her skirts.

"Are you ready to beard the lion?" Katherine teased, gesturing to the shop.

Pru laughed and nodded. "I suppose I have to face her eventually. Best to make sure she hasn't added something hideous to my trousseau."

Smiling, Katherine steeled herself to interfere once more should Pru think it was needed. For all that Mrs. Burwick had applauded Katherine's efforts in arranging the match between Pru and Lord Annandale, her gratitude only stretched so far. If Katherine negated her wishes one more time, she might find herself uninvited to the wedding. Not that Pru would allow that to carry on for long.

As she glanced down the street, Katherine caught sight of a familiar figure stepping out of the neighboring milliner's shop while donning her gloves. Elizabeth Verne exuded the same air of practicality as she had during the crisis at Lady Dalhousie's ice ball. Her hair was tucked neatly under her hood, her fur-lined pelisse fastened to the chin to ward away the chill as she took her bearings. As she met Katherine's gaze, she smiled.

"Katherine, dear!"

"Elizabeth," she greeted just as warmly. She beckoned the young woman closer. "So good to see you!"

Pru smiled, too, though her expression was a bit tight. "From yesterday, yes?" she muttered under her breath. Had Katherine introduced them properly in the chaos? She couldn't recall.

She did so now. "Elizabeth, are you acquainted with Prudence Burwick? Pru, I met Elizabeth Verne last night."

"Miss Burwick, it's wonderful to be introduced to you properly."

"And you," Pru said.

Elizabeth turned to Katherine. "How is Lady Bath? She mentioned as I was with her last night that you and she had attended the ball together."

Katherine nodded. Fortunately, she had insisted upon taking her own carriage, which allowed her to deposit Lord Bath and his grandmother at their London townhouse before she saw Pru safely home.

Her smile turning brittle, Katherine answered, "As well as can be expected after such a shock. Lady Bath is heartier than most give her credit for."

Elizabeth laughed. "I guessed that from the moment I saw her. You don't grow to be her age and do so much for your town without developing a spine of steel. Why, I heard she even commissioned a unique attraction for the town square in Bath and is working tirelessly to bring more interest to the town. She is quite a gem."

"Indeed, she is," Katherine agreed.

Elizabeth sounded as though she admired the old woman, a good sign. Once again, the notion ignited to match Elizabeth with Lord Bath. She was sensible, pretty, gracious. *And* she seemed to enjoy Grandma Bath's company. She might be the perfect match.

However, Katherine couldn't broach the subject in the middle of the street. She needed a more private location to gain Elizabeth's confidence first.

Not that many women would object to being matched with a marquess, but Lord Bath was a bit eccentric. His heart was in the right place, even if he happened to make decisions that Katherine, for one, did not agree with. However, he was always kind and friendly, and he cared immensely for his tenants in Bath.

"We're just finishing here," Katherine said. "Would you care to join us for a glass of elder wine to combat the cold?"

"Thank you," Elizabeth answered as she glanced over her shoulder. "I'm afraid I'm not alone... oh, there she is. Katherine, have you met Dorothy Fairchild?"

Please, let it be any other Fairchild...

However, fate was not nearly so kind. Mrs. Fairchild strode from the milliner's shop with purpose in her step. Although she was far shorter than Katherine, she held herself with her head held so high it was as if she hoped to outstrip her in height as well as matches made. The rival matchmaker joined them with alacrity, but she didn't seem at all pleased at the notion.

"We've met," Mrs. Fairchild said, her words clipped. "Lady Katherine, what a delight to see you."

She didn't sound delighted in the least.

"Allow me to tender my congratulations once more

on the fabulous match you made this September in Bath," Katherine said, her voice saccharine.

Mrs. Fairchild drew herself up proudly. "And you," she answered, nodding to Pru. "I see you've met my newest client, Miss Verne?"

Tarnation! Katherine's dreams of matching Elizabeth with Lord Bath shriveled and winked out. Mrs. Fairchild would certainly drip poison in her client's ear the moment they were out of sight.

As if to prove the thought, the older woman tucked away a strand of her auburn hair beneath her hood and asked innocently, "Who is your newest client? Or do you intend to see one all the way to the altar before taking another? I hear that might be quite a while."

Pru bristled. "Katherine and I are *friends*, I'll have you know."

Mrs. Fairchild pretended not to hear. She turned to her charge, whose forehead crinkled with worry as she looked around the group.

"Elizabeth, I'm afraid we're late for a meeting with your mother. We really can't tarry."

The young woman hazarded a smile at Katherine, but it disappeared in a flash. "So nice to see you again, Lady Katherine."

Confound it! Mrs. Fairchild seemed to have her hooks well into Elizabeth. How would Katherine ever find a way to pair Elizabeth with Lord Bath? It was impossible. Not without prying her away from Mrs. Fairchild for an evening or more, and then she might be seen as stealing a client.

Well, that would earn Katherine no favors from Mrs. Fairchild, that was for certain. Perhaps it was just as well that Katherine had a far more important matter upon which to focus her thoughts. She had a woman's murder to solve.

CHAPTER FIVE

For all Katherine's suspicions, the only way to prove that Lady Rochford had been pushed from the balcony was with Lyle Murphy's help. That evening at the monthly meeting of the Royal Society of Investigative Techniques, she found him gawking at Philomena Graylocke, the Duchess of Tenwick, as the charming woman delighted the crowds with a description of her latest invention, one her young son had purportedly aided her with.

Her sister-in-law, Lucy Graylocke-Douglass, the Marchioness of Brackley and intrepid author, stood by her side, beaming. The women, both in their thirties, were as different as night and day.

Philomena, with whom Katherine was friendly

given that she often attended Society meetings, had auburn hair and an impish smile. Whenever she spoke, she seemed to take her listener into her confidence and share a secret.

Lady Brackley, several years younger, had long ebony hair that seemed to spill from its pins and a gaze hungry for knowledge. Katherine had encountered her once before and found herself trapped in a corner all evening as Lady Brackley asked her endless questions regarding how she had felt visiting crime scenes as a child, of all things. If the questions had been research for a book, Katherine had yet to find it published.

Lady Brackley's first book, a romantic adventure about a princess-turned-pirate, had been rather entertaining, however.

Katherine elbowed her way past the horde of Graylocke admirers to Lyle's side.

"Are you planning on speaking with her tonight?" Katherine teased. Lyle had been half in love with the Duchess of Tenwick for as long as she'd known him, never mind that the woman was blissfully wedded to a very powerful man. As far as Katherine knew, Lyle had only spoken to the woman he so esteemed once. He'd turned scarlet and stumbled over his tongue.

At her words, Lyle jumped, his cheeks filling with color. "Katherine, you startled me."

"I didn't know this was an inventor's club," Pru muttered as she sidled in next to Katherine. She critically eyed the group clustered around the duchess.

"It isn't," Lyle snapped, jumping to Philomena's defense. "But inventions can greatly aid investigations. The duchess once designed a bullet-resistant corset that saved Lady Brackley's life."

Katherine smiled and added, "Perhaps someday, you'll submit to giving a lecture to the Society yourself."

Lyle rubbed his thumb across his red, freckled cheek, sheepish. "I'm not near the inventor she is. Besides, I'm happy to share my knowledge to help Sir John." Even though he was paid to patrol the streets and apprehend criminals, he readily shared his inventions with his colleagues on Bow Street and with Katherine.

"Perhaps you are, or perhaps not," Katherine said with a shrug. "I've never used a single one of Philomena's inventions when solving a crime. I've used more than one of yours."

Lyle's shoulders relaxed, and his chest puffed out, telltale signs of pride.

"Speaking of," Pru interrupted. "Don't we need Lyle's help?"

"Yes." Katherine laid a hand on Lyle's arm, squeezing. "If you don't mind me stealing you away for a moment."

Although he glanced once more at the duchess, he nodded and allowed himself to be led into a quieter corner near a fireplace that had a series of armchairs and low tables for more intimate discussion.

Katherine sat at an armchair and leaned close as Lyle did the same. Pru stood between them, silent, as she seemed bent on soaking in the atmosphere and studying every aspect. Whether she was impressed by the Society or not, Katherine couldn't tell.

"Have you heard of Lady Rochford's death?" Katherine whispered.

Lyle nodded, keeping one eye on the demonstration across the hall. "It's impossible not to hear of an unfortunate death in my line of work. She slipped off a balcony, did she not?"

"Slipped..." Katherine hesitated. "Or was pushed. Pru and I found no indications of ice or other hazards."

Lyle raised his eyebrows. "Did you find evidence of a struggle?"

"No." An image of the scraped finger bubbled up. "Well, maybe. She had a scrape on her finger. Is Bow Street investigating, by chance?"

Lyle shook his head, his face grim. "We received

the body, but I heard it was ruled an accident. She's to be buried this week, if she hasn't been already."

Katherine let out a breath. "She was pushed. I'm almost certain of it. However, no one would believe me if I suggested such a thing, not without proof. Can you help? I know you've been testing a method of calculation."

With a frown, Lyle removed a small leather-bound notebook from his pocket. He flipped it to a page scribbled with letters and numbers and turned it toward her. "You mean this? I'd need a lot of information. We haven't had many people who have jumped or fallen from pronounced heights of late, so I haven't had the opportunity to test the formula rigorously. I would need to know the height from which the victim fell, the positioning of the body, how far the body landed from the building—"

Pru rustled in her reticule and produced a page. Since Katherine didn't spy any handwriting on the back of it, it seemed that Pru had copied Katherine's notes onto a fresh page so as not to submit her letter to too much scrutiny.

As Lyle accepted the page, Katherine explained, "I took rough measurements while I was there. Some are measured based on the size of my feet."

Lyle harrumphed and dug into his pocket once more. "I'll have to see your feet. Are these the boots you wore?" He produced a measuring cord.

After hazarding a glance at the gathering, who now bustled around Philomena's form to congratulate or question her following the results of her demonstration, Katherine lifted her foot so Lyle could measure. "No, but all my shoes are nearly identical in size." Her cheeks heated as she submitted to Lyle measuring her foot for a more accurate count based on her rough measurements. She hoped she hadn't been too imprecise; her investigation hinged on the answer he deduced.

Never before had she been more grateful that Captain Wayland wasn't here—even if his absence was peculiar. As a detective himself ever since he had retired from the military after the Battle of Waterloo, Wayland was an avid, active member of the Society. Had he attended the meeting tonight, Katherine knew precisely what he would have said upon spotting Lyle measuring her foot.

"And here I thought you to be the only person obsessed with the size of people's feet. Is it a club?"

He had once caught her measuring suspects' feet—including his—in the hope of identifying the Pink

Ribbon Murderer. His feet had been much too big to fit with the boot print she had found, and unfortunately, every time she'd turned around, he'd been loitering nearby. Ever since she'd pursued investigations independent of her father's guidance, that seemed to be a common occurrence. Wayland, apparently, had nothing more interesting to do than try to glean information about her ongoing investigations.

Except, it seemed, this time. Wayland usually attended these meetings, but tonight he was nowhere to be seen. Not that she was looking for him. All the better. Perhaps she would finally be able to root out the criminal without his confusing presence.

The moment Lyle lifted the measuring cord away, she returned her foot to the ground. "Do you need help or peace?"

He cocked an eyebrow. "Do you have a familiarity with higher-level mathematics?"

"Peace, it is." Katherine latched onto Pru's arm and towed her away. "Find me once you're finished. I'll be circulating."

Lyle nodded absently, already lost in the realm of mathematics given his intense expression as he stared at the page, returning the cord to his pocket and pulling free a pencil instead.

"Come," Katherine said to Pru. "Let me see if I can't introduce you to some of the members of the Entrance Committee."

Unfortunately, the only member of the Entrance Committee in attendance tonight was an old, crotchety man who didn't look fondly on female detectives. Although the Society didn't prohibit the inclusion of women among their ranks, too many men for Katherine's tastes believed themselves above the female members. Pru would gain no favors by speaking to him. As the man to whom the elderly curmudgeon was speaking turned, Katherine stiffened.

Noticing her rigid stance, Pru wrapped an arm around Katherine's shoulders and steered her in the opposite direction. "Perhaps we ought to try speaking to someone else. It's best you don't box Mr. Salmon's ears and have us barred from the premises."

"He deserves more than to have his sarding ears boxed." Katherine seethed with hatred and anger. Unfortunately, Pru had a firm hold on her and refused to allow Katherine to so much as glance over her shoulders. Good thing too. If she had, Katherine might have given the dishonest detective a piece of her mind. But she couldn't, at least not in public. Katherine had only learned of his dishonesty when trying to uncover the identity of the Burglar of Bath, but to reveal Mr.

Salmon for what he was would mean she would have to endanger the reputation of another, more honest person. Katherine would not do that even if it meant letting Mr. Salmon take credit for a case that *she* had solved.

"Look, there's your friend Lady Tenwick. Let's say hello."

Although Katherine recognized the distraction tactic, she *had* hoped to find a moment alone with Philomena during the course of the evening. Before marrying a duke, Philomena had been an inventor of some renown, an independent woman and one to be esteemed. Katherine hoped that the duchess might be able to help her find independent living arrangements.

As they approached, Philomena smiled broadly. She held out her hands. "Lady Katherine, so good to see you!"

Katherine accepted the offering and squeezed her hands tight. "Phil, it's been too long. Can I introduce you to my friend Pru Burwick?"

The duchess smiled as she nodded at Pru. "It's lovely to meet you. Are you a new member?"

"An aspiring one," Katherine answered for her.

Phil nodded sagely. "Let me see if I can put a good word in the ear of the Entrance Committee. We need more women here, to even out the numbers. My sister-in-law, Lucy, is considering joining as well."

"Oh?" Katherine asked, turning her gaze toward the ebony-haired beauty. "I wasn't aware that you were so interested in investigating."

"I am." Lady Brackley's eyes gleamed. "In fact, I believe my next novel will be heavily influenced by the experience of the Society. Didn't I hear you were a matchmaker, Lady Katherine? I'm certain someone applauded you as the reason the Earl of Northbrook found his new countess."

If Lady Brackley cornered her and demanded every minute detail of that courtship, Katherine might scream. She forced a smile. "I am," she answered, choosing her words carefully. "But only insofar as it allows me access to the suspects of the crimes I solve. Unfortunately, a lady cannot stride up to near strangers and demand they answer questions. There is an unfortunate stigma regarding the investigative arts still, especially where it pertains to women."

"Is there? Fascinating," Lady Brackley said. She dug into her reticule and pulled out a notebook and pencil. "Do you mind if I ask you more on the subject?"

Tarnation. Katherine's smile felt as though it might flake away like weathered paint. "Actually, I'd hoped to get a moment alone with Phil to ask a question. It won't take long."

"Certainly," the duchess answered easily. "Perhaps it will be easier for us to hear each other over here."

She led Katherine away from her relative and Pru. Lady Brackley, who would undoubtedly make a very tenacious investigator should she ever take up the profession in lieu of writing, immediately latched onto Katherine's friend to quiz her about Lord knew what.

"What is it that you'd like to ask me?" Phil asked, her manner easy and approachable. That was what Katherine loved best about her. From the moment they had met years ago, when Katherine had yet trailed at her father's coattails with an eagerness to learn and emulate him, Phil had treated her as an equal, an individual. That alone had granted Katherine confidence at a time when everyone had looked down upon her for her youth and treated her as though the only thoughts in her head were those of her father.

"I'm looking for an independent residence. It's high time I stood on my own. Since you once lived independently, I hoped you might be able to recommend an appropriate neighborhood."

Katherine's needs were specific. She needed to live close enough to Mayfair to suit her family, but frankly the townhouses within those borders were priced higher than her budget. The only money she had to use, for the rest of her life, was the dowry her father had awarded her upon the successful completion of her first independent investigation. Although it was more money than many had at their disposal, she had to use it wisely. She had not only herself to support but Harriet too.

Philomena hummed under her breath. "I don't know of anything for sale, currently. To be honest, I inherited my father's house when he passed on. Though now that Morgan's brothers have all found independent lodgings for their families, we don't have quite so full a house anymore, and we don't have much need of two London townhouses. Would you be interested in buying my old house? It isn't far from Hyde Park, and it has the most darling little hidden room. I used it for inventing, but you might find good use for it in your investigations."

As tempted as Katherine was, if the house was as close to Hyde Park as Phil claimed, it was in the heart of Mayfair. Out of her reach. Although she had never stepped foot in the house, Katherine found herself saying, "Thank you for the offer, but I'm afraid it's a bit too big to meet my needs. The residence I'm hoping to find will hold only myself, my maid, and my dog."

She must have been correct in the estimation of its

size, for the duchess nodded in understanding, "Of course. I'll keep my ears open in case I hear of something smaller coming available for you."

"Thank you," Katherine answered, her voice warm. "I do appreciate it. And your offer, sincerely, I do."

Katherine was not lying in that. Now that she had a brother or sister on the way, perhaps her parents would cease to act like newlyweds and cooing at each other behind every corner. Then again, perhaps that was their nature. For her own sanity, it was time for her to find a house all her own to live in.

Her wandering gaze found Lyle, who still stared at the page, his eyebrows pulled together as he read over his calculations as if searching for errors. She excused herself and joined him. Pru seemed to be mired in Lady Brackley's impromptu interrogation, but she looked none the worse for wear. Katherine decided not to wait. She would inform Pru of the outcome of Lyle's calculations later.

Struggling to conceal the excitement churning within her, she reclaimed her earlier seat to Lyle's left. "You have that look about you. What have you found?"

With a sigh, Lyle set down the pencil. He folded the page and tucked it neatly into his pocket before he answered. "You're right, Katherine. Judging from the position of the body and the distance where it fell, Lady Rochford did not slip or jump. I conclude with about an eighty-five percent certainty, given the rough measurements"—he raised his eyebrows at her pointedly—"that she was pushed. This was murder."

CHAPTER SIX

The moment Pru breezed through the door of Dorchester House the next morning, her eyes gleamed. "What did Mr. Murphy have to say?" Without looking, she doffed her muff and cloak and handed both to the butler.

Katherine raised an eyebrow. "Hello to you too." She'd been expecting Pru to stop by. When Katherine had left the monthly Society meeting the prior evening, Pru had been deep in conversation with Lady Brackley and reluctant to leave. Philomena had promised to take her home later in the evening.

After stamping her feet on the runner, thereby clearing her boots of snow, Pru followed Katherine upstairs to the library, where Katherine had been making notes on the case. A silver tea service and two overturned teacups had been placed on the round oak table that sat between two chairs. "Tea?" Katherine asked.

"Only if you'll answer my question while you pour. I saw you speaking with him at length last night over the parchment I'd provided him."

Katherine perched on the edge of one of the velvety maroon armchairs and indicated for Pru to take the other. As she leaned back, a yelp prompted her to jump up again. Emma peeked her head out from behind the cushion, where she'd been resting. She glared at Katherine, her nose twitching at the interruption.

"Sorry, girl. What were you doing behind there? Are you hiding from Harriet again?"

The moment Katherine patted her head, the dog's disapproving demeanor disappeared. Her lips parted, and her pink tongue fell out one side as she raised her face, happy for the attention. Katherine plucked her out from behind the cushion and settled the dog on her lap as she met Pru's gaze once more.

"Do tell. Did Mr. Murphy conclude the matter to be murder?" Pru's eyes sparkled with the promise of a new case to investigate.

Katherine leaned forward and carefully overturned the teacups. Pru was so eager for information that Katherine couldn't help but tease her by delaying the answer. "You can call him Lyle. We are all friends."

"The only man I need to refer to by his given name is my future husband."

"Then why do you still refer to him as Annandale?"

"*Katherine.*" Pru batted away a strand of her dark hair.

She refused to relent. Her lips quirked at the corners as she slowly poured the tea.

"What has you so agitated?"

"Nothing." Pru fidgeted in her chair.

Katherine took pity. "Lyle confirmed it was murder. We'll have an investigation to conduct, just as you'd hoped."

Pru winced. Her teacup rattled in its saucer as she drew it onto her lap. "I didn't mean for someone to die for my entertainment."

"Of course you didn't."

Emma lifted her head upon hearing the conviction in Katherine's voice.

Stroking her pet absently, Katherine added, "What made you think I'd believe something so heinous about you? Did someone at the meeting last night imply as much?"

"Pardon?" Pru raised her gaze from the liquid in her teacup and blinked rapidly. "No. Of course not. It was a delightful event."

Something was clearly on Pru's mind, but Katherine knew the other woman would tell her when the time was right.

Pru pursed her lips as she lifted her teacup halfway to her mouth. She didn't drink. "Have you heard anything about Lord Rochford?"

As Katherine reached for her tea, she tried not to frown. "I don't know him well. He's of an age with Papa and doesn't run in my social circles. Why?"

"I meant, have you heard anything about him since the death of his wife."

Until Lyle had confirmed it was murder, Katherine hadn't wanted to devote too much time and resources into the investigation. The upset seamstress they'd encountered yesterday was only one example of the kind of upset they would spread if they started asking questions unduly.

Given Lyle's calculation about where her body had landed, the police were starting to look into the death as more than an accident, but still the general public was unaware of that. Once Katherine started asking uncomfortable questions, there would undoubtedly be some resistance.

"I haven't looked into Lord Rochford yet."

"Shouldn't you?" Pru asked. "I heard at the meeting last night that the culprit is almost always the husband."

Katherine frowned. "Were you discussing Lady Rochford's investigation?"

"Of course not. Lady Brackley was discussing the research she had done. Did you know she's writing a book?"

"She's written one. Several, I believe, though I've only read the first."

"Perhaps I'll borrow it, if you have it handy."

Katherine set her teacup and the saucer on the table and placed Emma on the floor. "Of course. I believe it's right over here."

Katherine scanned the leather spines lined up in one of the tall oak bookcases.

"Don't you think Lord Rochford ought to be the first person we investigate?" Pru asked.

"Did you find him disingenuous in his grief the other night?" Katherine asked over her shoulder as she moved to the next case.

"He seemed inconsolable... but that doesn't mean he didn't do it. He was at the ball, and he didn't appear outside right away. He would have had plenty of time to throw her off then run back down to the ballroom.

What if he threw her off the balcony in a fit of rage and later regretted it?"

Katherine paused, turning to look her friend in the eye. "The thought crossed my mind the other night, but that was before I knew she was pregnant. If she was carrying his heir, what possible motive could he have for killing her before the baby was born? Lord Rochford has waited a long time for an heir, so I doubt he'd take that gamble even if they did have a spat."

"It would account for how devastated he was," Pru countered. "Didn't you mention she had some kind of wounds? Perhaps there was a fight."

"A scrape on her finger. It really wasn't much and could have happened in any number of ways. Maybe the police will find more evidence of a fight."

A slim smirk ghosting across her face, Pru said, "What if the child wasn't Lord Rochford's?"

Katherine shook her head. "Let's not accuse Lady Rochford of infidelity without proof. She was a friend of my stepmother's. They were both trying to conceive, I'll have you know."

Katherine bent down to scan the lower shelves. Where had she put that darn book?

"Are we certain that Lord Rochford knew his wife was pregnant?"

That was a question Katherine hadn't considered.

Papa knew that Susanna was pregnant. Why wouldn't Lady Rochford have told her husband? It was a moment of joy and hope that an heir was on the way. Although if Lady Rochford had as long a history of miscarriage, as Katherine's stepmother did...

"If you were pregnant, would you tell Annandale?"

Pru's mouth dropped open as she straightened. "Don't be crass! Annandale and I haven't"—she paused to swallow audibly, her cheeks coloring—"anticipated our vows."

"I didn't mean to offend. After the wedding, wouldn't you want to tell your husband straight away?"

"I'd rather not answer that question," Pru answered, but dimples formed in her chin as she frowned.

Katherine abandoned her search for the book and turned to her friend. "Is something wrong?" She held Pru's gaze until the other woman's shoulders bowed in defeat.

"Annandale is due to arrive back in town this evening."

Katherine smiled. "That's good news, isn't it?"

"What if he's forgotten me?"

"He's sent you letters every week."

Pru shrugged, not meeting Katherine's gaze. "Perhaps he has, but what if he's romanticized our connection and forgotten the reality?"

"What do you mean?"

"He might remember me prettier and be disappointed when he sees me again."

Katherine nearly laughed, but the look on Pru's face told her that her friend was serious in her fear.

"Do you remember him handsomer than he is? Will you be disappointed when he comes back from Scotland with ice crystals in his beard?"

Lord Annandale, not one to follow the fashions of High Society and a bit wild at heart, as he'd confessed once to Katherine, wore a beard that he kept meticulously groomed, along with his auburn hair. If that hadn't repelled Pru, Katherine didn't know why her friend would assume that an unflattering dress or the way she styled her hair would move her fiancé to reconsider.

Aha! Katherine spotted the book on the bottom shelf, pulled it out, and returned to her chair.

"Of course not." Pru accepted the book from Katherine with a nod. "But he's devastatingly handsome, and you know it. Women would line up for miles for the chance to marry him."

"Because of his title and wealth," Katherine reminded her. "*You* are the woman he's shown his heart to. That makes you far more dear to him than some diamond of the first water."

Pru's mouth curved in a wry expression. "Aren't you supposed to tell me *I'm* a diamond of the first water?"

"Would you believe me if I did?"

Pru chuckled. "No." After a beat, she added, "With your taste in dresses, I have to wonder that you aren't blind."

"You're worried for nothing," Katherine assured her friend. "Lord Annandale will be delighted to be reunited with his bride-to-be. It is long overdue."

Pru looked down again at Emma, who panted happily at her feet. "Perhaps you're right."

"I know I am," Katherine answered with conviction. They exchanged a smile.

A sharp, relieved exhalation echoed from the doorway, making both women jump. Katherine turned to find Harriet there, her cheeks flushed, looking out of breath. She pointed a finger at Katherine.

Emma squeaked and dove beneath the table. She had been hiding from Harriet, after all. Katherine had wondered why Emma hadn't been wearing the ribbon Harriet liked to tie around her collar in a bow.

"You've returned," Katherine announced.

"Was Harriet away?" Pru asked.

Katherine nodded. "I sent her to Dalhousie Manor now that we know for certain Lady Rochford's death was murder. What did you discover?"

Harriet, braced against the doorframe as she caught her breath, held up her hand. "You said you would wait for me in the parlor. I ran all over the house, looking for you."

"My apologies. I was distracted. Your findings? Did any of the Dalhousie servants happen to see something?"

Harriet nodded. She took another gulp of air before answering, "They did. Knowing you, you'll want to speak with them yourself. I'd advise changing your dress."

Pru smirked. "That's good advice for Katherine on any day."

Ignoring her, Harriet waved her hand. "You too, Miss Burwick. You'll both want to wear something plainer, less conspicuous, or the servants will know you for high women in an instant."

"Me?" Pru pressed a hand to her chest. "I don't even have a lady's maid."

"You are going to be a marchioness," Katherine reminded her. "You're as lofty as I am in the eyes of the working class now." She winked. "Very well, Harriet, but we may have to borrow something."

Harriet looked at the pair and sighed. "I don't have anything nearly long enough to fit the two of you. Come, let's see what you have, Lady Katherine. Perhaps you have something that will do."

KATHERINE'S ANKLES WERE COLD. Her thin stockings were no barrier against the winter chill even with the scuffed ankle-high boots Harriet had lobbied one of the maids to allow Katherine to borrow. The dress Harriet had found for her was tight across the hips and loose across the bosom, the opposite of how these placket-front dresses were supposed to fit.

A dowdy brown, the sort of color she should consider investing in, for it would certainly ward away male attention, the dress ended at mid-calf. Coupled with a borrowed shift that reached no further, the outfit was as warm as the Arctic. Even though she'd insisted on a long cloak to cover her exposed legs, the walk from Dorchester House to Dalhousie Manor, ten minutes away, had chilled her to the bone. Harriet had insisted that, posing as they were as servants, they could not take the Dorchester carriage.

Pru looked no more pleased, clad in a threadbare black cloak and a dress that might once have been green but had yellowed with far too many washes. Hers, at least, fell properly from the empire waist just beneath her breasts, though it, too, fell short of the tops of her boots.

"I don't see why this is necessary," Pru grumbled as they stamped their feet while waiting for someone to answer Harriet's knock on the servants' door. The servants' entrance was located around the side of the house where, if Katherine squinted, she could see the vague shapes of the ice sculptures still standing in the garden out back. The gravel walk was covered in a fresh layer of ice. Unlike with the front steps, this walk hadn't been freely salted to discourage falling. Katherine clung to Pru for balance.

"I already told you," Harriet answered over her shoulder. "The women would find speaking to an earl's daughter too intimidating. They'd never think she would believe their tale over that of a peer. Even if one of the servants would recognize your faces, they will never make the connection to who you really are in these clothes."

"We could have left Katherine at home."

Katherine straightened and tugged her arm away. "This is my investigation too, or had you forgotten?"

Pru merely shrugged, unconcerned and clearly uncomfortable.

Thankfully, the door was soon opened by a short, mousy woman who blinked often. "Harriet," she greeted, her voice as timid as her demeanor. "Are these the friends you spoke of?"

"Yes. Thank you for waiting for me, Peggy. We won't keep you from your duties long."

Peggy stepped aside, glancing nervously over her shoulder as she waited for the trio to enter Lady Dalhousie's manor. Once they did, she shut the door and announced, "Not here. We have too great a chance of being found out. Come upstairs."

Peggy led them up four flights of stairs and down a narrow corridor past a line of closed doors to a tiny room with a window no wider than Katherine's forearm. It was set into the slanted wall, gazing out into the sky dappled with clouds. The bed, neatly made, held the maid's nightgown, neatly folded on the white linen. Aside from the bed, there was little space to sit. In fact, once the door was shut, there was scarcely any place to stand. A short, narrow chest of drawers and a nightstand were the only other furnishings.

Peggy indicated for Harriet to take the bed. When she declined, Peggy perched on the edge herself. She paid no attention to Pru or Katherine.

Harriet stepped closer to the maid. "It's all right,

Peggy. Tell them what you told me. Tell them what you saw the night Lady Rochford died."

Instead of answering, the maid looked down at her hands. She wrung her skirts and worried her lower lip. "It might have been nothing. Thoroughly unconnected."

"Peggy." Harriet put her hand on her friend's shoulder. "Please. It might be useful."

After a few more rapid flutters of her eyelashes, Peggy looked at no one in particular and confessed, "I went up to fetch more candles for the ballroom, as we were running low, and her ladyship wouldn't much like it if her ballroom was doused in shadows."

Katherine exchanged a glance with Pru as she chose her words carefully. "Is that unusual?"

"Oh, no." Peggy shook her head. Strands of her hair clung to the side of her mouth. She didn't appear to notice.

The fact that she was so consumed by her own thoughts likely played in Katherine's favor. The house-maid glanced at the floor so often, it was a wonder she hadn't yet noticed that Katherine and Pru's dresses didn't quite fit.

After a moment spent clenching her fists tight in her skirts, Peggy continued, "But on my way to fetch the candlesticks, I spotted Lady Rochford's driver on the third floor of the house, in the same wing as she—" The maid shook her head, her cheeks draining of color. "He had no right to be there, but he's known for chasing the maids, so I gave him a wide berth and let him be. What if I..." Her eyelashes fluttered again, and Katherine saw a glint of what she thought was moisture.

"You did nothing wrong," she assured the distraught woman. "Even if Lady Rochford's driver had some hand in the murder—and that is by no means guaranteed—what do you think he would have done to a woman who got in his way? You did right."

"Even better by telling us," Pru added.

"How close was this to the time when Lady Rochford went over the balcony?"

Peggy worried her lip again. "I don't remember. I'm terribly sorry."

"It's fine," Harriet comforted. She patted the woman's shoulder again. "Take a moment and breathe. It'll come to you."

"Try not to think of the fall," Katherine advised. "You said you were going up to fetch candles. Lady Rochford hadn't fallen at that point, had she?"

"Dear Heavens, no." Peggy pressed a hand to her chest. "I remember when she did. I heard the scream."

"And where were you at that time?"

She blinked hard. "Upstairs, with an armful of candles. I dropped them and came running at the sound."

"Is that when you encountered Lady Rochford's driver?"

"No, that was on the way up. I didn't see anyone when I came down again. Except..."

When she paused, Katherine took a small step forward. She tried her best to look approachable. "Except for who?"

"No one... inside. But as I passed a window, I saw a figure exiting the servants' entrance, the one by which you entered."

"Did you recognize the person?"

Peggy shook her head. "I'm afraid not. It was too dark, and they had the hood of their cloak up. I think it was a woman—the cloak looked feminine. Black, but it had an ermine fur trim around the hood and hem. It wasn't the cloak of a serving girl."

"Did she go around to the front, where the drivers might have been waiting with the carriages?"

"I hurried down the stairs and didn't see where she went. The drivers all wait in the livery down the street, where it's warm."

Katherine frowned. If that was the case, then it was doubly odd for a driver to be found on the third floor of the house. What could Lady Rochford's driver have been doing here? Chasing skirts, like Peggy suggested, or something more sinister?

"Can you think of anything else unusual that you saw or heard that night?"

Wiping her eyes, Peggy shook her head. "No. I'm sorry. I knew I wouldn't be of much use."

Harriet squeezed the maid's shoulder. "You've been a wonderful help. Thank you. I'm going to sneak down to the kitchen to say hello to Gertie before I leave. I'll show us out, so you don't have to worry about manning the door."

Nodding, Peggy lifted her gaze toward Harriet and gave a watery smile. "Try not to be seen. Her ladyship is still bemoaning the ruin of her ice ball. I don't think she'd take kindly to knowing there were visitors in the house."

"We'll keep to servants' corridors," Harriet assured her.

As they bundled into the narrow corridor, Harriet warned with her eyes for them to remain silent. They would speak of their findings later. She shut the door, leaving Peggy in peace to collect herself. The moment the door was closed, Harriet whispered, "My friend in the kitchen, Gertie, saw someone as well. Since we're already here, you might as well hear the tale from her."

Katherine nodded. "Thank you, Harriet. I know you don't care for investigating. We appreciate the help."

With a small sigh, Harriet muttered to herself as she passed. "As if I could sit idly by with a murderer on the prowl."

Katherine frowned. Perhaps her enthusiasm for investigation was rubbing off on her maid too.

They retraced their steps through the house until they reached the door by which they had entered. From there, Harriet led the way down a marginally wider corridor toward the kitchen. The heat of the ovens soaked into Katherine's bones as she neared, a comfort. Unfortunately, Harriet stopped shy of the door. She shooed Katherine and Pru into the larder and promised to return shortly with her friend.

Pru whispered, "Are we looking at the driver now instead of the husband? Perhaps he pushed Lady Rochford on behalf of the baron."

Katherine shook her head. "It's suspicious for him to be in the house, I'll admit, but we mustn't jump to conclusions. I've done that before, and it's clouded my judgment."

"But it's worked out in the end. We need an angle, a suspect to investigate."

"And we'll have one," Katherine assured her. "But I must do this right, for Susanna's sake."

"Then how would you have us proceed?"

Katherine held up a finger. "First of all, by hearing what this friend of Harriet's has to say. It's possible the two tales will conflict horribly."

Pru frowned. "You mean the way Peggy's did? She all but announced that she thought Lady Rochford's driver to be the murderer then turned around and confessed to watching a woman flee the scene of the crime!"

"Peggy saw Lady Rochford's driver in the house. But how much time had passed between then and when she was pushed off the balcony? Peggy admitted that she can't recall. It might have been ten or fifteen minutes, for all we know, or it might only have been five. Unless someone else is willing to admit they saw him on the third floor, we cannot know for certain."

"And the woman fleeing the house?"

"She might be a suspect, but again, the timing is suspect. Peggy claimed she heard the scream and saw the woman out the window as she ran downstairs. Would there be enough time to push Lady Rochford and make it all the way to the servants' entrance in order to have been seen by Peggy?"

The ajar door swung open to reveal Harriet next to a motherly woman near her height. Harriet ushered her inside and shut the door behind them once more. "Gertie, these are the friends I was speaking to you about. I'd like you to tell them what you told me, if you'd please."

Rather than acting timid or upset at the prospect of confessing what she'd seen, the woman narrowed her eyes and studied Katherine and Pru from head to toe. She lingered near Katherine's ankles, where her stockings showed above her boots. The urge to cover herself was nearly overwhelming.

She met Gertie's gaze plainly.

"Your friends, you say?" the cook asked.

"I am her friend," Katherine declared. "We'll take only a moment of your time."

"You must be cold, dressed as you are. Did Harriet say you served at Dorchester House with her?"

Katherine gritted her teeth. From the corner of her eye, she noticed Harriet shift in place. She clasped her hands in front of her and spoke firmly. "I do not, but we've crossed paths there a time or two."

The grooves around Gertie's mouth deepened as she made a suspicious noise. "Your master cannot afford to give you new clothes?"

"I had a recent growth spurt. You know how it is, as long as it fits 'round the middle..." Katherine tugged on the material uncomfortably tight over her hips. "Harriet told me you saw something unusual the other night?"

For a moment, she feared that Gertie would keep whatever it was she had seen to herself. The woman's lips tightened, and her eyes narrowed as she studied Katherine once more as if to gauge whether she was trustworthy. Next to her, Pru tensed.

Katherine waited, trying to keep her stance relaxed and her expression open. Despite the nerves stinging beneath her skin, she didn't press Gertie further. Instead, she waited for the woman to reach her own conclusions.

At last, the cook admitted, "I saw a woman, cloaked, shortly after the time of the accident."

"A black cloak?" Pru asked, her voice loud.

Gertie frowned. "No. Royal blue. I'm quite certain. She passed by the light of the scullery as I was washing up. I saw her through the window."

Katherine asked, "Did you recognize her?"

"No," the cook answered after a moment's pause. "I never saw her face."

"The cloak, did it have ermine trim?"

Gertie's frown deepened. "No. Are you looking for someone in particular?"

Merely hoping to get the story straight.

This proved Katherine's earlier point on witnesses being unreliable. One woman saw a black cloak with ermine trim. One saw a blue cloak with no trim. Could be the maid imagined the trim or the cook didn't see it. Neither had seen the woman's face. Gertie undoubtedly had seen the person more closely, given that Peggy had glanced out a window on the second or third floor when she'd seen this fleeing figure.

Wait... "Is the scullery near the servants' entrance at the side of the house?"

"No. The scullery is near the back. Closer to the main street. The servants' entrance is on the side street." Clearly exasperated, the woman turned to Harriet. "Did you want to hear my tale or concoct your own? I don't have time for this. I have chores to be about."

As the woman turned and strode from the room, leaving the door open in her wake, Harriet opened her mouth.

"It's fine, Harriet. I trust she told us all she told you?"

The maid nodded.

"Then all we have to do is piece together the truth of the matter."

Pru frowned as she mulled over the problem. "I do

see what you mean about unreliable testimony. What color was the cloak?"

"I don't think it matters at the moment so much as the fact that two people have confirmed seeing a woman fleeing the scene of the crime."

"But... if she was seen coming out the servants' entrance and then going past the scullery, that means she didn't go toward the livery, because that is in the opposite direction. Where was she headed?" Harriet asked.

"Good question," Pru said. "Is this mysterious woman, whomever she may be, still our only suspect? We were told outright of the unusual presence of a man near the site of the murder at a time when he *could* have done it."

Katherine scouted to ensure that the corridor was clear before she whispered back. "We'll have to follow that lead as well. We can't afford to discount any of the clues."

"And Lord Rochford? Even if he wasn't specifically seen on the third floor, he might still have done it. His driver might have been scouting to ensure that he wasn't interrupted. They could be working together."

"It's possible," Katherine answered, her voice tight. "Let's wait and discuss this outside, where we won't be overheard."

Fortunately, the larder wasn't located far from the door they'd used to gain entry. Harriet led them there directly. Although they passed a young footman going about his chores, he didn't stop them. He merely nodded at Harriet and continued past.

Outside, Katherine gathered her cloak close around her shoulders and followed in Harriet's footsteps as they departed Dalhousie Manor and set out down the street. The sludge thrown by passing carriage wheels made for slick footing. As a carriage passed, she tried to pull her cloak around her ankles to save them from the spray. The cold flecks that splattered her stockings chilled her.

"So, what of the husband?" Pru asked when they reached the corner of the street. "Are we to interview him next?"

Katherine acknowledged, "It might be wise. Perhaps we can discover who in his household had driven the family to the ice ball that night. He might have more than one driver."

Harriet shook her head. "Baron Rochford has only one."

"How do you know?" Pru accused.

Pausing in her step, Harriet skewered her with a wry look. "I'm Lady Katherine's abigail. What do you think I do when she's at events? I wait with the drivers and the other ladies' maids." When Pru didn't question her further, Harriet turned to Katherine and continued to walk. "I know you well enough to know your next question. Yes, one of the footmen *could* conceivably have taken the driver's place for that evening. But Peggy's description of the man matches Rayner, the driver. He has a reputation with women."

Katherine frowned. "He's never given you trouble, has he?"

"Nothing I can't handle."

Katherine held her gaze for a moment more before nodding. Years ago, when Lyle had taught Katherine some defensive maneuvers in case she found herself in an undesirable situation, he had also instructed Harriet. Harriet had taken great pleasure in executing these moves on Lyle in the most precise and painful of manners. He had underestimated her. Katherine tucked away a smile at the memory.

"Very well. The driver is Rayner. If he's around Lord Rochford's home when we call, we can interview him as well."

A flicker of unease crossed Harriet's face. "I'll ask for you to question him without me present. We had a bit of a misunderstanding a few months ago, and as a result, he doesn't much care for me. I think you'd be more likely to discover the truth if you asked him yourself."

Katherine nodded. "We'll approach him on our own, then."

"Make sure you tell him you're Lord Dorchester's daughter. He won't give you any trouble then."

She frowned. "Is he so much of a predator?"

"Not a malicious one, like some. He wouldn't force a woman to accept his attentions, but he does make it abundantly clear when you've caught his interest."

Katherine almost hoped that Rayner was the murderer, simply so that by shutting him away, she would be able to save the women in Mayfair some grief.

"What do his womanizing ways have to do with the murder?" Pru asked. "Unless... Do you think Lady Rochford could have been having an affair with her driver?"

Pru seemed awfully attached to the idea that Lady Rochford had been unfaithful. If she had been the type, wouldn't Katherine's stepmother have mentioned it as a possibility as to the motive of her murder?

Katherine chose her words carefully. She didn't want to discount any theories without just cause, but she didn't want Pru to run off chasing flights of fancy, either. "It may be possible. Let's learn more of the situation before we dash to any conclusions."

Harriet flung out her arm, preventing them from crossing the street as a driver led a team of four at a quick trot. While she checked for further dangers, she said, "I think you're approaching this investigation the wrong way."

Pru scowled.

On the other hand, Katherine knew her maid to have a quick mind. What had she seen that Katherine had discounted? "What do you mean?"

"You're counting everyone as a suspect when there are several you can discount from the beginning. An entire ballroom watched Lady Rochford fall from the balcony. Who was among them? Was her husband? Was anyone conspicuously absent?"

Katherine couldn't recall where he'd been, only that he'd run out sometime after Lady Rochford fell. However, her breath hitched as she recalled that she *had* been looking for one man in particular. One man that she hadn't seen in the ballroom at the time of the death.

"Katherine?" Pru asked, touching her arm lightly. "You have that look about you, like you've thought of something. What is it?"

"There is one person I know was missing from the ballroom, but it can't be him."

"Who?"

Katherine took a deep breath before she admitted, "We couldn't find the Marquess of Bath at that time. His grandmother exited into the cold and was ushered inside by someone else. But he's a good man. I know he is."

Pru looked grim. "You said yourself we cannot discount any possibilities."

"Is he even acquainted with Lady Rochford?"

"There's only one way to find out," Pru announced. "We'll have to ask him."

CHAPTER SEVEN

"Will you be leaving the dog outside?" asked the butler as he peered down his long nose in the doorway of Lord Bath's townhouse in Mayfair. Since it was located a mere two blocks from Dorchester House, Katherine had taken the opportunity to walk Emma. She needed the distraction in case Grandma Bath should decide to take up the cause of matching her with Lord Bath.

"Thank you, I'll bring her inside with me. Lord Bath is acquainted with her. Is he at home?"

The butler, more ancient perhaps than Grandma Bath, shifted in place, though not a sliver of discomfort showed in his expression. Katherine swore she heard his bones creak.

"It is highly irregular for a woman to call upon my lord."

Katherine gritted her teeth. "What of Lady Bath, then? I'm sure she will love to see us."

The butler gave no outward indication that he had heard her speak. Not the twitch of a muscle betrayed his curiosity, but his eyes took on a gleam of interest. Katherine's instincts clamored, telling her that he wanted to know who the esteemed marchioness would be. However, it would be against proper decorum to question an earl's daughter on the matter. "Proper Decorum" appeared to be his middle name.

He glanced over her shoulder toward Pru.

"Miss Burwick is acting as my assistant in this matter. She is engaged to the Marquess of Annandale."

It was difficult to tell, given the miniscule changes in his expression, but Katherine thought that he looked a bit relieved.

Emma whined and pawed at the butler's polished boot. When he glanced down, stoic, she wagged her tail and tilted her head as if to show off her pink bow.

"Is Lady Bath at home?" Katherine asked again. She half feared this was a waste of time.

Fortunately, the butler took a small step back into the foyer and said, "This way. May I take your pelisse, milady?"

Katherine unbuttoned it quickly and handed it over. She followed suit with her muff and warm fur-trimmed jockey cap. As she undressed, Emma tugged on the leash, attempting to pull Katherine farther into the house. Fortunately, she had the lead firmly looped around her wrist. Emma wouldn't steal anything today, try though she might.

With his arms piled with their outerwear, the butler instructed a passing footman no more than fourteen years old to show them to the room where Grandma Bath awaited. The young man led them to a cozy parlor on the second floor. The walls, surprisingly plain, were an inoffensive shade of cream that matched the furniture. As Emma crouched to jump onto one pristine cushion, Katherine lunged to catch her, dropping the leash.

Her haggard footfalls trampled the footman's announcement of their arrival. Grandma Bath, standing over an enormous open trunk set beneath the window, turned just as Emma wriggled from Katherine's grasp and knocked into a delicate hip-high vase set next to the chair. Katherine tripped over her feet and landed on the floor. The vase thunked against her rear as it fell, unharmed. Her front and forearms smarted from the impact.

Grandma Bath let out a loud harrumph. "Still clumsy, I see."

Katherine sighed. By searching for certain clues in her investigations, she had garnered an unwarranted reputation for clumsiness. "I am not—"

Emma, concerned, trotted over and started licking Katherine's face. She clamped her lips shut to ward away her dog's tongue.

"Hugo, fetch Katherine a caudle from the kitchen to help her mend."

Warm wine mixed with egg yolks, honey and saffron? Katherine had never understood how that was supposed to fix her ailments. If anything, she expected it to *make* her violently ill.

Fending off Emma with one hand, she said, "No need. I'm fit as a fiddle. If someone will remove the vase from my backside so I don't break it, I will happily rise."

The footman performed that chore, but when she managed to get her feet beneath her after securing Emma's lead once more, she found the young man red in the face from contained laughter. A flush crept up her neck and into her cheeks, but she pretended not to be bothered.

"I know what will cure those lumps!" Grandma Bath turned and rummaged in the trunk. This close to the chest, Katherine peered over the old woman's shoulder and found that it contained shelf after shelf of carefully arranged stoppered bottles no bigger than her palm. Each appeared to have been unwrapped from the white handkerchiefs now wedged between the glass containers to ensure they didn't break.

Katherine tightened her hand on Emma's leash in case her dog decided one of these vials would make a tasty snack.

"Here you are! Drink this!" Grandma Bath beamed as she thrust one of the squat bottles into Katherine's hand.

It didn't *look* like a caudle. In fact, the clear liquid inside seemed harmless enough. She still didn't trust it.

"What is it?"

"Healing water from the springs, of course! You've been there, so you know the curative powers of our waters."

Katherine looked at the trunk, dubious. "Why do you have so many bottles?" If she had wanted to bring some of the waters from Bath, she could have done so in a single, larger container.

"I'm giving away the bottles as samples. Once more people know of the healing properties, they will flock to our grand city. Everyone will profit!"

Gingerly, Katherine held out the bottle. "Perhaps you ought not to waste it on me."

"Nonsense," Grandma Bath exclaimed overly loudly. Katherine fought back a wince. "We need you in tip-top shape if you're to find a match for Ernest. Drink up, now. Or would you prefer the caudle?"

Katherine broke the seal on the vial with her fingernail, removed the cork, and drank the lukewarm water. It didn't leave her with a magnificent feeling at its end, but it was a sight better than whatever caudle Grandma Bath cooked up. She handed over the empty bottle.

"I feel much improved," she lied.

"You see," Grandma Bath said, beaming. "I knew you would. Our waters are most helpful. Why don't you sit while you wait for the full effect?"

Half afraid of what the old woman would offer her if she did not, Katherine sat. When Emma tried to jump up onto the pristine divan next to her, she caught the dog in mid-lunge and turned her onto her back in her lap, dirty paws in the air. Emma squirmed, but when Katherine started scratching her exposed belly, the pug stilled.

Silent, Pru sat next to Katherine. Once Grandma Bath was settled, she sent the footman, Hugo, to the kitchen to fetch the tea service. The moment he vacated the room, she turned to Katherine with a gleam in her eye.

"Tell me, how goes the matchmaking endeavor? Are you here with good news?"

Good news? Surely she didn't expect for her grandson to have fallen head over heels in love during a single evening. Lord Bath was more practical than that. Not to mention, he seemed to have standards for his future wife that he hadn't yet shared with Katherine. How could she match him when she didn't yet know the sort of woman he desired?

Although Miss Verne, in her opinion, was a good contender.

"I'm afraid I don't have any news regarding match-making. I'd hoped to speak with Lord Bath this morning if he's at home. Your butler refused to say."

Narrowing her eyes, Grandma Bath harrumphed. "No news? Have you been making any attempt to match him at all?"

She'd only been hired three days ago! Katherine bit her tongue. "Of course I am—"

"Of course. I see your dilemma."

Although she was certain she would regret asking, Katherine rubbed her temple and said, "I beg your pardon?"

"You want Ernest for yourself. That's why you've

been dragging your heels when it comes to finding potential matches."

Pru snorted. "Oh, is that why? Katherine, you should have said something."

Katherine glared at her friend.

To her client, she said, "I am not dragging my heels. The events of the ice ball did not make an atmosphere conducive to falling in love."

Grandma Bath exchanged a glance with Pru. She didn't look convinced.

What did Katherine have to do? Paint a sign on her forehead reading *"I do not want to marry Lord Bath"*? She needed to match him with someone, anyone, as soon as possible. Grandma Bath didn't seem likely to practice patience.

But given that Lord Bath had been missing from the ballroom when Lady Rochford fell... Katherine battled her own conscience. History had proven that Lord Bath had a good heart and did things for the right reasons. But he also crossed lines that others would not. *Could* he have been responsible for Lady Rochford's death? Only if it had been an accident, and even then she didn't want to believe it could be so, as he would have confessed immediately.

"I'll find his perfect match," she vowed. "All I need is a little time to find a woman worthy of him."

Grandma Bath lifted her eyebrows. "You needn't look too far, my dear. I know someone with a sensible head on her shoulders."

Pru stifled a chortle behind her hand.

Katherine stepped on her foot. That cut off the sound of her mirth quickly.

Fortunately, Katherine was saved from further conversation on the topic when Hugo, the footman, returned. He carried the tea service in two hands, but on the corner of the tray was a piece of parchment held beneath the weight of an ink bottle and pen. He set the tea service down on the table.

"Here you are, milady. Abigail sent along the letter she was writing for you. She said that you wanted to have it out in this morning's post, but it's only half done, milady."

Grandma Bath frowned. "Is it? I thought I'd finished it. Can you read out what we've written already, Hugo?"

The young footman kept his gaze averted as he carefully picked up the letter. It was crosshatched over another letter, Katherine noticed, the new writing perpendicular to the old. The boy squinted as he tried to make out the script.

"Dear Jane," he read. "I pin... pine for ev-er-y-one dreed—drade—"

He seemed to shrink with every mistake he made in reading the letter aloud. Katherine set her pug on the ground, fisted the leash, and stood to read over his shoulder. "Dreadfully," she corrected, pointing at the word. "I know, those letters make an odd sound in some cases. They never seem to follow the rules."

His cheeks flushed with shame as he held the letter out to her. "Would you like to read it, milady?"

"Forgive me, it's not my place." She took a step back and bent to pat Emma, who basked in the attention. "If we caught you at a bad time, we'll be happy to continue on our way. I'd like to speak with Lord Bath, if he's in."

Once again, Grandma Bath ignored the request. "It won't take but a moment. Hugo is much improved since he first started in the household a year ago. Aren't you, son? I've been teaching him better reading and writing skills little by little. My eyes aren't what they once were, and I can't tend to my own correspondence. I do wish there was free education for everyone. I would see to arranging it in Bath, but I haven't the stamina or energy for such a time-consuming endeavor. Katherine, you seem the enthusiastic sort about reading."

Katherine straightened before the old woman somehow managed to appoint her the governess for all of Bath. "I'm afraid I haven't the time to linger. I must speak with Lord Bath. Is he in his study or at the club?"

For a moment, Grandma Bath's expression hardened. Emma whined, pawing at Katherine's ankle. The curve of the dowager's lips turned sly, and her half-lowered eyelids softened. "Ernest is in his study, tending to estate business. It's on the floor above us, overlooking the garden. But dear me, it looks as though Emma needs to take a walk. Miss Burwick, would you kindly see to that while Katherine conducts her business with my grandson?"

Katherine cursed under her breath. It was as plain as day that Grandma Bath conspired to arrange for Katherine to be alone with her grandson.

Pru would never fall for that trick.

As she crossed to the door, Pru plucked the leash from Katherine's hand and led Emma away. She had a twinkle in her eye as she called over her shoulder, "Of course, Lady Bath. I'll meet you out front in a moment, Katherine."

Tarnation, Prudence!

Fuming, Katherine gawked at the door, unable to formulate words.

"Would you like Hugo to show you the way?" Grandma Bath asked.

"Please." Katherine bit off the word. Even if Grandma Bath had ulterior motives in sending her to the study, Katherine needed to speak with Lord Bath and find out if he knew Lady Rochford.

The moment the young footman escorted her to the room in question and announced her presence, he left her there and shut the door. Katherine stared at the dark wood and stifled a sigh. *Is that necessary?* Grandma Bath must have whispered a word to him as they'd left, though how she'd managed it without Katherine hearing when she was more than halfway to deaf, Katherine didn't know.

"Katherine." Lord Bath greeted her warmly. As movement stirred at the corner of her eye, she turned to greet him. He neatened the pile of papers on his desk before he stood. "This is a surprise, I must admit. Has something happened to your father?"

Lord Bath must not have been expecting to entertain, for he was only half dressed in his shirtsleeves and waistcoat, no jacket or cravat around his throat. His wide cuffs were unbuttoned, flapping in the air as he straightened his desk.

"Nothing has happened to Papa. I came to visit your grandmother and thought I would come up to see you as well." Katherine tried to sound conversational, not wanting Lord Bath to know she was interrogating him. He wasn't actually a suspect; she just wanted to assure herself that he couldn't have done it.

"Well, it is lovely to see you although a bit unusual." His eyes narrowed. "Is my grandmother up to something?"

Katherine looked away. "No, not at all. Why do you ask?"

"It's just that she's been going on about finding a wife, and we did just attend the ice ball together…"

Either Lord Bath thought Katherine was interested in him, or he'd caught on to the fact that his grandmother had hired her to find him a wife. But the mention of the ice ball was a convenient segue into what she really wanted to ask him.

"Did you know Lady Rochford?"

"No," he said sharply, the word following close on the heels of her question. "Why would I? I'm rarely in London, save for Parliament sessions."

"Were you in the ballroom when she fell?"

"Yes. Yes, I was. Terrible thing. That scream. Ghastly."

"Indeed. I'm surprised that you let your grandmother rush out into the snow to witness it."

Lord Bath started. "You are? I mean… I didn't… I might have been in the loo or playing poker."

"Of course. Who can remember where they are

every minute?" Surely one would remember where they were when they heard a bloodcurdling scream. And if Lord Bath had been in the ballroom, he never would have let his grandmother rush outside. So why was he acting so cagey?

Yip!

The sound of Emma's bark drew Katherine's attention to the window. Outside, Emma tugged the leash in one direction while Pru tried to drag it another.

"Oh, you brought your adorable dog." Lord Bath squinted out the window. "And Miss Burwick. It does seem like she needs your assistance."

"I can see that," Katherine said. "I'd best be going."

Katherine gave the parlor on the floor below a wide berth as she hurried to collect her things from the butler and rejoin Pru, who was still in a tug of war with Emma.

Pru held the leash out to Katherine, glad to be rid of it. Katherine tugged and looked sternly at the pug. "Stop it."

Emma obeyed, and Katherine started down the street.

Pru hurried along beside her. "Well? What did he say?"

"I don't know if you deserve to know, being as you abandoned me to his presence alone."

Her friend chuckled. "Grandma Bath seemed so adamant. I didn't want to disappoint her."

"It wasn't funny."

"To the contrary, I'm highly amused." Pru glanced at Katherine. "So, tell me what you learned."

"Lord Bath was not in the ballroom. Though at first he claimed he was."

Pru frowned. "So he lied to lead you astray?"

"I'm not sure. He claimed he wasn't keeping track of exactly where he was at all times." At the corner of the street, Katherine paused. "Do you think he's capable of killing Lady Rochford? He told me he's never met her."

"I don't know," Pru said. "I'd like to think not. He dotes on his grandmother. He genuinely cares for his tenants. Would that sort of man resort to murder?"

"We don't know that the murder was premeditated. It might have been an accident."

"He said he didn't know her," Pru pointed out. "How could he push a stranger off a balcony by accident? It makes no sense."

She checked that the way was clear before she crossed the road, giving Katherine no choice but to follow.

The moment Katherine stepped alongside her

friend once more, Pru asked, "We need to discover the identity of this cloaked woman."

"I agree. Even if she isn't the murderer, she might have seen something and fled before she was noticed."

"And Lord Rochford," Pru added. "We can't forget him. It's almost always the husband."

For once, Katherine hoped she was correct. If so, Katherine might be able to tie this investigation in a neat little bow before it grew too dangerous.

CHAPTER EIGHT

K atherine adjusted the collar on her pelisse, wishing she'd thought to wear something with a hood. Her ears burned with cold. She and Pru had taken her father's coach to Lord Rochford's town-house. The driver, rather than wait, had deposited them at the door and rumbled off toward the shared livery at the corner of the street. None of the houses in this part of Mayfair was quite large enough to accommodate a livery on the grounds.

Using the large brass knocker, Katherine rapped on the door for a second time.

"Perhaps Lord Rochford isn't at home," Pru mused. It had been her idea to visit immediately, before afternoon waned into evening. She held the expensive posy of flowers that they had stopped along the way to purchase. They couldn't simply enter Lord Rochford's home and begin questioning him without pretense. Therefore, they had arrived under the guise of offering their condolences, using Katherine's tenuous connection between Lady Rochford and her stepmother.

"Even if he weren't at home, his butler would answer the door." Was something sinister afoot in the house?

Just as Katherine contemplated strolling along the perimeter and peeking into the windows to see for herself, the door was wrenched open by a haggard matron dressed in a smeared apron and simple frock. Her graying hair escaped her coif, flying around her face like a chaotic halo.

"May I help you?" she asked, her voice terse and her expression hard.

"I'm Lady Katherine, Lord Dorchester's daughter, and this is Miss Burwick. We're here to call on Lord Rochford and offer our condolences. Is he at home?"

Although Katherine was tall enough to peer over the woman's head and into the house, nothing she saw offered any explanation for why this person was answering the door rather than the butler. The foyer and corridor were neatly made up, with a single portrait of a beautiful, dark-haired woman that Katherine didn't recognize hanging on the wall.

"His lordship is not in a fit state to entertain, I'm afraid."

Drat, that put a damper on Katherine's plan.

"Are you certain? My family was friends of Lady Rochford's. My stepmother isn't fit to venture to offer her condolences personally, so she instructed me to pass them along for her. Sending a posy with a footman seemed too impersonal." Katherine hadn't told her stepmother of her plans to interrogate Lord Rochford, and she hoped Susanna had not already come to give condolences. That would be rather awkward indeed.

The woman stared at them for a long moment then stepped aside grudgingly. "I'll see if his lordship has raised himself far enough from his cups to see you. Wait here."

Katherine exchanged another glance with Pru. Left unattended in the foyer of a baron's home? A housekeeper that talked about her master being in his cups?

"This is highly irregular," Pru muttered.

Katherine couldn't agree more. Uncertain whether or not to unbutton her pelisse, she decided to keep it on in case they were summarily ejected onto the street.

She and Pru waited in silence, the only sound the rustle of their clothing as they shifted position.

A moment later, their patience was rewarded when the matron returned, looking defeated. "He's awake," she muttered under her breath. "Which is more than I can say for this time yesterday. I had to throw water on him to rouse him so he could tell his daughter the terrible news. Would he resign her to learning of the death of her stepmother in the news rag? She deserves the dignity of being told the news in person, not by letter."

A daughter? Katherine frowned. "Does his daughter not live here, then?"

The woman shook her head. "No, milady. She's Mrs. Dillinger now, grown and married, and thank Heavens too. She didn't need to see the way his lordship's second wife slowly wore him down. He was even in love with this one, can you believe?" She raised her gaze to the portrait on the wall, her gaze disapproving.

Lucky thing the housekeeper had a loose tongue. Katherine was shocked, as most servants never talked out of turn. If they did, her investigations would be so much easier. No more pretending to be a maid or cook so that they would gossip to her. Come to think of it, most barons never entertained in the bowels of the house, either. Apparently things at the Rochford house ran a bit differently than most. Tentatively, Katherine asked, "Was he not in love with his first wife?"

"Not near as much as he should have been. Lady Rochford was angelic!"

Interesting that she still referred to the baron's first wife as Lady Rochford, when the recently deceased Lady Rochford had held that title for years. Although it seemed that the servant had an unceasing loyalty to her first mistress, Katherine wanted to be certain. After all, the woman painted a very different picture of the most recent Lady Rochford than the one Katherine's stepmother had given.

"Was the second Lady Rochford a poor mistress?"

The matron's mouth twisted in distaste. Eventually, she admitted, "Not horrid. But she wasn't as gracious or kind as Her Ladyship. And she had no right to conceive."

Ahh, so Lord Rochford, and his entire household, *did* know about the baby. The driver likely knew about it too, then. If there had been an affair and the baby belonged to him, then perhaps he had argued with Lady Rochford...

Pru frowned. "Isn't that the aim of the wife of a lord, to provide him with an heir?"

Katherine raised an eyebrow at her friend. Pru was

soon to marry, but she didn't seem the type to remain in the bedroom or nursery for the rest of her days. She liked investigating too well. Still, Katherine supposed that didn't mean she wouldn't welcome a pregnancy... It was a matter between her and Lord Annandale, something that Katherine had no right to speculate about. They were a long way from marrying, in any case.

The matron scoffed, turning toward the corridor. "If it had been a boy, the baby would have inherited everything and robbed her ladyship's daughter of her rightful due. She is his heir, if you ask me, though the crown doesn't see it that way."

Katherine knew that well. If her new sibling was male, as her father and stepmother hoped, her father's title and estates would fall to him upon Papa's death. Katherine had known from the time she could walk that she would never inherit. She had her dowry, which Papa had already released to her on the merit of her solving the Pink Ribbon Murders, and that was quite enough for her.

Had Lord Rochford's daughter been allotted as hefty a dowry? Her father wasn't as rich as Papa, being a baron with less extensive estates than the earldom Papa managed. However, he had only one daughter to provide for rather than the five Papa had bequeathed dowries upon.

"If you're set on giving your condolences to his lordship, I suggest you don't tarry. It won't be long before he starts reaching for the brandy again."

Clearly, they weren't going to receive any more information from her. Katherine nodded stiffly and, with her pelisse still on, followed the woman down the corridor into a parlor.

It smelled to high Heaven in there. The cushions from the armchair had been thrown across the room. A vase lay smashed on the floor, flowers strewn all over the oriental carpet. Lord Rochford sat in that wing-backed chair, a brooding master. His hair was disheveled, the gray strands sticking up at odd angles. His weathered cheeks were covered in a thick layer of stubble. His jacket was absent; there was no sign of it in the room. He wore his waistcoat unbuttoned, and his shirt was pulled from his breeches. Katherine didn't want to contemplate the stains on the white linen. He was clearly a broken man.

"Lord Rochford?" Katherine said tentatively. "I'm Lady Katherine, Lady Dorchester's daughter. She sent me to give her personal condolences for this loss. The news has impacted her greatly."

Opening his eyes, the man passed a hand across his

chin before he waved a hand toward the settee to his left. He didn't even speak. Shoulders hunched inward, Pru scurried like a mouse and laid the posy of flowers on the table next to him, beside a tumbler with a sheen of amber liquid on the bottom.

Tentatively, Katherine perched on the edge of the settee, not too close. She breathed through her mouth, determined to make this quick. Pru settled next to her.

"My stepmother was devastated to hear of Lady Rochford, especially considering..." Katherine politely refrained from mentioning Lady Rochford's pregnancy outright.

He scraped his hands over his face, his hairy knuckles for a moment obscuring his eyes and muffling his voice. "Fate robbed me of two beloved members of my family in one fell blow. Oh, Celia. How am I to survive without her?"

Gently, Katherine asked, "Do you know why she was up on the balcony?"

"I haven't the foggiest notion." Emotion clung to his voice, tears he refused to shed. Wearily, he added, "She told me she had to visit the withdrawing room a moment. Perhaps the morning sickness—she got it in the evenings—sent her out of doors for a bit of fresh air. But why the balcony? Why not the garden? I guess she wanted the privacy." His voice caught, and his hands trembled, then he sobered for a moment. "Do you know they won't even give me her things. Said I had to wait. How cruel."

So the police had spoken to Lord Rochford. Apparently they hadn't let on that they suspected her death might not be an accident. But they also had not returned her belongings, so that must mean they were still investigating.

Despite the stench of brandy drifting from him, Katherine's heart clenched. It did appear as if he'd loved his wife dearly.

"Would anyone have accompanied her? Her maid or a footman, perhaps?"

Or her driver?

Katherine didn't want to paint Lady Rochford in an adulterous light. Besides, they didn't yet know that she had been unfaithful. Or that it was with the driver. Perhaps his presence in the house was entirely unrelated.

"I don't know. She would have had to send for her maid, but I don't know if she would have. Celia was so independent, she insisted she didn't need help with simple tasks. Most days she fashioned her own hair if she didn't plan to leave the house."

So her maid wouldn't have followed her around with a bourdaloue, a small ceramic cup for her to relieve herself into. But that still didn't explain why the driver, Rayner, had been found in the house.

Lord Rochford looked on the precipice of falling apart, and Katherine couldn't ask any more questions without raising suspicion. Taking pity on him, Katherine said, "Forgive me for bringing up such horrible memories. My deepest condolences to you, sincerely. I'll show myself out."

He made no move to stop her from leaving, so she stood. Pru gave her a sharp glance but followed without a word. They traversed the empty corridor in silence. Only once they'd exited into the bitter cold did Pru hiss a protest. "You didn't ask him whether or not he knew of anyone who might wish her harm."

"The family doesn't know that anyone considers this to be a murder. From what Lord Rochford said, the police have kept Celia's things, but he didn't mention that they'd told him foul play was suspected. We must tread carefully to ensure that it remains that way. We don't want rumors of murder to get out. Let the killer think they got away with it, and they may make a mistake. Besides, the servant who answered the door was rather helpful."

"She appeared to hate Lady Rochford, if you ask me."

"Yes. The first such person we've come across. She

seemed afraid that Lord Rochford's daughter would be robbed of her inheritance if Lady Rochford carried the baby to term."

"Lord Rochford's daughter won't get a penny of it, anyway," Pru countered. "I have no doubt that Lord Rochford has a cousin somewhere waiting for him to cock up his toes so he can inherit. I had no notion that he had a daughter, which means he hasn't gotten the crown's permission to bequeath his estates to his daughter when he passes by special remainder. If there's no heir, the crown will seize everything."

It was a sorry truth. Katherine frowned as they continued walking toward the livery. She held her hands over her ears to warm them. "You seem well versed in inheritance law."

"My father is dead," Pru pointed out. "I'm his only child. I know precisely the plight Mrs. Dillinger will face when her father perishes."

Katherine paused in mid-step. "Did the crown seize your family's holdings?"

"They would have if Papa had been the earl. He has an older brother. My uncle dictates our allowance now. Papa never touched Mama's dowry, so she'll bequeath it to me upon marriage."

"That's unnecessary. I'm certain Lord Annandale has more than enough money."

Pru nodded. "Undoubtedly, but he might not have looked twice at a woman who had nothing. Besides, Mama says it's good for me to have some money of my own, in case the worst should happen."

For all that she drove her daughter mad with the way she insisted on controlling the wedding, clearly Mrs. Burwick loved her daughter. She wanted what was best. Even if she mistakenly thought that to be atrocious buttons on her wedding gown.

Katherine touched Pru's arm. "You and Lord Annandale will have a long, happy life together. I'm certain of it."

Pru smiled weakly. "I'll have to remember to stay away from balconies, then, won't I?"

They continued walking. Pru wrapped her arms around herself and glanced back at the house. "What now? I truly expected the murderer to be Lord Rochford, but he seemed so distraught."

Katherine pointed to the livery. "Now we interview the Rochford driver, Rayner."

They reached the livery shortly, and none too soon. Despite the hands clapped over her ears, her skin burned from cold. The braziers in the stables provided some measure of warmth to chase away the icy temperature.

The moment he spotted her, the Dorchester driver

jumped up from where he was playing cards with two other men, one of them presumably Rayner. "Forgive me! I thought someone would ring for me to ready the horses."

Katherine waved her hand. "Don't worry yourself. I wanted to visit the livery so I might see the Rochford carriage. I spotted it the other night at Lady Dalhousie's house. Who is the driver?"

A handsome man with a slightly crooked nose stepped up and bowed. "That would be me, my lady. How may I serve you?"

Katherine drew herself up. "I'd like to see the carriage, please. I'm looking into purchasing one of my own, and I couldn't help but admire the shape." Though a convenient excuse, it also had a ring of truth. Once Katherine had her own townhouse, she would need her own carriage.

The driver, Rayner, led her and Pru down the line of stalls toward the conveyances parked in the rear of the building. Although Katherine's driver levied a suspicious glare at Rayner as they departed, he didn't follow. They had some modicum of privacy for Katherine to ask her questions.

As they reached the carriage in question, a tall coach with wheels that reached just below her shoulder, Katherine pretended to admire the fancy vehicle.

Although she would need a carriage, she cared more for the functionality than aesthetic appeal.

Rayner ran his hand along the side of the conveyance slowly. "I'm sure this will meet with your delicate feminine sensibilities."

Pru balled her fists. She looked as though she wanted to strike all notions of feminine sensibilities out of Rayner's head. Katherine couldn't much blame her, but they needed information, not violence. She stepped between her friend and the driver.

"It was much to Lady Rochford's taste, was it?"

"It was indeed. Closed from prying eyes, doesn't jostle the passenger unduly... unless you crave that sort of thing."

Was he leering at her? Katherine gritted her teeth, resolving not to strike the man herself. Certainly he couldn't entertain the notion that she'd made up this excuse to be alone with him! Well, she had, but certainly not for a salacious visit.

Now Katherine understood precisely why the maids in the Dalhousie house feared to be alone with him. He was a predator, and it seemed one that overstepped his bounds. But she needed information, which meant that however dearly she wanted to put him in his place, she must refrain.

She feigned innocence at his intentions. "Such a

terrible thing happened to Lady Rochford the other night. Were you nearby when it happened?"

"Nearby?" He stiffened. His demeanor changed in an instant from flirtatious and accommodating to closed off. That, if nothing else, told Katherine that he was keeping a secret he didn't want to tell. "I was with the carriage, as was my place."

"But surely you might have been able to see the garden?"

"No." His voice was hard. "All the carriages were lined along the front drive, to keep as many as possible from blocking traffic on the road. I learned of the tragedy only when a footman was dispatched to call me forth."

"Is that so?" Pru asked from over Katherine's shoulder. "Why, then, did I hear word that you were inside the house, trying to seduce one of the maids?"

Rayner crossed his arms. The hardness in his eyes mirrored his posture. "You must have been mistaken. I wouldn't shirk my duty."

To keep them from coming to blows—or worse—Katherine linked her arm through her friend's and led her away. She ended with a sharp but polite, "Thank you for showing us the carriage. We must be off."

"But—"

Pru didn't know when to end an interrogation.

Leaning closer, Katherine lowered her voice to a hiss. "Let it be. You'll draw suspicion."

Her friend pulled a face. "We shouldn't have to deal with this nonsense of having to hide the investigation in the first place."

"In an ideal world, we wouldn't. But at the moment, our only advantage is that the murderer thinks himself safe because the death is thought to be an accident. Let's not reveal our cards before we're ready."

Pru's mouth puckered, but she said nothing more as they approached their driver, who was busy readying the horses for their drive home. Once he and another hostler fetched the pair to the carriage, Pru leaned forward and said, "Do you think the driver might have killed Lady Rochford? We have witnesses placing him in the house. Now I'm not sure who I suspect more, the driver or the husband."

"Rayner is clearly hiding something." With a smile, she reassured her friend, "Never you fear. Whatever it is, we will discover his secret. In the meantime, there is one other person that might have information we can use. Lord Rochford's daughter."

CHAPTER NINE

B y the time Katherine and Pru had toured Hyde Park once, the crisp edges of snow crunching beneath Emma's eager footsteps, Katherine had begun to suspect that the information Harriet had provided was false. Normally she wouldn't suspect the gossip Harriet gleaned to lead them awry, but they had scoured Hyde Park for an hour. If Mrs. Dillinger took to walking her dog here every morning at half eight, they had certainly missed her. By Katherine's estimate, it was now after nine in the morning.

"Perhaps we should call on her like we did her father yesterday."

"That would be a very poor idea. We have no connection to Mrs. Dillinger. I've never even seen her." The only means she had for recognizing such a woman was by the description of her person and the hope that should their dogs cross paths, they would be able to exchange introductions. Thus far, in the crisp winter air, they hadn't crossed paths with a soul. It was as though Hyde Park lay in a pocket of deathly silence. If not for Pru, Katherine might have found it too eerie to traverse alone.

"We must do something," Pru said between gritted teeth. She rubbed her hands up and down her arms despite the thickness of her cloak. "Something other than walk in circles. I feel as though my nose is going to fall off."

Katherine shoved her hands deeper inside the ermine muff, the leash dangling out the end. She'd borrowed the muff from her stepmother. The ermine matched Susanna's cloak, a cloak likely similar to that which Peggy reported having seen. Though given what they'd heard from the cook and Peggy's nervous condition, Katherine was suspicious she actually did see a woman in an ermine-trimmed cape. However, it would be very convenient if Mrs. Dillinger showed up wearing one.

"Perhaps we'll get more information and try again tomorrow. If Harriet can discover her usual route or the gate by which she enters or leaves, we can arrange to cross paths with her."

"We should have done so today," Pru grumbled.

Privately, Katherine agreed. However, she had only thought to do such a thing after they had entered Hyde Park. She'd forgotten how large it was.

A tremendous bark shook the air, making Emma's hackles rise. She shrank back, searching for the source as Katherine turned to do the same. A grey Irish wolfhound burst from the crux of the paths, a leash strained tight as it pulled a harried woman behind. With every ground-eating step, she dug in her heels. The hood of her cloak fell across her face, obscuring her expression as she was inexorably pulled nearer. The dog gave another shattering bark.

"Bonbon, no! Stop! They don't care to make your acquaintance."

Although the woman's shout was breathless, having little effect on her pet, Katherine recognized it instantly. Elizabeth Verne seemed flustered and not at all herself. Katherine bit back a smile, knowing full well what a handful Emma could be when she had a mind to misbehave. She could only imagine the effect when amplified by one hundred pounds.

Lest her pug get the idea to run or trip them in the leash, Katherine leaned down to snatch her off the ground. Emma's small legs kicked through the air as she twisted to look the wolfhound in the eye. She growled, her hackles stiff. Apparently, she hadn't yet noticed the hound's vigorously wagging tail.

As the wolfhound slowed to meet them, Elizabeth regained control over her pet and drew herself up. "Sit," she said with the approximation of a harried schoolteacher.

The hound whined, ears back, as it looked over its shoulder at her.

She transferred the leash to one hand and used the other to point at the ground.

Mere feet away from them, the wolfhound turned to give them a forlorn look before it sat.

"Stay," Elizabeth added, a note of warning in her voice. When the hound didn't look in danger of running amok, she straightened her cloak and cast them an apologetic look. "I'm terribly sorry. She's friendly, I promise. A bit too friendly, if I'm honest." As she finally seemed to look up to see who stood in front of her, her eyes widened. "Oh, Katherine!"

Katherine held up her hand, hoping to stall whatever apology would fly from the other woman's lips next. Emma squirmed in her other hand, wanting to be let down. "Is she friendly toward other dogs?"

"Oh, yes," Elizabeth answered, nodding vigorously. However, she also tightened her hold on the leash, as if she feared the wolfhound would fly beyond her control once more. "She adores making friends."

Deciding to take her at her word, especially after the wolfhound began thumping her tail so vigorously against the ground that Katherine felt the vibrations even through the packed snow, Katherine set Emma on the ground. "Go say hello, girl."

Emma seemed tentative, but once the wolfhound had stopped making the air ring with her barks and no longer strained to get nearer, she had stopped growling. After a moment of strained silence, Emma grew curious and took a step closer. The wolfhound's tail waved so vigorously that a plume of flakes billowed from the ground. Elizabeth wrapped the lead around her wrist.

"Gentle," she cautioned her gargantuan dog.

This time, Bonbon behaved as Emma inched nearer. She leaned her head down to sniff noses with Emma. When the pug seemed satisfied enough to give a little wag, the wolfhound decided to investigate the pug's short tail more vigorously.

Katherine relaxed marginally, thankful that the pair didn't seem to be at odds. Emma was usually well behaved among other dogs, but with her reaction to the wolfhound's introduction, she had been cautious.

She turned her attention to Elizabeth. "What a surprise to find you here. A pleasant one, I might add."

Elizabeth grimaced, but she hid the impolite expression behind a gesture to adjust her hood once more. "Bonbon gets... overly excited when she smells another dog. I thought it best to walk her early, before anyone else thought to rise."

At the very time Mrs. Dillinger usually walked her dog. Katherine pursed her lips. "Are we the first people you've encountered?"

"With dogs? Yes." Now that the pair had finished their introductions, Elizabeth shortened the leash and stepped closer. "I did happen across a robust old man, who informed me he does ten tours of the park every day, rain or shine."

Ten? That seemed excessive given its size, but Katherine decided not to comment. She turned, beckoning Elizabeth forward. "Pru and I were about to take our leave of Hyde Park. Would you like to walk with us toward the gate?"

"Of course," Elizabeth said brightly. She fell into step on Pru's far side and said to her, "I don't believe we've had much opportunity to talk. How was your dress fitting the other day?"

A bit too far away to add to the conversation without effort, Katherine contented herself with listening. It didn't escape her notice that Elizabeth had chosen to separate the two dogs.

She attended to the conversation with only half an ear as she assessed Elizabeth's capabilities. Gracious, beyond a doubt, and skilled in diplomacy for immediately striking up a conversation with Pru to cover the fact that she was separating Emma from Bonbon, minimizing the risk of something amiss occurring. Both were excellent qualities in a potential marchioness, not to mention that Lord Bath had always seemed particularly fond of Emma. His adoration of dogs boded well for matching Elizabeth with him.

If Katherine still intended to match him. She didn't believe him capable of murder, but...

As they passed through the Queen's Gate onto Kensington Road, a shadow detached from a building across the road. Several carriages and carts trundled past, necessitating that the lanky figure, bundled in a greatcoat, pause for the conveyances to pass. Eventually, he reached their side of the street and unwound the scarf around his cheeks far enough for Katherine to identify him.

Mostly. One side of his face sported a mottled blue bruise. It looked fresh.

Katherine nearly dropped Emma's leash in her alarm. She fumbled for it. "Lyle, what happened?"

He shrugged, the movement making him wince. "Some excitement on shift, that's all. I came by Dorchester House as soon as I could extract myself from the matter. Harriet suggested I might find you here."

Katherine nodded. Then, noticing Elizabeth's curious glances, she recalled that the woman would have no notion of who Lyle was. "This is Lyle Murphy, one of Sir John's Men who operate out of Bow Street. Lyle, this is Miss Elizabeth Verne, a friend."

"Nice to meet you," Elizabeth said politely.

Lyle returned the greeting with an inclination of his head. Judging by the flush creeping up his neck, he had succumbed to his usual tendency to become tongue-tied in the presence of a beautiful woman.

Luckily, Elizabeth didn't linger. "Thank you for the company, but I fear I must take Bonbon home before she decides to chase some other poor, hapless creature. Good day."

Murmurs of goodbyes echoed hers as she turned to leave. Only once she was out of earshot did Lyle turn to Katherine. "Harriet said you were searching for a Mrs. Dillinger?"

"Yes. She is Lord Rochford's daughter." Had Lyle seen her? "I hear she bears a strong resemblance to her father. Tall, though not quite as tall as me or Pru, brown hair, a curvaceous figure. Harriet told me she walks her dog every morning at half eight. Have you seen her?"

Lyle's mouth puckered, pulling the bruise on his cheek tight. He winced. "Yes, I believe I have. A woman matching that description ventured to Bow Street to fetch her husband, Mr. Dillinger." He frowned. "Perhaps I digress. The excitement of last evening was in finally uncovering the location of an illegal pugilists' ring, in no small part thanks to the contributions of your father these past weeks. Last night, we descended en masse to arrest the lot. I spent half the night interrogating those arrested in an attempt to discern which were the leaders and which the spectators." Raising one eyebrow in an expression of chagrin, he gestured to his face and added dryly, "The fighters were self-evident, as you can see."

"You must be exhausted," Katherine exclaimed. "Whyever did you come to see me? I value your help, but I'd rather you were abed."

"The entire endeavor still has me flushed with energy. I'd hoped to tire myself by applying myself to the suspicious death."

"The murder," Pru corrected, propping her hands on her hips. "And didn't you say we could find Mrs.

Dillinger at Bow Street? We must depart at once before she slips away."

"Not much chance of that," Lyle answered, weary. He rubbed his forehead. "Last I left her, she was making a fuss at Bow Street in an effort to have her husband released. He was one of those arrested at the pugilist match, but we haven't yet been able to determine if he was a leader or a spectator. Given how soused he was when we brought him in, I imagine that it was the latter, but we must be thorough. It will be at least an hour before he is released."

When Pru continued to glare, he raised his hands in surrender. His gloves left an inch of skin showing between the hem and the cuff of his greatcoat. He must be as cold as ice. How long had he been waiting near the gate?

"Let us return to Bow Street, if you're so adamant." He looked as though the very notion threatened to drain the energy from him.

Katherine reached out to touch his arm, offering her support. "Don't worry, we'll take the carriage rather than walk. And I'll inform you of the latest developments in the case along the way. Thank you."

He returned her smile with a nod of gratitude. "You know I'm happy to help you in any way I can."

THE COURTS at Bow Street were housed in a grand three-story brick edifice with doors facing the corner of the street. The carved façade loomed over Katherine, Pru, and Lyle as they entered by the heavy, plain wooden door. Inside, the lobby housed myriad concerned citizens begging for the release of their loved ones.

Mrs. Dillinger, haranguing a harried-looking clerk, was easy to spot. She shared characteristics not only with her father's proud bearing and build but also with the delicacy of her mother's features that Katherine has espied from the portrait hanging in Lord Rochford's foyer. Her mouth twisted in distaste, Mrs. Dillinger turned away and stormed toward a seat in the corner of the room. Although two other women stood nearby, they took small steps away from Mrs. Dillinger and whispered quietly.

Lyle pointed a finger at the woman in question. "There she is."

The best way to uncover motive was to question Mrs. Dillinger, but how to go about it? As a friend, perhaps?

Pru pursed her lips. "I can't fault her for wanting to see her husband freed."

"Maybe I can endear us to her by discovering the state of the investigation regarding her husband. He wasn't particularly coherent when I questioned him earlier. Perhaps he's sobered up," Lyle offered.

Katherine nodded. "Good idea. Let's introduce ourselves."

As they crossed the room, the other occupants gave them curious looks. However, they must have been found lacking any form of titillation, for Katherine soon found herself ignored. She wasn't unhappy to see the loiterers returning to their conversations. The only person to whose attention she wished to recommend herself was Mrs. Dillinger.

Fortunately, the woman's behavior had cleared several seats nearby for Katherine and Pru to occupy. They chose the ones on either side of their suspect.

She, on the other hand, only had eyes for Lyle. She narrowed them, her lip curling. "You."

"I'm not here to antagonize," he said quietly.

"Then leave."

Katherine sat taller. "Madam, perhaps you ought to listen to him. He is an officer of the court."

"He's a filthy Bow Street Runner who looks to rip a man from his wife for profit!"

Although Katherine—and, undoubtedly, Lyle—had met with some prejudice when informing others that her dearest friend worked on Bow Street, she had never come across someone so vile. Lyle, on the other hand, didn't bat an eyelash. His demeanor stiffened, his shoulders thrust back in the customary way he approached suspects. His expression looked as stiff as a mask, but the eyes were far less cold than he likely intended. If Katherine were to hazard a guess, she would say he was hurt by the woman's unfounded accusation.

"He can help you," Pru snapped. "But he won't lift a finger on your behalf if you continue to insult him."

Mrs. Dillinger gnashed her teeth. Her eyes filled with a film of water a moment before she blinked it away. With the way she clenched her hands, Katherine half expected her to darken the bruise on Lyle's cheek.

Instead, she loosened her hold and said, "If I was wrong, then I beg forgiveness. I overstepped." She looked between Katherine and Pru, avoiding Lyle's gaze. "All I want is to be reunited with my husband so I can go home. I've been here far too long."

Lyle nodded, his movement stiff. "I'll speak with my colleagues and inquire as to the status of your husband."

"Thank you." Despite his help, Mrs. Dillinger still refused to look at him. "His name is Roger Dillinger."

That, Lyle already knew. He turned on his heel

and entered a door leading deeper into the building, offering a nod to the clerk along the way. Katherine envied him the ability to leave.

Perhaps she is grieving. After all, everyone grieved in their own way. Lord Rochford had fallen deep into his cups. Mrs. Dillinger might choose to hide behind her hatred. But if so, she could prove a valuable asset. A woman who suspected others of wrongdoing might be able to point them toward other suspects. For Susanna's sake, Katherine didn't want to overlook any possible angle in this investigation.

At all costs, she must prove that she could solve this murder.

"Dillinger... You wouldn't, by chance, be related to Lord Rochford, would you?"

Mrs. Dillinger stiffened. She cast Katherine a wary glance from the corner of her eye. "And if I am?"

"If you were, I would offer my condolences over the loss of your stepmother. Such a terrible tragedy."

Mrs. Dillinger looked down at her hands, now folded neatly on her lap. "Thank you."

"I hope your father is well. I'd heard he was rather broken up about it."

Mrs. Dillinger glanced sharply at Katherine. "Of course he was."

"Were you at Lady Dalhousie's ice ball with them?"

Mrs. Dillinger straightened in her chair. "I was at home that night."

"With your husband?" Pru asked helpfully.

Mrs. Dillinger shook her head, her shoulders slumped inward in defeat. "My husband was out at one of the pugilist matches. Last night wasn't the first he attended. He has a... taste for them."

Color stained her cheeks, almost as if she was embarrassed to admit the fact.

"Too bad. It might have been nice if you were there to comfort your father." Katherine lowered her voice and added almost as if to herself, "I wonder what she was doing up on that balcony."

Mrs. Dillinger tsked. "I would have no idea."

"I imagine she stepped out for fresh air. Maybe after an argument—seems she must not have been paying attention to fall over the railing—and, of course, your father did not accompany her."

A furrow formed in Mrs. Dillinger's brow. "Why are you asking all these questions about my stepmother? Do you not share everyone's belief that her death was an accident?"

"Of course we do," Katherine assured Mrs.

Dillinger. "If the authorities have ruled it an accident, far be it from me to disagree."

As far as Katherine knew, the authorities hadn't ruled it as anything yet, but apparently Mrs. Dillinger didn't realize the investigation was ongoing.

Unfortunately, her questions seemed to have aroused Mrs. Dillinger's suspicions. Looking concerned, she asked, "You don't think it was a *murder*, do you?"

"No... I... "

Mrs. Dillinger carried on in a quiet, willful voice. "If you're looking at my father, you'd best look somewhere else. He adored Celia down to his marrow. It was sickening the way she used him, but he never saw a single flaw. Besides, Papa isn't the sort to resort to violence to solve his problems... even if she didn't appreciate his kindness enough not to stray."

Katherine glanced at Pru. Apparently Mrs. Dillinger had no qualms about bad-mouthing her stepmother to strangers. She might as well dig further. "Do you mean to imply that your stepmother was unfaithful?"

Mrs. Dillinger drew herself up again. "I suspected she was. I'm not sure if father knew."

At that moment, the door leading farther into the building opened. Lyle walked out, accompanying Mr.

Dillinger. The man must have been officially deemed a spectator and not a leader of the match. The moment Mrs. Dillinger espied her husband, she dashed up to greet him, snatching a scarlet cloak from the seat behind her.

Lyle met Katherine and Pru halfway across the room, not far from where Mrs. Dillinger greeted her husband with worried queries as to his health and treatment. When Lyle rubbed a hand across the reddish stubble lining his jaw, he looked weary to the bone.

"Did you discover anything?"

"She doesn't believe her father killed his wife," Pru answered, her voice dismissive.

Katherine raised a finger, beckoning them toward the exit before she resumed the conversation. "Or maybe she does and was trying to persuade us otherwise. It seemed like once she thought we were trying to imply it wasn't an accident, she got a bit defensive of her father."

"She was the one to tell us of Lady Rochford's unfaithful behavior," Pru reminded her. "That, if anything, only points toward Lord Rochford as the suspect, especially if his wife was with child."

"That was after I brought up the question of why she was on the balcony. We already know she was expecting," Katherine answered. "What we don't know is whether or not the child was his. I'd rather not suspect one of my stepmother's friends of infidelity, but if what Mrs. Dillinger told us is indeed true, then we might have stumbled upon a motive after all. We had had some inklings of infidelity before this."

Pru nodded. "Oh, yes. With her driver, wasn't it? He had appeared to be hiding something..."

"We won't know for certain until we discover what that something was."

As they exited the courts, Pru suggested, "We shouldn't discount Mrs. Dillinger, either. If she suspected her stepmother was unfaithful, she may also have suspected she was with child. Not to mention she was accompanying her to the seamstress to have her dresses let out. Mrs. Dillinger may not have wanted a stepbrother to inherit."

"Why not? She couldn't inherit it, and besides, she has a scarlet-red cloak. I think someone would have seen."

Pru raised her eyebrows as Katherine hailed the Dorchester carriage waiting down the street. "She may have thought she could inherit, or maybe something is in the works. And a woman can own more than one cloak, Katherine."

CHAPTER TEN

"Do I look all right?" Pru asked as she smoothed down the front of her understated buttercup-yellow dress for the twentieth time.

Katherine assessed her from the mirror on her vanity, where Harriet was busy with her hair. "You look smashing."

Pru didn't seem inclined to accept compliments at the moment. She fiddled with the cuffs of her gloves. If she continued on like that, she would tear them to shreds before the evening began.

The sole reason Katherine had accepted Pru's invitation to accompany her to the opera was in order to prevent such nervous behavior. Lord Annandale had returned to town after his extended journey, and Pru was fretting herself apart at the seams. They needed a distraction.

"So. She had a lover," Katherine said, referring to the murder investigation.

Harriet stopped with her hands in Katherine's hair and hairpins sticking out of her mouth. "Lady Rochford had a lover? I hadn't heard that. I wonder if Lady Dorchester knows."

"Let's not ask," Katherine begged. "At least, not yet. She's grieving enough over her friend, and I don't want to upset her into—" She sealed her lips shut a moment before she spilled the news that her step-mother was pregnant. Harriet was quite the gossip with the rest of the household, and Susanna had begged her to wait until the official announcement.

"Into?" Harriet asked with a coy raise of her eyebrows that made Katherine suspect she already knew. News travelled fast among the servants.

Still, she refused to divulge the information, just in case. "Knowing that Lady Rochford might have had a lover means little if we cannot identify the man."

"Which is precisely why we should ask Lady Rochford's friends. If her husband doesn't know, perhaps one of her friends had some inkling."

When Katherine didn't answer, Pru crossed to stand next to her, arms akimbo.

"The lover might be the killer, you know."

"It's possible," Katherine conceded.

"If the child was his and he didn't want that knowledge spreading..."

Katherine pursed her lips as Harriet put the last few pins into place. She felt as though she could walk through a windswept moor and not a hair would come loose.

"I don't know if I agree with that theory. Her husband, who would have to either publicly claim the child as his heir or denounce him and his mother altogether, seems to have a stronger motive."

Pru pointed a finger at Katherine's reflection. "You are the one so adamant that his grief is genuine and not born of guilt."

So she was. Each suspect they pursued left her more confused. Perhaps the next would offer some clarity. They didn't have the full picture yet, and until they did, speculating was just that—guesswork.

"All set," Harriet said. She stepped back with a smile. "Now, let's add a dress to those underclothes, or you'll scandalize the breadth of London. What do you say to your new pink dress?"

Katherine turned on the stool, wrinkling her nose as she followed Harriet's progress to the wardrobe. Emma, taking the movement to indicate that playtime was about to resume, hopped down from the bed, her tail wagging.

"I'd say you are a great deal fonder of pink than I am."

The ribbon around Emma's neck attested to that much. As the pug reached Katherine's calf, she rubbed her neck against Katherine as if to add her agreement to the conversation. Katherine leaned down to scratch beneath the ribbon in case it itched.

"Choose a gray or beige."

Harriet looked as though she'd rather chew off her arm. "Lady Katherine, you're going to the opera! If I were going, I'd want to look my best."

"I shall look my best. In the gray or beige."

Pru chuckled. "I can't believe I ever asked you for fashion advice. You'll fade into the walls next to everyone else."

That was the point.

"What of the lavender instead?" Harriet begged. "You'll still look as though you're mourning your squandered youth, I promise."

Katherine bolted to her feet. "I am not mourning my youth! I'm only twenty-five. I'm still young."

Pru attempted to hide a fit of giggles and failed. When Katherine turned to glare at her, too, she asked, "When will I ever convince you to dress fashionably?"

Katherine didn't attempt to claim she did so now. "Never," she vowed. "I'm perfectly content presenting myself the way I do. I have no need to peacock."

"You are pretty," Harriet agreed, "but you would look even more splendid if you wore something to complement your complexion."

"And don't you dare say green," Pru added.

The pair were worse than a gaggle of geese with the way they cackled. Katherine chewed on the inside of her cheek to keep her expression even. She did *not* look sallow in green, despite what Pru seemed to think. In fact, she'd gotten a compliment once when she'd worn that color.

From Captain Wayland. A man who, despite his seemingly good intentions, had managed to finagle his way into her past two investigations under the guise of helping. Although he had proven helpful, she didn't trust him. Papa had always been at odds with him, something about his methods for solving crimes. Katherine hadn't found any such distasteful methods, but she trusted her father implicitly. Wayland must be hiding something.

Which was why, his good opinion of her green dresses or not, she was happy that he had made himself scarce during this investigation. She didn't need his interference.

Harriet dangled a delicate lavender dress in front of her. With the short sleeves, it was better suited to summer than it was to winter. However, Katherine decided to admit defeat. She doubted that either woman would let the subject rest unless she made some small concession.

"It's very thin," she said cautiously, testing her theory. "I'll be cold."

"You have gloves that will reach almost to your nose, and you're wearing thick enough undergarments that a few brisk moments in the open air won't lead you to your deathbed."

Katherine fought the urge to roll her eyes at her maid's sarcasm. Harriet was sometimes more practical than she let on with her preference for frippery. Katherine did, indeed, have gloves that reached just above her *elbow*, thank you very much, not to her nose.

"Very well," she muttered under her breath. "If you think it would suit."

Harriet beamed. "It will match very well with your fox-fur pelisse."

That, at the very least, was warm. Katherine inclined her head to indicate that she would wear that one.

Pru added, "A hint of cosmetics wouldn't be amiss."

Although this conversation was helping to mitigate her nervousness, in that, Katherine refused to give way. She would not wear cosmetics. Heaven forbid that someone assume she was casting off her independent lifestyle and searching for a husband! Her days of dealing with fortune hunters were best left in her past.

She had far more important things to worry about than romance, in any case.

———

"You're certain I look all right?" Pru asked again as the carriage pulled to a stop. Although Annandale had presumably offered his escort, Pru had decided that she and Katherine would meet him at the King's Theatre in Haymarket instead.

"Stop worrying," Katherine chided. "He hasn't seen you in over a month."

"Precisely," Pru answered, glum. The light from the streetlamp slanted in through the coach window and onto Pru's fallen expression.

"He'll be delighted," Katherine answered.

Pru took a deep breath and threw her shoulders back. She muttered something that sounded, to Katherine's ears, like, "I know someone, at least, will be."

Katherine didn't know what to make of that statement.

Pretending not to hear, she waited for the driver to open the door before she descended the steps he'd laid to the street. The grand opera house loomed over them, well lit by lamps in sconces bracketing the doors. The front entrance left little room for carriages to linger, and once Pru had stepped down, the driver departed posthaste. Another carriage lumbered into place within seconds, one of a long line. Katherine beckoned for Pru to follow.

"Did Lord Annandale mention where he'll be meeting us?"

"The lobby," Pru answered. Her breath frosted in front of her face, but she didn't seem to feel the cold. Anxiety had taken root too deeply.

Katherine, on the other hand, was eager to enter the establishment so she could ward off the biting chill of the air. She should have worn mittens along with the elegant gloves tonight, for extra warmth. She rubbed her hands together and turned toward the theater.

"Come, then. Let's not tarry."

Pru followed mutely next to Katherine as they entered the opera house. A doorman opened the door for them as they arrived. Katherine inclined her head to him and entered, taking a moment to get her bearings.

The crowd moved like the shifting light on a multifaceted gem. The colorful garb of the ladies was offset by the muted tone of most gentlemen. The chatter swelled as theatergoers greeted each other and exchanged gossip. Even in a crowd this large, Katherine expected to be able to spot Lord Annandale easily. A large bear of a man, he had auburn hair and usually sported a beard, caring nothing for fashion.

Pru latched onto Katherine's arm and tugged her into a corner while they searched for their escort for the evening.

"Perhaps Lord Annandale hasn't arrived yet."

"He ought to be here. When he wrote, he said he would be here an hour before the opera began. You took so long to dress, we're a few minutes late."

Katherine glared at her friend. "It was the traffic, not I, that rendered us tardy. And I would have been ready to leave far sooner if I'd only been allowed to wear the clothes I wanted."

Despite Katherine's heated response, her friend didn't appear to be listening. Standing on her tiptoes, Pru scanned the crowd.

"There. I've seen them."

Them?

Pru latched onto Katherine's arm and towed her forward.

Perhaps she'd misspoken. Yes, she must have. Pru had only mentioned Lord Annandale being in attendance when she'd coaxed Katherine into accompanying her. Despite reasoning this much to herself, Katherine battled a sinking feeling in her stomach.

The feeling only intensified into that of a swarm of bees as she spotted the two men standing head and shoulders over the crowd around them.

Lord Annandale was tall and unmistakable despite the topper shielding the color of his hair. The man next to him was even more distinctive. His back was turned, only a small sliver of his short-cut brown hair peeking beneath the brim of his hat. But the way his wide shoulders filled out the emerald-green jacket or his military-straight posture... Katherine didn't delude herself for an instant into thinking that he was any other man.

She pulled free of Pru's hold to fiddle with the neck of her pelisse, hoping to hide the feminine, delicate lavender fabric beneath.

Unfortunately, Pru noticed. She smirked. "I'd wager you wish you'd worn a more fetching gown now, don't you?"

Katherine scowled. "Quite the opposite. I do not care what—"

Ignoring the response, Pru lifted a hand to hail her fiancé. All remnants of her earlier nervousness had melted away, replaced by a broad, eager smile at the sight of him. Yes, Pru was just as lovesick as Lord Annandale. Had she concocted the tale of her nervousness in order to trick Katherine into attending tonight?

No, her fear had been altogether too real. Katherine didn't believe Pru would toy with her emotions in such a way. She'd been genuinely worried for her friend.

For her scheming friend.

She took an instinctive step back, wanting to cry off, but Lord Annandale noticed Pru's wave. A smile pulled at his cheeks. From the way he looked at her, despite the people yet standing between them, the rest of the world might have melted away. It would have been endearing if Katherine hadn't been in danger of spending the evening with her father's rival yet again.

Captain Wayland turned. His eyes, which she'd spent enough time in his company to know were hazel, scanned the crowd before coming to rest squarely upon Katherine. At this distance, she couldn't decipher the expression behind that gaze, but his unknown intentions didn't stop a shiver from coursing down her spine.

Of revulsion. A shiver *of revulsion.* Of course that was what it was. It could not be anything else. She wiped her palms on her dress, forgetting for a moment that she wore gloves.

Fortunately, Pru was far too preoccupied to notice the lapse. Her friend all but floated toward her fiancé, ignoring everyone in her path and wake. Reluctantly, Katherine followed, trying to compose herself. Her friend was not yet married, and she had undoubtedly listed Katherine as her chaperone tonight when informing her mother where she would be.

"Och, lass, how I've missed ye."

Katherine had never seen Pru flush that particular shade of pink. She almost seemed to glow as Lord Annandale lifted her hand to his lips. Preoccupied as they were, Katherine had no choice but to greet Wayland.

His eyes still hadn't left her person, though he hadn't made any attempt to greet her. Was he waiting for her to make the first overture? In the past, he had always been more polite.

She inclined her head. "Wayland, it is..." She paused, choosing her next words carefully. "Unexpected to see you here."

A small smirk played at the corners of Wayland's lips, emphasizing the cleft in his chin. "Didn't Miss Burwick inform you? I accompanied Annandale to Scotland."

Katherine bit the tip of her tongue. Knowing that Wayland was out of town had been a balm to her conscience. She shouldn't expect to see him crop up in the middle of her investigation. Now, after his return, his interference in Lady Rochford's murder was all but guaranteed. She'd hoped that he would immediately find another investigation to consume him. Preferably one far from London.

"Pru informed me of your absence, yes."

His smile grew. "So you've been talking about me while I was away."

She turned her shoulder to him, fighting the blush that mantled her cheeks. "No more than necessary, I assure you."

To her relief, Annandale and Pru had stopped cooing at each other long enough to notice others around them. Katherine smiled at the smitten marquess. "Welcome back. I trust your journey wasn't too inconvenient?"

He raised an eyebrow. "You mean with the blighted snow north of Hadrian's Wall?" He shuddered. "I'd sooner forget it."

Katherine bit her tongue to keep from pointing out that winter had hardly even arrived. It would be a long season before they saw spring again. She gestured to the curtains separating the lobby from the staircase leading above. "Then let's do our best to forget it, shall we?"

Annandale offered his arm to Pru, who latched onto it with a flush of color in her cheeks. She looked up at him adoringly, her smile seeming to light the room.

Unfortunately, this left no course but for Katherine to accept Wayland's arm. They followed in Annandale's wake as he cut a path through the crowd to the private box he had reserved, pausing now and again to greet an acquaintance. At first, the silence between Katherine and Wayland writhed like a living creature. She felt every minuscule flexion of the muscles in his forearm acutely, though she tried not to show how she noticed.

As Annandale paused to greet a fellow Scotsman, Wayland leaned down to whisper, "I hear London has been quite eventful since we last parted."

If he was fishing for information about her investigation, she would not oblige. Who had informed him of it, in any case?

"That depends on your definition of eventful."

Her quip didn't appear to penetrate his casual, collected mien. After a moment's pause, he whispered again as they continued to walk. "Miss Burwick's latest letter to her intended mentioned a murder investigation."

"There are plenty of those in London."

"*Katherine,*" he said, drawing out her name in a way that made the muscles constrict in her chest.

She swallowed hard before raising her gaze to meet his. His warm hazel eyes were curious—too curious by far. He might have made it a habit to step into her investigations, but that didn't mean she had to facilitate it. There was a reason her father abhorred him so, and though she wasn't exactly sure quite what that reason was, it would behoove her not to forget about it.

No matter how helpful Wayland *appeared* to be.

"I'd like to know the details of this investigation."

"Yes, I imagine you would, wouldn't you?" She raised her chin at the challenge, daring him to offer her something in return. She wasn't going to spill the details in good faith, even if he might eventually learn them through Annandale. Katherine didn't imagine that Pru and her future husband kept any secrets from one another.

Lord Annandale and Pru disappeared behind the swish of the curtain, the staircase revealed beyond them for only a moment. Wayland stopped walking, his expression shrewd. He stared down at her, not seeming to care about the stares they drew. She braced herself for his renewed persistence. Typically Wayland only investigated for payment... or so she'd thought. But the last investigation he'd done for free, for his own satisfaction apparently. This investigation had no reward, so hopefully he would look for a more profitable investigation elsewhere.

His gaze skated across her cheeks, mouth, chin to take in the high collar of her pelisse. She bit back the urge to turn and bolt. Could she use her chaperone duties between Pru and Annandale as an excuse? The way he looked at her, like a nut he wanted to crack to discover the juicy secrets hidden within, caused webs of nervousness to bloom in her stomach. She battled the urge to rub away the discomfort.

After what felt like an eternity, he resumed walking toward the staircase. "If you have no wish to tell me, then keep your secret." His voice was flat, as if he didn't care one way or another.

Katherine nearly stumbled over her feet before she recalled how to use them. He was admitting defeat? That wasn't like the Captain Wayland she knew at all. It wasn't a trait he'd displayed while fighting against the French, and it wasn't one he'd ever shown her when he dogged her investigations, either. It had to be a trick... didn't it?

They'd nearly caught up to Pru and Annandale, who, given the color flushing her complexion, must have paused their descent for a private conversation, when they passed the first landing. Lord Annandale had continued on, so Katherine intended to do the same.

"Oh, Lady Katherine."

Katherine recognized that voice and paused. Wayland, in true gentlemanly form, took his cues from her and didn't try to tug her along. They both peered into the corridor toward the gaudily dressed woman who waved her hand.

Lady Dalhousie picked up her jewel-bright skirts and quickened her step to meet them at the landing. Footsteps to Katherine's right indicated that Pru and Annandale, curious, had decided to backtrack to learn what the fuss was about. The old matron, the hostess of the ice ball where Lady Rochford had been killed, patted her feathered turban and the aquamarine-and-diamond necklace adorning her neck. The backs of her gloves were painted with a waterfall scene rather reminiscent of the necklace.

"Lady Dalhousie, it's so nice to see you again."

"Lady Katherine. So good to see you without your

latest client. Or do you have a new one?" Lady Dalhousie raked Wayland with a long, lingering look from top to toe as if she had a personal interest in seeing him married.

Although he barely shifted his position, he grew stiff with unease. If Katherine hadn't been touching him, she might not have noticed, what with his penchant for exact posture at all hours.

"No, I'm afraid I don't have the pleasure of finding Captain Wayland a wife."

Wayland twisted, one eyebrow cocked as if to call her wording into question. Perhaps she ought not to nettle him, or she might find herself teased in return.

She frowned. "Though, how did you uncover my latest client? When I was hired, it was with the understanding that discretion was needed, lest he balk."

At that, Wayland's eyebrows rose even further. He brimmed with curiosity, though he didn't speak a word of it.

"Lady Bath told me, of course," Lady Dalhousie said, as if she and the elderly dowager were great friends. Given the disdain Grandma Bath held for anyone who showed a lack of sense, Katherine highly doubted that were true. However, they must have had some sense of camaraderie in order for Grandma Bath to inform her of a supposedly clandestine endeavor.

Lady Dalhousie leaned in and chided, "Tut, tut. I must say, if you're to match him, choosing a married woman isn't the right way to be going about it. Even if her husband has one foot in the grave."

Katherine's temples throbbed. "I beg your pardon? I'm not matching Lord Bath with a married woman. That would be an exercise in futility."

Not to mention morally indecent.

"No?" Lady Dalhousie pursed her lips. "Perhaps I was mistaken..."

From the look on her face, flushed with excitement, she had a tantalizing bit of gossip to divulge.

Pru, however, had no patience to tease it out of her. Without a trace of her formerly lovesick demeanor, Pru demanded brusquely, "What would lead you to make such a misunderstanding?"

Lady Dalhousie didn't need any further gossip. Without bothering to lower her voice further, she confessed, "Why, I saw Lord Bath follow Lady Rochford into the stairwell not ten minutes before her terrible accident!"

Her chest suddenly burning with unease, Katherine exchanged a look with Pru. She didn't look any more pleased to hear the news than Katherine felt. In fact, she was rather nauseated.

If Lady Dalhousie noticed the unease her confes-

sion caused, she thrived on it rather than trying to mitigate it. "I had heard one titillating rumor that Lady
Rochford's death was no accident at all. Perhaps you
should rethink your choice of client as well."

Katherine hastened to say, "The authorities
consider it an accidental death."

Lady Dalhousie tsked. "And they have never been
known to take a bribe?"

Katherine drew herself up. This vapid woman was
tarnishing the good name of men who worked tirelessly to keep people like her from harm. She opened
her mouth, a scathing comment about the integrity of
the Bow Street Runners despite the derision earned
from that name on the tip of her tongue, but Wayland
shifted beside her. He laid his hand atop hers. When
she tilted her face up to meet his, his expression was of
stone, his eyes blazing. He shook his head.

Civilly, though with a touch of ice that told her he
was not as unaffected as he seemed, Wayland
answered, "Which is the more likely outcome, madam?
That Lady Rochford suffered a terrible accident, or
that she was murdered and the breadth of London has
conspired to keep it a secret? I haven't heard a whisper
of a murder, myself. Who was the source of that
gossip?"

Lady Dalhousie, never one to enjoy being put in

her place, pressed her lips together and fussed with the fit of her gloves. "I suppose I must concede the point. I still think it is highly irregular for a marquess to follow a married lady into a stairwell!"

A hush quaked through the crowd. Turning, Lady Dalhousie murmured, "Oh dear. The program must be starting. If you'll excuse me."

Katherine muttered a polite goodbye, but the moment the woman's back was turned, she removed her hand from Wayland's sleeve. When she turned to her friend, she was relieved to discover that Pru hadn't fallen back into Lord Annandale's orbit. She looked just as serious as Katherine felt.

Of a mind, the two women fell into step as they ascended the staircase to the next row of boxes. Pru leaned close, her gaze accusatory. "Didn't you tell me that Lord Bath claimed not to know Lady Rochford?"

Katherine frowned, biting the inside of her cheek. *Lord Bath is a good man,* she repeated to herself, but the words seemed to have lost some conviction. He'd looked her in the eye and sworn that he had no association with Lady Rochford, that her inquiries into his whereabouts near the time of the baroness's death were unfounded. "That is precisely what he told me."

Had Lord Bath played her for a fool?

CHAPTER ELEVEN

W hen in London, Lord Annandale lived in an understated townhouse remarkably close to St. James's Square. Although the area was home to multiple respectable edifices, Katherine would not have allotted any to the use of a marquess. One more way in which Lord Annandale's tastes continued to shock and scandalize those of polite society.

Upon consideration, the stucco-sided townhouse likely made the perfect second home to a lord not often in London. It was no secret that Lord Annandale preferred his estates in Scotland. As Katherine craned her neck back to take in the plain five-story townhouse, no different from any of his neighbors in the row, she felt a pang at the thought that Pru might be whisked off to Scotland for the rest of her days. What of their friendship, their investigations?

"Katherine?"

Shaken from her reverie, Katherine feigned a smile and turned to her friend. Behind Pru, the driver shut the door on the coach, the Dorchester crest prominent against the glossy black siding. As he returned to the high seat and urged the horses to lumber away, presumably to find the nearest livery to rest out of the unseasonable winter chill, Katherine focused her attention on her friend.

"Yes, Pru. Are you concerned about calling on Annandale here?"

Pru gave Katherine a peculiar look. Although it wasn't polite to call upon a gentleman in his home, Pru had never had qualms about tarnishing her reputation. Besides, she and the gentleman in question were to be married. Katherine was a chaperone. Apparently Katherine must be more rattled than Pru had thought by the notion of losing her friend so soon after building a camaraderie with her.

"We have business to discuss with him," Pru pointed out.

Not that anyone outside of their circle knew that. Upon hearing at the opera the previous evening that Pru had entangled herself with a murder investigation,

Lord Annandale had insisted upon learning the particulars. Pru trusted him, and Katherine trusted her friend's judgment.

Trying to hide her trepidation, Katherine indicated the neat steps to the plain wooden door. "Let's not tarry out in the cold, shall we?"

Pru hesitated. "Do you not think we should share the details with him?"

At times, her friend had an uncanny ability to guess her thoughts. "If you're confident in revealing your investigative nature to him, then I have no qualms in sharing what we know. He might have some insight we hadn't considered."

Pru smiled, looking radiant. Katherine would much rather that than worrying her friend over their impending separation.

Despite the difference in their social statuses, Pru took the lead in mounting the steps and rapped smartly on the door. After a moment, it was opened from within by a large, shaggy man who Katherine recognized.

McTavish, Lord Annandale's personal valet, grinned from ear to ear. "Och, lass, you're a sight fer me poor, deprived eyes. His lordship is some surly without ye near."

For a confusing moment, Katherine thought that

McTavish might embrace Pru in the middle of the doorway, never mind that she was destined to marry his employer. His blue eyes twinkled with good humor, and his voice was thick with warmth.

He brushed aside a wayward lock of his ginger mane and beckoned them inside. "Come on in, lass, before you freeze yer peaches off."

Katherine decided that she didn't care to know what part of her anatomy he referred to as her *peaches*. She found herself greeted with as much warmth as Pru as McTavish shut the door and collected their outerwear.

"His lordship has near about worn the carpet thin in the drawing room," McTavish confessed. "Ye'd best join him before he gets it into his mind that I'll steal away his fine lass." The valet winked, making Pru blush. He turned his attention to Katherine. "Doona worry, yer lad is beside himself waiting for ye as well."

What in heaven could he mean by *that*?

If he noticed her confusion, McTavish took it in stride. "Can I offer ye a wee mite to wet yer whistle, milady?"

"Tea will suffice," Katherine answered with a polite nod. "Thank you."

McTavish ushered them toward the nearby stairs leading to the first floor. As she and Pru reached the bottom step, he craned his neck back and hollered, "Lorna! Bring a wee dram for the ladies."

Katherine winced from the strength of his voice.

No less loud, a woman's Scottish burr echoed from farther in the house. "Stop yer flirting and do it yourself, you overgrown louse. I've work to be done!"

Katherine should have suspected that a man as eccentric as Lord Annandale would keep an unconventional staff. Nevertheless, she couldn't hide her shock at the open animosity between the two servants.

When McTavish caught her looking, he winked. "She gets a wee bit jealous when I find a new flower to praise."

Baffled, Katherine asked hopefully, "Your wife?"

McTavish roared with laughter. "A lone wolf like me? I've more flowers to pluck yet, lass. Run along up, lasses. I'll be up before long with yer tea."

Katherine sincerely hoped that no *dram* of spirits would find its way into her cup. With McTavish as its server, she didn't dare predict the outcome.

As he loped down the corridor, whistling a jaunty tune, Katherine turned to the staircase once more. Were they expected to peek into every room on the first floor until they came across Lord Annandale?

Pru giggled. "You'll get used to him."

Katherine wasn't so sure about that, so she simply said, "Why don't we find your betrothed?"

Pru gathered up her skirts and took the steps two at a time.

At the top of the stairs, a short, undecorated corridor ran the length of the townhouse, punctuated by open doors. Pru paused for only a moment before she started down the corridor in search of the drawing room. "Love?" she called, blushing as she glanced over her shoulder toward Katherine.

Katherine smirked but didn't comment.

"In here," Lord Annandale boomed, his voice only slightly muffled by the walls and distance.

Pru followed the sound to the room facing the street, a smile spreading over her face. She crossed the threshold without hesitation. Katherine followed, only to stop short in the doorway.

The drawing room, as expected, was a cozy affair with several overstuffed armchairs punctuated with tables, a plush carpet underfoot, and an unwelcome man at the window. Katherine gritted her teeth. Now McTavish's quip made sense. Wayland stood gazing out the window at the street below.

What in tarnation was *he* doing here?

Despite the accusatory glare Katherine leveled at Pru's back, her friend didn't appear to notice her

displeasure. Instead, she and Lord Annandale gravitated toward one another, shutting the rest of the world
away as they greeted each other. Never mind that they
had parted mere hours before, after midnight. Frankly,
Katherine was surprised to see both men out of bed at
such an early hour. Emma might not be inclined to let
Katherine sleep in the mornings, but given their late
night, for both men to be so fresh at ten of the morning
was nothing short of a miracle.

As Lord Annandale bestowed a kiss on Pru's
knuckles and asked after the quality of her sleep,
Katherine gave them a moment's privacy by vacating
the doorway and choosing the chair farthest from
them. Unfortunately, it was also the chair closest to the
window, where Wayland stood. Despite his curiosity
the evening before, this morning he acknowledged her
only with a reserved nod before turning to look out the
window again.

Should she be insulted? Katherine rearranged her
skirts. She'd worn green, though certainly not because
she thought *he* would be in attendance.

"I hadn't known you were invited," she said softly,
knowing he would hear. She didn't turn to look at him.

The rustle of his movement was overly loud in her
ears. Once again, Wayland had found a way to insert
himself into one of her investigations, and this time,

she didn't even have the luxury of hiding information from him. Her only solace was that, with everyone believing this was an accident rather than a murder, there would be no reward. Since, as far as she knew, Wayland only solved murders so he could gain the reward money, he had no incentive to take the information she'd gathered and use it to solve the murder himself. She wouldn't have to suffer his company for long.

"If it makes you feel better, pretend I'm not here. I have business with Annandale after this is concluded."

Katherine turned, frowning. Wayland's expression as he continued to peer out the window was every bit as aloof as his voice. What was he waiting to see happen on the street below? Were they due to be interrupted by someone else?

Katherine opened her mouth to ask, but at that moment, McTavish arrived bearing a silver tea tray. "Here we are," he said, not out of sorts at all for the fact that he had had to fetch it himself. Serving tea to guests was not typically the job of a valet.

Then again, nothing about the man seemed typical.

Pru turned away from her betrothed, wearing a bright smile. "Now that we're all here, perhaps you'd like to hear of the investigation thus far?"

Reflexively, Katherine checked Wayland's reaction. Not a hint of curiosity penetrated his impassive expression. They might have been discussing the weather, for all the interest he showed.

She turned back to find both Scotsmen peering at her intently. Lord Annandale rested his hands on Pru's shoulders as he stood behind her. McTavish paid more mind to Katherine than he did to the tea service he was sloppily pouring out.

"Yes, lass, I'd be some interested to learn what ye've gotten yourself into."

Her cheeks flushing with color, Pru looked up over her shoulder and into Annandale's open expression. "It's nothing I can't handle." She flexed her fists, as if readying for a fight. Katherine did not envy Annandale if he thought to curb Pru's investigative activities.

"Katherine, would you care to do the honors of explaining?"

As McTavish offered her a dainty little cup filled to the brim with what looked to be too-weak tea, Katherine frowned. "Perhaps we ought to wait until McTavish has returned to his duties. This information is of a sensitive nature."

The man puffed out his chest as he divvied up the rest of the cups and beckoned his employer to sit. Lord Annandale chose the seat next to Pru, to no one's surprise. His valet took up position at his elbow before he announced, "I'm nae loose of tongue, milady. Ye can trust me."

Pru added, "If McTavish would like to be included, I trust him. You share information with Harriet all the time."

Harriet was often vital to Katherine's investigations. She didn't know McTavish beyond the two times she'd interacted with him. Nevertheless, she could see that no one in the room would be budged on the subject. Even Wayland, who, after conducting investigations of his own, must know the value of discretion, didn't leap to her defense. In fact, from his bored expression, he was still monitoring the street.

"Very well," Katherine said reluctantly. She inclined her head to her friend. "Pru, feel free to interrupt if you think I've left out anything vital. I'll be as succinct as I can in the matter."

She sipped her tea—little better than flavored water. She set the cup down and dusted her hands on her knees before she began.

"On this past Tuesday, November the fifth, Lady Rochford was pushed from a balcony during Lady Dalhousie's ice ball. Although it is widely believed that her fall was an accident, my friend Lyle Murphy—you may recall him from Bath, where his invention helped with our search for the jewel thief—has mathematically proven that she was pushed. This is based off positioning of the body, distance from the balcony where she fell, and so on."

Katherine paused, looking at each person in turn. Pru appeared more interested in watching her fiancé's expression than in contributing to the conversation herself. McTavish looked intent, and Lord Annandale appeared worried but attentive. Clearly, he waited to hear more.

To ease his mind, Katherine added, "We are investigating under the assumption that someone targeted Lady Rochford intentionally, not that there is a madman on the loose, pushing women from balconies and decrying the results to be accidents."

Lord Annandale reached out to hold Pru's hand, resting on her knee, but otherwise didn't respond.

Katherine carried on. "The servants at Lady Dalhousie's manor informed us of several rumors. As best we can piece together, a cloaked woman fled the scene by exiting the side door and then running around back."

"A cloaked woman? Can ye not find anything as to her identity?"

"No," Katherine admitted, "as we haven't found

the cloak. It is a dark shade and might have ermine fur around the hood."

"Might?" Lord Annandale added, drawing out the word.

For a man who claimed to want to know the particulars, he seemed intent on interrupting her. Katherine stifled a sigh and tried to gentle her tone as she added, "If you have any experience in questioning gossips, you'll know that the story evolves from person to person. We must take the information at its core. There was certainly a woman, and she was certainly seen at the side exit and passing the kitchen door, but we have conflicting stories as to what she wore and the timing, so it may not be relevant to the murder."

"But using the side door is highly irregular," Pru added. "If she meant to walk around back, why not choose a door closer to the back where she could access the street quickly?"

To Katherine's surprise, it was not Wayland but McTavish who leaped to her defense. "If her carriage had a seal on the door, she may nae have parked it on the lit street. Better an alley, and if she did nae wish to be seen, to take the door least traveled."

Perhaps he was more astute than she'd given him credit for. Inclining her head to him—which earned her a wide, devilish grin—Katherine acknowledged the possibility. "Which brings me to the other gossip we heard while questioning Lady Dalhousie's servants. Her driver, Rayner, was seen on the same floor where Lady Rochford fell. Pru and I approached him—"

"Ye did what, now?" Lord Annandale interrupted, straightening in his seat.

Pru shushed him.

Katherine raised her eyebrows as she tucked her hands neatly into her lap. "We followed a lead. We are professionals, Lord Annandale."

She thought she caught a snatch of a chuckle behind her, but when she glanced over her shoulder, Wayland looked as composed and ignorant of the conversation as ever. Why was he here? Surely, if he truly had business with Annandale, he could have returned later.

Returning her attention to the lord, who glanced dubiously at his future wife, Katherine steeled herself. Would Lord Annandale prove to be one of those narrow-minded men who didn't trust his wife farther than he could throw her?

Still holding his fiancée's hand, he addressed Pru, not Katherine. "I don't like ye to put yerself in such danger." His Scottish burr thickened nearly to match that of McTavish's. "What would have happened had this Rayner thought to kill you next?"

Pru stiffened. She started to pull away her hand, but Lord Annandale threaded his fingers through hers, stalwart. In a soft voice that barely carried to Katherine's ears, Pru hissed, "Is this what our marriage will be like? You telling me what I can and cannot do? I'm sensible enough to make my own decisions. I have an aptitude for investigation, and I intend to put it to good use."

"Nay, lass," Annandale answered, stroking his thumb across the back of her hand. "I'm worried for ye is all. I'd feel a mite better if ye'd consider having me along. Fer protection, as it may be."

With a pensive look, Pru lowered her gaze to stare at their joined hands. "I don't need your protection, but if you'd like to help with the investigation, I certainly wouldn't turn you away."

Did Pru just ask Annandale to join their investigative team? Although it stung a bit that Pru was offering before so much as speaking to Katherine regarding the notion, Katherine tried to remind herself that they were in love. Better Lord Annandale was welcomed into the group than that he lurked behind them in a cloak and gaudy hat.

Katherine raised her voice to cut into the semiprivate conversation. "Please don't mistake questioning a suspect with taking unnecessary risks. Not only am I capable of defending myself, and Pru too, if necessary —don't make that face, Pru; Lyle has taught me some very useful tricks for fending off unwanted attacks— but we were in full view of my driver at the time, who would have intervened in a heartbeat. As I have said, we are *professionals*."

"In any case," Pru answered quickly, likely hoping to defuse the situation, "Rayner admitted nothing. The way he insisted he was in his carriage on the front street is highly suspect. We have a witness who interacted with him, not merely saw him from a distance. He must have been inside."

"We will uncover the truth of the matter," Katherine assured her friend. "One way or another, it always comes to light. But he is not our only suspect. Lady Rochford was with child, and we have reason to believe that she was unfaithful to her husband."

McTavish clasped his hands behind his back. "It's the husband who pushed her, then."

Katherine considered her words carefully. "Of course, we cannot discount the possibility, but he seemed to be genuinely mourning the passing of his wife. He was nearly insensible."

"Guilt could render a man in such a way," Pru muttered under her breath, bringing up that same opinion she had voiced earlier.

The only acknowledgment Katherine gave to its merit was a curt nod. She addressed McTavish again with a more likely theory. "If Lady Rochford was indeed carrying another man's child, it is possible that she chose that evening to end her association with her paramour or bring her condition to his attention."

"You think Lord *Bath* is the father?"

Aha! Wayland was listening, after all. Of course, he'd heard Lady Dalhousie mention that Lord Bath had followed Lady Rochford up the stairs shortly before she fell.

Katherine rounded on him, meeting the sardonic raise of his eyebrow with an expression of equal disbelief. "Of course not. The marquess doesn't leave Bath except when Parliament is in session, and Lady Rochford would have had to be several weeks along in order to know of her condition." When he opened his mouth, no doubt to ask how she would know of such a thing, she jabbed her finger in his direction. "I have sisters. And nephews."

His mouth curved in a smirk. He turned his attention to the window once more. "Forget I said anything."

If only it were so easy. Now that she knew he was listening, the hairs on the back of her neck rose in awareness when she turned around, as though he were also watching her. Why was he interested in this case? He couldn't be. Perhaps he had tired of watching the street.

Lord Annandale, a smirk almost hidden by his beard, asked, "Lady Dalhousie seemed certain she saw Lord Bath with the victim shortly before she died. Are ye sure it mightn't be him?"

"As the father of her child, yes, I am certain." Katherine released her breath slowly, trying not to show how beleaguered she was that a man of Lord Bath's caliber was a suspect at all. She knew him to have his heart in the right place, so what could have moved him to commit murder?

Nothing, she hoped. But she couldn't prove it, so she couldn't discount him. "Unfortunately, at the moment, I cannot discount him as a suspect. He informed me he had no association with Lady Rochford; why then would he be seen following her? I couldn't find him in the ballroom shortly before she plummeted from the balcony." Katherine grimaced. "He might have been going up the stairs after her, but perhaps it was for some other reason. But he's a good man, and I haven't been able to find a motive for him to have wanted her dead."

"What of this Rayner lad?" McTavish asked. "He

was seen nearabouts too. Do ye think he might be the lover?"

"It isn't beyond the realm of possibility," Katherine said with a shrug. "He was close-lipped when we spoke with him. As I said, he denied being in the house."

"And yer certain he's lying?"

Pru interjected, "We have a witness who spoke with him. I believe she knows a womanizer she had best keep her distance from when she sees one."

The valet seemed eager to take this witness at her word too. With a grin, he cracked his knuckles against the opposite palm, one hand at a time. "Why don't ye give me this Rayner's direction? I'll find the truth for ye."

"How?" Katherine asked, full of trepidation. He looked a tad *too* eager, in her opinion. However, no one —not even Wayland, still standing impassive by the window—seemed to have any qualms about his going.

McTavish winked. "I have ways to loosen the tongues of men. Don't worry your wee pretty head."

CHAPTER TWELVE

K atherine was worried. She wanted whatever information McTavish might be able to glean from Lord Rochford's womanizing driver but was concerned about exactly how he was going to go about getting it. It consumed her during the night as she tossed and turned to such an extent that Emma had opted to sleep on the floor. It had distracted her during church, and even after, when Susanna had imparted her happy news to the family. Katherine so rarely sat down with the whole family that she should have been solely focused on them, not consumed with doubt and guilt over her decision to employ McTavish's methods, whatever they might be.

The happy exclamations resounded as her grown sisters, Elise and Lydia, embraced their stepmother and tendered their congratulations. Elise, a round five-foot-two and almost never found without her twin sons on either hip, resembled Papa strongly in the cut of her chin and the blue-gray color of her eyes. Lydia, three inches taller and willowy in build, more closely resembled the mother Katherine remembered less and less as years wore on. If she were to recall the image of her mother now, she would think only of Lydia, with her oval-shaped face and sly green eyes.

Susanna wept openly as she embraced her step-daughters. They knew the struggle their stepmother had endured in order to conceive. She had been trying for an heir since before Elise had married, yet three years ago after several years of marriage, Elise had shared the happy news of her pregnancy. Susanna had celebrated with her, and it warmed Katherine's chest to see the favor so warmly returned.

Katherine had never seen the family so happy. It formed a counterpoint to the sour mood Katherine couldn't seem to shake. Had she erred?

Not wanting to diminish the moment, she slipped away, hoping to escape alone to compose herself. However, as she entered the dim, cool corridor, footsteps clicked behind her. She released a breath and turned with a feigned smile.

Papa. Her smile fell away at his look of concern.

"Shouldn't you be celebrating, Papa? I'm certain your sons-in-law would like to tender their congratulations."

He raised his bushy eyebrows. "They'll still be waiting in the drawing room in a moment. I'm more concerned about you. Is everything all right, kitten? You haven't been acting like yourself today."

Kitten was a term of endearment he'd used for her far more often when she was young, particularly when she fell ill. She wasn't a child anymore.

"I didn't sleep well, that's all." It was the truth, although not all of it.

Papa had been an investigator for far more years than she cared to contemplate. No doubt he saw through the partial truth with ease. He laid his hand on her back, between her shoulder blades. "Come. Let's sit in the study a while, just the two of us."

Although she wanted to protest further, what she craved more was his good opinion. Had she made a terrible mistake? If she divulged it to him, would he think less of her? She didn't think it was possible for him to wrest her dowry from her now that he'd put it in a trust with her as the sole person with the power to touch the funds, but money meant far less to her than her father's approval. She brooded, trying not to show it in her posture as she preceded him to his study.

The room was dark and cold, no one having antici-pated its use today. Papa lit a candle from the tinderbox but didn't bother to yank the bellpull to summon a servant to stoke the hearth. Instead, he brought the candle to the table between their favorite chairs, where they sometimes sat in the evenings and played chess. Once she found a residence of her own, that would occur far less, but then, he would have a new baby to occupy him. Katherine took her customary chair, trying to compose herself.

"I can tell you're out of sorts. You seemed happy for me and Susanna when we broke the news to you earlier. Perhaps now it is finally sinking in."

Katherine sat straighter, frowning. "Whatever can you mean?"

"Don't bluff, dear girl. You aren't as skilled at it as you think."

Katherine had no idea what she was supposed to make of *that*. When Papa reached out to take her hand, she made no effort to draw away. She waited for him to speak.

Furrows formed in his forehead as he stared at her over the lit candle. "Are you feeling left out now that the focus is on Susanna and the pregnancy?"

"No, of course n—"

"Do you fear the child will be male?"

Katherine clasped his hand tightly. "I hope he will be. For both your and Susanna's sake. Papa, whatever are you asking of me?"

"If you harbor ill will toward Susanna, I think it would be better to let it into the open so we can discuss it. I won't begrudge you your emotions, but please don't hide your discontent from me."

Katherine shut her eyes for a moment. With all the excitement surrounding the murder, she'd scarcely had any time at all to contemplate the child on the way. First, she had to make certain that Susanna carried the child to term, and a shock like the death of her dear friend hadn't helped. But she'd been in good spirits today. Being surrounded by family made all the difference.

"I'm not hiding any discontent." She hesitated then shook her head. "Though it is peculiar how I'm faced with that very possibility in my current investigation."

"How so?" Papa asked. He retracted his hand and stroked his chin.

"Lady Rochford was pregnant, and her stepdaughter didn't seem the least bit pleased at the notion. Neither did the Rochfords' housekeeper. Both seemed not to accept Lady Rochford as the rightful baroness, never mind that the last is long dead. The feelings you describe—it wouldn't surprise me if that had been Mrs. Dillinger's reaction to the news."

"And you believe she might have harmed her stepmother because of them."

Katherine propped her chin on her fist as she leaned forward, thinking. "I have other leads yet to pursue, as well. I haven't discounted her."

She had found Mrs. Dillinger's apparent animosity to be peculiar. Stepmother and daughter were meant to attend a dress fitting together, which bespoke a certain closeness. Could Mrs. Dillinger's method of grieving be to remain angry with the deceased so it hurt her less? Or was her animosity really worry about her father being the killer, or maybe just grief? Papa had taught Katherine over the years that everyone grieved differently. No one way was invalid, but some ways were healthier than others.

This had been especially poignant when Katherine had been mourning the loss of her mother.

"Is that what troubles you?"

"Not precisely." Katherine lowered her gaze to her lap and smoothed a wrinkle from her skirt. "Lady Rochford's driver was seen in the house during the ball, near to where she fell. However, he denies being there."

"Is your witness reliable?"

Katherine hesitated. She recalled the young woman, frightened to speak out for fear of the ramifications. She also recalled the fear and distaste upon confessing how Rayner would accost any maid in his vicinity. A woman who so detested a man like that certainly wouldn't be mistaken about his identity.

Unless she'd hoped to use Katherine's investigation as a means to remove such a man from being dangerous to the women he accosted. Tarnation! Katherine hadn't considered that. She fought back a cringe as she admitted, "I thought my witness to be reliable and the driver to be lying. So much so that I accepted an offer for a man to pry the information from the driver's lips... by means left unspoken."

Her stomach tightened as she spoke the words. She shouldn't have given McTavish permission. If she'd only thought that the maid, however innocent seeming, might have had an ulterior motive...

Papa would tell her to consider the information from all angles and jump to no conclusions. She braced herself for his chastising words.

She wasn't disappointed. A shadow falling across his face, Lord Dorchester admonished, "Violence is never a valid method of uncovering the truth. Weak men will tell any lie in order for the pain to stop. They are unreliable, at best."

Although she'd braced herself for the look in his eye, Katherine couldn't contain the tears that gathered along her lower eyelashes. Shame swept through her, so overwhelming that she could feel nothing but the heat in her face and hear nothing but the ringing in her ears. She picked at the edge of her fingernails as she tried to compose herself.

Violence *wasn't* the answer. He'd taught her that from the start, which was why she'd been so reticent to allow McTavish to perform his interrogation, even if he hadn't specified his methods. But she'd thought herself desperate, for Susanna's sake, to solve the case as quickly as possible.

Katherine frowned. She raised her head. "Are those the methods you so despise Captain Wayland for using? You've never been specific."

In this case, Wayland hadn't seemed interested in joining, but in the past, she hadn't been able to tear herself free of his influence. Presumably, in another investigation, he would be nipping at her heels again in an attempt to siphon information.

Or would he? His demeanor had changed since he had returned from Scotland. In Bath, he had been warm, friendly, even... amorous. No, that near-kiss had to have been her imagination, after all. If he had made an overture then, he would have done the same thing upon returning to London. He hadn't.

She was better off without his confusing presence distracting her from her investigations. So she told herself, but she couldn't stifle her curiosity. Why did Papa abhor him so?

Papa donned a cool, aloof expression, as if they spoke of an offensive piece of furniture that needed to be removed. "Why do you ask? Has he been violent toward you?"

"Toward me? Never, Papa!"

The words escaped Katherine's mouth without her permission. She winced, heat scalding her cheeks as she awaited a reprimand.

Papa's blue-gray eyes sharpened. "Then you've been spending time with him?"

"Of c-course not." Sard it, why couldn't she control her sudden stutter? She swallowed and tried again. "Our paths have crossed once or twice, but I haven't encouraged the association. I would certainly never deign to work with him. But I am curious."

"Your curiosity will get the better of you, Katherine," Papa said as he moved to stand. His expression was impassive, though she thought she caught a slight upward quirk of his lips.

"My curiosity is the very quality you've praised all these years. It is the very thing that makes me an adept investigator." She took a deep breath and serenely stood despite the tremor in her knees. "And you haven't answered my question. Why is Wayland so terrible?"

Papa studied her for a moment. Whatever he found in her expression, it didn't loosen his tongue. "Trust me, kitten, you aren't ready to hear my opinion of Captain Wayland."

Katherine pressed her lips together. His answer was confirmation in itself of her worst suspicions. Wayland *was* using her—as perhaps he had done with Papa without her learning of it. Whatever his crimes, they were grave indeed. And she had best cut her association with him.

Even if she couldn't quite conceive of what Wayland might have to gain from his behavior thus far.

CHAPTER THIRTEEN

The longer Katherine contemplated her father's words, the worse she felt. Not only because of her acceptance of McTavish's help but also because of Wayland. She would never admit as much aloud, but his charm had been working on her, at least a little. She hadn't believed that he was capable of violence, or any other heinous act, but Father hadn't denied it.

She couldn't return to her family while feeling so out of sorts, so she collected Emma and hurried to Hyde Park. The crisp winter air should have cleared her head, but as she brooded along the walks, she drowned in her father's words and her own shame.

At least, until a resounding bark punctuated the air.

"Bonbon, no!"

Katherine turned and froze as the excitable wolfhound barreled down the path to meet them, towing Elizabeth along behind her. Bonbon looked so eager to renew her acquaintance with Emma that Katherine couldn't help but smile.

She checked on her pug's reaction to the much bigger dog but didn't find Emma exhibiting the typical signs of fear. Perhaps she'd gotten over her initial shock and now thought Bonbon a lumbering boor for calling out whenever she espied them. Regardless, Bonbon took advantage of the moment to sniff Emma thoroughly, a greeting Emma cautiously returned, nose to nose.

"I'm terribly sorry," Elizabeth apologized, out of breath. "I hope you weren't too startled." Grimacing, she wrapped the leash around her fist a few more times to shorten it.

"Not terribly startled, I assure you," Katherine answered. "I know she's friendly. Even Emma is happy to make friends this time around."

The smile the other woman gave was nothing short of relieved. "And how are you today? I admit, I'd hoped it might be another hour yet before any brave ladies ventured out into the cold to walk their dogs."

"More likely, they've given over the task to servants on a day like today." Were it not for her muff and the warmth of her cloak, Katherine would not have been tempted to walk farther than the end of her street. "I'm well, thank you for asking. I hope you are as well?"

Elizabeth nodded. "Very well, thank you for asking. All this exercise does me good, even if Mrs. Fairchild seems to have other opinions."

Katherine's teeth clenched at the thought of her would-be matchmaking rival. "Don't listen to her. If walking Bonbon brings you pleasure, you ought to continue to do it."

The corners of Elizabeth's mouth tipped up in a bright smile. "My thoughts precisely."

"I was just on my way out," Katherine said, reminded that her family yet awaited her at home. "Would you care to walk with me?"

Warily, Elizabeth studied the two dogs. "They appear to be getting on well enough."

"They'll be fine. If there's any trouble, I'll lift Emma and walk with her under my arm."

After a moment's hesitation, Elizabeth nodded. "Very well. It would be my pleasure to join you. Were you walking in this direction?"

The pair continued to stroll along the path leisurely as their dogs found particularly interesting spots along the path to smell. For a short while, they held the sort of banal chitchat that easily flew out of

Katherine's head, especially as she was considering another dilemma.

She should not try to poach Mrs. Fairchild's client out from under her. No, indeed, it would be morally wrong and earn her the other woman's undying enmity. Not that she didn't have that already...

Still, Katherine found herself asking, "How are you liking Mrs. Fairchild's tutelage?"

Despite her earlier comment, Elizabeth showed no sign of distaste. In fact, her expression was perfectly composed, her voice even as she asked, "Are you asking because you believe you would make me a better matchmaker?"

"Dear me, no!" Katherine exclaimed. Even if she had a lord in mind for Elizabeth, she was a detective first and a matchmaker only when strictly necessary. "Call me curious, that is all. Does she have anyone in mind for you?"

"Several potential matches, in fact." Elizabeth paused in her step, looking down. "If you ask me, she is overreaching. I know she secured a prince for her last client. That success is in large part why my parents chose to employ her. But I haven't any need for a prince. In fact, if I'm honest..." She trailed off, worrying her lower lip. Then, with a firm shake of her head, she resumed walking.

Katherine fell into step next to her. "If you're honest?"

Elizabeth sighed. After tucking a strand of her golden-brown hair behind her ear, she gave Katherine a sideways glance. "Perhaps I'm peculiar, but I feel as though you'd understand. I feel as though I'd make a far better governess or schoolmistress than I would a lord's wife."

"You ought to marry Lord Bath," Katherine blurted. She winced the moment the words left her mouth.

Elizabeth looked scandalized. "Katherine, not you too! I thought you of all people would understand a desire to submit to a pursuit other than marriage."

"I do," she hastened to answer, holding her hands aloft in surrender. Emma paused in her step to peer up at her mistress, confused. "Believe me, I understand that desire. But the moment you said schoolmistress, my imagination ran wild with my tongue."

She paused, her breath fogging in front of her face. To buy herself time to collect her thoughts and express herself rationally, she adjusted her hood. Elizabeth's incredulous—and perhaps in no small part disappointed—expression didn't alter while she waited to hear a response.

"The Dowager Marchioness of Bath has commissioned me with the task of finding her grandson a wife. No easy task, considering that he insists he is well enough off without one. But when you confessed to your aspirations..." Katherine reached out to clasp Elizabeth's hand, beseeching her. "You could attain them if only you marry Lord Bath."

Elizabeth looked dubious. "I could become a governess if I first became a marchioness?"

"I'm explaining this badly, aren't I?"

The shorter woman laughed. "You certainly aren't explaining it well."

"Let me begin again. Lady Bath has expressed a fond wish to open a school in Bath to provide an education for all her citizens, not only the well-to-do. However, she's lamented that she hasn't the energy to organize or enact it. If you were to marry Lord Bath, you could work in conjunction to bring such a project to fruition. You would be perfect!"

Elizabeth laughed. Shaking her head as though she addressed a willful child, she said, "Then perhaps I ought to offer my services as an educator. To ask me to marry Lord Bath in order to run a school is ludicrous!"

Yes, put that way, it was. "Why is it so ludicrous that you marry him? He cares very deeply about his tenants, he dotes upon his grandmother, and he is fond of dogs. He would make you a very fine husband, I imagine."

"He's a marquess," Elizabeth exclaimed. "My family couldn't scrounge together a title if we tried. Or rather, we have one on a distant branch of the family, and it's been generations since my family could tie itself to it directly."

"Lord Bath is rich and powerful enough that he doesn't need a woman from a titled family to be his wife. Someone without such connections but with greater aspirations to better his people would be a much better fit." Katherine held up her hand to stall the inevitable protest. "Lord Bath is known to be eccentric. The daughter of a peer would be most unhappy with the way he carries on, you know, actually caring for the people in his care."

She paused for a heartbeat, waiting for her friend to respond, but Elizabeth remained mum. She didn't appear to be enthusiastic about the idea, but at the very least, she was no longer openly protesting it. As the final nail in the coffin, Katherine cajoled, "Pru was recently engaged to the Marquess of Annandale, and her father was only a second son. They're incomparably happy, by the way. I have quite the eye for these things."

Elizabeth still seemed reticent.

"Is it Lord Bath himself that you object to? Do you not find him handsome?"

"I don't know that we've been introduced."

"No?" Katherine raised her eyebrows. "That's odd. Mrs. Fairchild is acquainted with him. Unless..." She sighed. "She will likely object to the match on principle. We had a bit of a falling out when Lord Northbrook married my client instead of hers. Perhaps, if you'd care to set your cap for Lord Bath, you ought not to tell her. Not until we're certain the match will be going forward."

They reached the edge of Hyde Park. Elizabeth looked ready to bid Katherine adieu, but Katherine wanted to continue her conversation. She had a good feeling about Elizabeth and Lord Bath. "Where is your direction? I'll walk with you partway home."

Although Elizabeth at first seemed reluctant, she graciously accepted Katherine's company. Once they had settled into a desirable pace, Katherine persisted. "Meet with Lord Bath once or twice. That's all I ask."

Elizabeth pressed her lips together. "I wouldn't presume to ask for his introduction."

"Of course not. I'll have him seek out yours. He's my client, so he'll do as I request."

"And then?" Elizabeth tipped her head forward charitably. Perhaps she was warming to the prospect.

"And then we'll see if you might suit. If you don't like him, I certainly would never try to force you to marry him. I orchestrate love matches, nothing less."

Elizabeth laughed, incredulous. "There are precious few of those going around."

"Oh? You doubt me?" Katherine smirked. "My sisters, Lady Banning and Lady Pevensey, beg to differ. As do Pru and Lord Annandale. I assure you, they cannot stop cooing at one another. Quite the sight, considering his stern exterior."

"I don't believe you work miracles. I also know that I have few remaining childbearing years left in me, and that makes me unattractive to a man, especially one who has yet to sire an heir. The best way to indulge my love of children is to educate them."

"You can do both," Katherine countered. She paused and put her hand on Elizabeth's sleeve. "Don't undervalue yourself. We have enough men around to do that for us, don't you think?"

Elizabeth smirked and shook her head again. "You are peculiar, Lady Katherine."

Katherine tried not to show how much the bemused statement stung. "I am also correct. And stubborn. I won't see you home until you've promised to meet Lord Bath and give me your opinion of him."

"Very well. If that is the only thing that will

appease you, I will do so." Elizabeth pointed down the street away from where Katherine needed to travel in order to return home. "Shall I bid you adieu?"

Katherine nodded. She leaned forward to clasp her friend warmly on the arm. "Thank you for the company. Good day!"

The momentary triumph from having begun the match for Lord Bath was quickly overshadowed as Katherine recalled how he had lied to her when she had last questioned him. Or had he? Lord Bath could become preoccupied with things. It was wholly within reason that he might not have been paying attention to where he was when Lady Rochford fell. There would have been no reason to if he wasn't the killer. And just because Lady Dalhousie saw him go up the stairs just after Lady Rochford did not mean he had gone up there to push her off the balcony.

He might have had another reason. Perhaps one he didn't want to tell Katherine lest it get to his grand-mother. She needed to speed up the investigation so she could prove Lord Bath's innocence. She frowned, brooding about her next course of action as she strolled with Emma along the street toward Dorchester House some minutes distant.

On the juncture of two streets, the door to a public house opened, spilling an appalling amount of chatter and revelry for a Sunday afternoon. Out stumbled two men. One, with ginger hair and his arm slung around the shoulders of the second man, was unmistakably McTavish. He roared a drunken ballad that would soon have him removed by the authorities for disturbing such a peaceful neighborhood, his arm slung around Rayner's shoulders. Both men grinned, their cheeks ruby from drink.

That was McTavish's means of loosening the driver's tongue? Tarnation, Katherine had been worrying herself to shreds over nothing. As McTavish turned his prey toward Lord Rochford's townhouse and the work he was undoubtedly shirking, he caught Katherine's eye and winked.

Whatever the means, McTavish seemed to have learned something of use. Katherine needed to extricate herself from her family obligations as soon as possible so that she could learn what he had to say.

CHAPTER FOURTEEN

"I'm missing a delicious Sunday dinner for this, I'll have you know," Lyle grumbled as they strode together along the narrow street to Lord Annandale's townhouse. Convincing him to accompany her to learn more about the murder investigation had been difficult, all the more so when his mother and siblings had tried to insist she stay for dinner with them instead. The word *business* was apparently not uttered during a Murphy Sunday dinner.

"I know. I'm sorry. I'll make it up to you. We can have dinner at the most expensive eatery you'd like."

Lyle shrugged. His hands shoved into his pockets and his collar uncurled against his neck for warmth, he looked the picture of surliness. If any criminals recognized him, they would no doubt scatter immediately.

"Did Bow Street get a chance to look at Lady Rochford's body for more signs of struggle? Has the investigation turned up anything else?" Katherine had been insistent that Lyle accompany her so he could hear the information McTavish had discovered firsthand, but also she wanted to know what the police had uncovered.

"The only thing we found was the scrape you mentioned. It likely happened as she grappled onto a spindle, trying to stop the fall on her way over. Which seems to indicate she did not jump."

"We already knew that." At least the police would take it more seriously now. Though they were taking their sweet time about investigating.

"Lord Rochford seems appropriately upset. Though he was unusually interested in her belongings and accusing us of not handing everything over."

"That's odd. Did you keep something?"

Lyle looked at her sharply. "Of course not."

"It doesn't sound like you've made much progress officially. Maybe McTavish will have something of use for you." She stopped in front of Annandale's townhouse. "This is it. Number twenty-four."

"This is an odd place for a marquess to live."

"He is an odd marquess."

Again, McTavish opened the door and ushered

Katherine and Lyle inside. This time, judging by his bloodshot eyes and the slight wavering of his hand as he accepted her cloak, he was suffering the effects of the drink. He pointed upstairs and said simply, "They're up waiting."

Pru was already there, seated alongside Lord Annandale as they chatted with a third person. The back of the man's head was facing Katherine, but no one could mistake that height.

What *was* Wayland doing here if he had no interest in the investigation? Suspicion knotted in Katherine's gut. If this had been her house, she would have cast him out.

But it wasn't, and he was a friend of Lord Annandale's. Perhaps it was mere coincidence that she found him yet again in the room when she had clues to discuss.

"More business, Captain Wayland?"

He and Lord Annandale stood to greet her. Katherine didn't keep them standing long but led Lyle into the room and chose a seat so the men could also sit. There was a scarcity of chairs. When Wayland remained standing to greet Lyle, she hoped that he would take himself off. Instead, he offered his seat to Lyle and moved to stand behind Katherine.

"Annandale isn't often in London. You can't blame my taking advantage of his presence while he is."

Katherine turned to Lord Annandale. "Thank you for letting me know the moment McTavish returned. I'm eager to hear what he has to say."

"Pretend I'm not here," Wayland said as he meandered to the mantel, where he poured himself a finger of spirits, though he didn't raise the tumbler to his lips.

No problem on Katherine's part, as she was already pretending he wasn't there. "Has McTavish informed you of his findings?"

Lord Annandale nodded. He reached over to clasp Pru's hand. "He said his piece ere he staggered in, but he wishes tae inform ye of the particulars himself."

Lyle adjusted his position in his chair. "How certain are we that the information this man has procured is accurate? Some men tell wild tales after a pint or two."

"I trust his judgment," Lord Annandale answered, his eyes hardening like steel.

At that moment, McTavish staggered in bearing a tray not of tea but of pastries. Seedcake, turnovers, biscuits, even sloppy-looking sandwiches adorned the tray, which he deposited on the table. "I hope ye don't mind serving yerselves." He raised a hand to his head as though in pain.

On his heels, a trim woman with a thick braid and a dour expression arrived with the tea and a jug of juice. She laid both neatly on the table and curtseyed to Lord Annandale. "The tea has another five minutes to steep, milord." Her Scottish burr, although present, was far less pronounced than either Annandale's or McTavish's, as though she took pains to hide it. "Would anyone care for some juice?"

Katherine and Lyle volunteered, each receiving a small cup of the deep-red juice a moment later. The maid's expression turned surly as she poured out a third and held it out to McTavish. "Drink it. Ye deserve this." She curtsied again to the room before backing against the wall, where she presumably waited for the tea to steep so she could pour it.

McTavish downed the contents of his cup with a flourish and grimaced. "I see ye sweetened it yerself, Lorna."

She scowled at him but didn't answer.

Tentatively, Katherine tasted hers. Not the sweetest of juices, but she wouldn't go so far as to say it was unpleasant. When she was halfway done, Katherine leaned forward to help herself to some of the food. Lyle, given his complaints on the walk here, was hungry but too polite to admit it.

"Allow me, milady," Lorna said as she bustled forward. "What catches yer fancy?"

Katherine chose a sandwich and a pastry and coaxed Lyle into asking for the same. Even Wayland took enough interest in the offerings to accept a slice of seedcake.

When she noticed the captain at the mantel, Lorna turned to glare at McTavish as though it were his fault. "Go fetch the man a chair. Or need I do everything in this house?"

Wayland held up his free hand. "I won't hear of it. I'm perfectly happy to stand."

Chafing under Wayland's unwanted presence and the tension straining the room between the two servants, Katherine forewent small talk and addressed McTavish directly. "What did you learn from the driver, Rayner?"

McTavish grimaced as Lorna refilled his juice cup but drained it again. "Rayner was inside Lady Dalhousie's house shortly before the murder."

"I knew it!" Pru exclaimed.

Annandale shared a smile with her.

Even Katherine couldn't help but grin with triumph at the confirmation.

At least, until McTavish added, "But he was nae with Lady Rochford. He snuck in fer a bit of a romp with his ladylove."

Lorna gasped in the process of pouring the tea. If McTavish had been closer, she might have struck him, if her expression was any indication. "Doona be crass!"

McTavish held up his hands in surrender. "No word of a lie."

"Could the lover have been Lady Rochford?" Katherine asked.

McTavish shook his head. "Nay, 'tis some sweet maid by the name of Ellie. Works fer—"

"Mrs. Fairchild," Katherine completed. Her rival in matchmaking couldn't seem to hire a virginal woman, for all her propensity of insisting on the highest moral caliber in her clients. Katherine hoped the poor girl fared as well as Mrs. Fairchild's last lady's maid, who had found herself carrying the elderly Duke of Somerset's child and been hastily married to make the child legitimate should he be the heir.

Somehow, Katherine doubted that Rayner was the type of man to take responsibility for his actions. "If that is the case, why didn't he admit to that from the start? With the upheaval in the house, I doubt he would have been reprimanded even if he had looked to his own pleasure before his duty."

"Och, well, the lad helped himself to a jewel he found on the floor while there. Wee fancy thing, 'tis, worth a pretty penny, but now considering the circumstances, he's a bit off on trying to sell it."

No doubt he was. If it belonged to Lady Rochford, that would certainly raise a few questions. Could it be the "belonging" that Lord Rochford had accused the police of keeping? "Did you see it? Perhaps the owner lost it near the time of Lady Rochford's death."

"And if we know who the owner is, we'll have another suspect," Pru added. She leaned forward, her eyes gleaming with enthusiasm as she clasped Lord Annandale's hand.

Lyle drummed his fingers on the armrest of his chair. "It will take some investigating to find the owner unless the gem is particularly noteworthy. We might waste more time following that lark than we will be rewarded for, and we have no idea when it was dropped."

"No?" Pru questioned. "Surely the floor was cleaned thoroughly before the ball. Therefore it must have been dropped sometime after the cleaning and before Rayner found it near the time that Lady Rochford fell from the balcony. It couldn't have been there for long."

"I'm not saying it isn't worth looking into, simply that we shouldn't rest our hopes upon it." He straightened his collar and said to the valet, "McTavish, how well can you recall the jewel? If you can describe it well enough for me to draw it..."

McTavish winked. "Oh, I can do ye one better than describing it. I convinced the lad to give me the trinket so as he wasn't caught with it." The burly valet dipped his hand into his pocket and emerged with a closed fist.

Wayland stepped closer as the valet presented his fist to Katherine. He uncurled his fingers to reveal an earring, a white pearl stud surrounded by intricate braided gold. Her ears rang. She knew precisely who the earring belonged to.

It can't be!

She snatched the earring from McTavish's hand and curled her fist around it, hoping to prevent her companions from identifying the stud. Not that any of them knew her stepmother well enough to identify it as hers, but Katherine didn't want to take the chance. How did Susanna's earring find its way into Lady Dalhousie's house the night of the murder, the same night Susanna had claimed to remain at home alone?

Susanna had been a friend, confidante, even surrogate mother since Katherine's own had died. She didn't believe her stepmother was capable of murder, not even of getting into a spat with her dear friend on the balcony of a ball and accidentally pushing her over.

No, Susanna had been so shocked to learn of her friend's death. So shocked, in fact, that Papa had been afraid of her miscarrying the baby. Actually... she'd been unduly shocked. Katherine had thought she'd overreacted a bit.

And Susanna had a cape with ermine trim.

Unable to think straight with so many pairs of eyes upon her, Katherine stood. "Thank you for looking into this, McTavish. I'll take on the task of searching for the earring's owner. I'm afraid I cannot linger. Good day."

"I beg your pardon?"

Katherine ignored Pru's outburst.

"Katherine?"

And Lyle's too. He was a grown man and capable of finding his own way home.

Katherine blinked away the tears stinging her eyes as she stepped out of the Annandale townhouse and into the crisp air and light falling snow. She welcomed winter's chill bite, a distraction from the cold turn of her thoughts.

Turning toward home, she set out. If she reached a street with more traffic, she might be able to find a hack willing to take her home, as she and Lyle had opted to walk instead of ride. However, exertion seemed a welcome distraction despite the close of night around her. Her footsteps crunched in the hardening crust of snow piled along the edges of the road. Her cheeks burned, and her tears threatened to freeze to her lower eyelashes. One more reason why she couldn't afford to cry.

"Katherine, what's gotten into you?"

She stiffened at the voice, steeling herself a moment before she turned to face Wayland. Why had he followed her when no one else had? He didn't even appear to care for the investigation, let alone how Katherine cared to spend her time.

They stood between the two nearest buildings, each lit with a lamp out front to supplement the light of the gas streetlamps at the junction of the street. Around them, the snow seemed to muffle the sounds of London, and the desertion of this residential neighborhood made it feel as if they were the only two people in the world.

"Nothing's gotten into me, Wayland. I'm going home, is all."

"You can't possibly think to walk all the way. Where is your carriage?"

"I don't have a carriage," she said, her voice clipped.

"Your father's carriage, then."

"At home, I imagine. Lyle and I walked from his residence."

Wayland lifted his eyebrows. For a moment, it seemed that Katherine had rendered him speechless. All the better, but she couldn't stand about and take in the sight. Her nose was already numb from cold, and tendrils of ice seemed to creep up her legs beneath her skirts the longer she stood there. Turning on her heel, she continued walking.

His long-legged stride caught up to her within seconds. "I've never seen you so abrupt, especially among friends."

Katherine didn't know what sort of answer he wanted to hear, so she wisely said nothing at all.

He persisted, "McTavish did well in uncovering what he did."

"You're right. He did."

For a moment, Wayland's presence at her right dropped away. She didn't dare to hope that she'd lost his interest. He quickened his stride and caught up to her once more.

"You aren't angry with him for another lead you cannot hope to follow."

Katherine clenched her jaw. She didn't dare to admit that she could, indeed, follow the lead. She had to know the truth for herself before she could confess the facts to her friends. "I am not angry with him, but I will be with you if you persist in this line of questioning. I'm going home. That shouldn't be the cause for such scrutiny."

"If you were acting even remotely like the woman I know, it wouldn't be."

Katherine clenched her hands, fighting the urge to box his ears. Wayland was not precisely a friend. Come to think of it, he must be an enemy, or at least her father thought so. But did she think so? Was she being too hard on him?

Wayland stepped into her path, cutting off the light from the streetlamp mere feet away from him. His expression plunged into darkness, his silhouette limned with the tendrils of light. "You can't think to walk home. You'll fall ill."

"What does it matter to you?" She crossed her arms. "If you have business to discuss with Lord Annandale, you'd best return and see it through."

Posture rigid, he turned toward the light then back to face her once more. "I am a gentleman. It is my duty to ensure that women don't succumb to frostbite if I can help them."

Katherine wanted to argue, but the chill had settled into her bones by now. Earlier, when Katherine and Lyle had arrived, the sun had still shone in the sky and lent the day some warmth. The temperature had plummeted upon the advancement of evening, and the flakes of snow blistering against her face with the unwelcome breeze didn't help much, either. She would be foolhardy to walk all the way home.

But to accept a ride from Wayland, of all people? If her father saw his family's seal on the carriage so soon after he'd warned her of Wayland's character, he might revoke his confidence in her judgment.

"If it will allay your fears, I intend to find myself a hack as soon as I reach a busy street."

"No need," Wayland said, his voice clipped. "I sent McTavish for my carriage with instructions to send it after me. If we wait, it'll be here in a moment."

Katherine was tired. Far too tired to fight this battle, not when she had another to wage upon returning home. "Very well. I'll accept a ride home, but only to the corner of the street. No farther."

When Wayland shifted to the side, the light slanted over his confused expression. "Why not to your door?"

Was he serious? "Have you forgotten that our families are at odds?"

"Ah, that." Wayland was silent for a moment then let out an exasperated sigh. "Very well. If you're intent on being stubborn, I'll deposit you at the corner."

Katherine nodded, appeased.

"*If* you tell me what's made you act so uncharacteristically at the moment."

That she could not do. Wayland might have proven himself helpful in past investigations, but she couldn't trust anyone with this. She met his gaze, stalwart. "I'm reconsidering the clues of the investigation, that's all. You have no interest in that."

Tilting her chin up in defiance, she waited for him to admit otherwise. He'd inserted himself into her investigations from the very first time she'd ventured to solve one on her own. He'd even feigned interest in her —interest he didn't currently seem to indulge—in order to learn more about the Burglar of Bath. He *had* been feigning interest, hadn't he? Because the way he was looking at her right now seemed to indicate...

However, they were interrupted by a carriage. Wayland held her gaze a moment more before he opened the carriage door for her. Did he expect her to jump up without the steps?

The driver, fortunately, had more sense. After tying off the reins, he jumped down and retrieved the steps from the boot of the carriage in the back. He laid them beneath the door. Katherine couldn't escape Wayland's hard gaze or his proffered hand. She accepted his assistance to step into the carriage, where a fur rested on the forward-facing seat. When she settled there and draped the fur over her legs to give herself something to do, the warmth sank into her cold bones, making her sigh in relief. The fur must have been heated next to a brazier while the team of four was hitched to the carriage.

As the driver tugged on his forelock and motioned for Wayland to enter the carriage, instead he took a step back. His expression cutting, Wayland ordered, "Take Lady Katherine home and return for me here." He lifted his gaze to hers for only a moment before he added, "I have further business to discuss with Annandale."

Katherine didn't protest as the door was shut in her face, shrouding her in darkness. At least she didn't have to abide his presence any longer.

But a small part of her wondered at the vast change in demeanor. He'd never shown any qualms in accompanying her before. What had changed?

CHAPTER FIFTEEN

B y the time Wayland's driver deposited her in front of Dorchester House, the early evening had deepened into a winter night. A lantern lit over their door meant that the staff yet awaited her return, or that of her father. Katherine didn't know whether she should hope for the latter.

After she handed off her garments, she retreated into the sitting room, where she was told a fire awaited her. She accepted the offer of tea and asked for Harriet to bring it. Perhaps before Katherine confronted her family, she would speak with her close friend and maid in order to garner her opinion. Once again, Katherine dipped her fingers into her reticule and emerged with the earring.

She swallowed hard, curled her fist around the

piece of jewelry, and strode into the sitting room. This room, allotted to family use, was warmly decorated in splashes of red and gold. A fire crackled behind a fire screen, shading the settee from its scorching warmth. Susanna perched on the edge nearest the fire, her hands resting on her stomach. As Katherine stopped short in the doorway, she glanced up.

"Katherine, you're home."

Her heart thundered so loud, she scarcely even heard her stepmother's greeting. "Forgive me, I didn't mean to intrude."

Indeed, she'd wanted to speak with Harriet before ever confronting her stepmother.

Straightening, the woman frowned and patted her black hair. "What are you nattering on about? This is your home, too, for as long as you want it. You aren't intruding."

Tentatively, Katherine took another step inside. The back of the earring bit into her palm, anchoring her to the moment. "Is Papa at home?"

"No. He left for a meeting to arrange his next job." Susanna rearranged her skirts. "You've never balked at being alone with me before. What's wrong? Is it the baby?"

"It's not the baby."

"Then what?" Susanna patted the seat beside her. "Please, come sit."

Numbly, Katherine crossed the distance to sit next to her stepmother, leaving a foot of space between them. The warmth of the fire soothed her but not enough.

Trying to don the impersonal observant state that aided her as a detective, Katherine raised her gaze to meet her stepmother's. "Where were you last Tuesday night?" Perhaps, without Papa around, this time she would receive the correct answer.

Susanna's delicately arched eyebrows pulled together. "I was at home."

Perhaps not. If Susanna was going to insist on lying to her, that left only one course of action: to present her with evidence that she could not deny.

Katherine opened her hand between them. "This found its way into my possession."

"My earring!" Susanna's face lit up with a smile as she took it out of Katherine's hand. "I thought I'd lost it. Actually, I'd suspected Emma might have stolen it again," she added with a laugh.

"She didn't." Katherine's voice was flat. "It was found in Lady Dalhousie's house. On the same floor where Lady Rochford plummeted to her death."

Susanna turned white, the glow from the fire

giving her complexion a sallow look. She clasped one hand to her stomach, the other around the earring, which she pressed to her chest. She didn't say a word.

"Tell me the truth," Katherine demanded. "You should have done so from the very beginning. Why were you at Lady Dalhousie's ice ball? It wasn't to socialize, or I would have seen you."

Susanna's chin trembled, her eyes filling with tears as she brought both hands to cover her stomach protectively. "I didn't harm my friend. I would never..."

A wash of guilt turned Katherine's insides cold, but she held firm. Her stepmother still hadn't given her a definitive answer. "I withheld this evidence from my friends, my companions in this investigation. I am putting my reputation on the line for you, Susanna. *Tell me*: why were you there, and why haven't you told Papa of it?"

"It was for the baby," Susanna whispered. The tremor in her lips muffled her words, as did the catch in her voice from emotion. Tears welled at the corners of her eyes, overflowing to drip down her face unimpeded.

Katherine steeled her spine, trying to appear unaffected. Her resolve crumbled in minutes. She loved Susanna with all her heart. Shuffling closer, she slid her arm around her stepmother's slender shoulders and offered her comfort.

"I don't mean to distress you. Please, I only want the truth."

Susanna sniffled and offered her a watery smile. "I know. You're a good girl, Katherine. You always have been. And a good detective. I should have known you would uncover my presence at the ice ball."

Still emotional, Susanna cried into Katherine's shoulder. For the moment, Katherine allowed her the solace, but even if it broke her heart, she couldn't allow her stepmother to sidestep the question again.

"Did you meet with Lady Rochford at the ice ball?"

"Yes." Susanna lifted her head, sniffling. Her eyes were round and red rimmed. "But she was alive when we finished and parted ways."

"Finished with what, precisely?"

Susanna twisted her skirts in her hands. "It's been seven years since Margaret was born," she said, her voice small. "Seven years, and four pregnancies in between. None lasted past three months."

The agony in her voice was plain. To say that she hadn't known of Susanna's difficulties in conceiving would be a lie. Katherine was far too good a detective not to realize that her stepmother had miscarried more than once. She hadn't counted the number to four, however. "I'm sorry. I'm certain that won't be the case this time."

"Celia had trouble too. So when Lord Bath came to town..."

Katherine stiffened. "Lord Bath?"

Susanna nodded and wiped her eyes. "Bath has healing waters. We thought they might help with the pregnancy, to keep us from losing our babies. I arranged it all by letter, and he assured me he brought a trunkful of water if I'd care for it. He only had two vials on him at the time, one for me and one for Celia, but we were arranging to obtain more."

"That's why you were at Lady Dalhousie's ball? And why Lord Bath was seen following Lady Rochford upstairs?"

Susanna nodded, still a bit tearful. "We met on the third floor. I didn't want to be seen, and Celia didn't want to be parted from Lord Rochford for long. It was only long enough for Lord Bath to give us the vials. Please don't tell your father. I hadn't wanted him to know of my fears. I know how it weighs on him every time I miscarry and go into doldrums."

"I won't tell," she said softly. "However, I must make certain that you're telling the truth this time. Do you still have the waters?"

"No. I drank them." Susanna clenched her hands in her skirts, looking ready to wring them apart. She brightened as she lifted her head and exclaimed, "But I spilled some on my cloak! The black one with the ermine trim. I don't know what is in those waters, but it left a crystallized white stain that I haven't been able to get out."

At last, Katherine had found the cloaked woman, but it gave her no peace. "I'll look in the closet before I go up. Don't strain yourself getting up. Can you tell me something else? How did you gain access to the house without being seen?"

"I went in the servants' entrance, of course. I exited the same way. I instructed the carriage to wait around the side, where the servants accept deliveries, so it wasn't far, and scarcely anyone was around to see."

Katherine nodded. Susanna was telling the truth. The maid had seen the ermine-cloaked woman go out the side door, and Susanna would have no way of knowing that. Except the cook had seen the cloaked woman near the scullery. That in the opposite direction, but perhaps the snow made her take a circuitous route. "And did you have to go past the garden to get to the side street because of the snow?"

Susanna frowned. "No. I don't think so. I'm not

sure where the garden is. I followed the path the servants follow."

Katherine closed her eyes, trying to remember the path. Did it pass the scullery? It must since Susanna was admitting to being there, and Lady Rochford would not have been wearing a cloak as she came from the ball.

"And Lady Rochford? You said you and she collected the waters from Lord Bath at the same time. But she would not have come from outside."

"That's right. Celia was attending the ball," Susanna said. "I provided the introductions, as she had never met him before."

"After you took the waters, did you leave him alone with her?"

"No. He walked down after me. Celia was going to the withdrawing room, except..." Susanna's expression clouded. "She mustn't have made it. I heard someone yell. I thought it was Lady Dalhousie being dramatic about something as usual, but now I wonder if it was... if it was..." Susanna buried her face in her hands and sobbed.

Katherine clasped her stepmother's hand. "Thank you for telling me the truth. I am so, so sorry for your loss."

Susanna nodded, weeping openly. "Me too,

Katherine. She was my dearest friend. Please, bring her justice. She deserves that much."

"I will," Katherine whispered, her heart breaking. "I have only one more question. I've uncovered rumors that Lady Rochford might have had a lover. Do you know if those rumors have any merit?"

Susanna's eyes widened. "Celia? No, she was trying to conceive the baron's heir! But..." Her lower lip trembled, and she bit into it.

Katherine squeezed the distraught woman's hand. "You've thought of something."

"A few months ago, I was searching for houses for sale around St. James's Square—for you, dear. You'd have the garden to walk Emma, and I believe your monthly meeting takes place on Pall Mall Street, not far..."

"It's a wonderful idea," Katherine said, mustering a warm smile. In fact, it was even more ideal than Susanna knew. Once Pru was married, she would reside mere blocks away.

When she was in London.

"What happened while you were near St. James's Square?"

Retracting her hand, Susanna leaned forward and used it to cover her face. It muffled her voice as she confessed, "I saw the Rochford coach around the corner from Norfolk House, on Charles Street. When I left my carriage behind to see if Celia was in and say hello, I saw her hurrying down the lane with her cheeks flushed and her hair a bit disheveled, I thought from the wind. But she refused to acknowledge me when I called out and jumped straightaway into her carriage and left before I reached it. She seemed... she seemed as though she might be avoiding me."

Susanna dissolved into fresh tears, and Katherine eased her arms around her stepmother's shoulders, pulling her close once more. "I promise, I will find the person who did your friend harm. They will pay for the sorrow they've caused."

The murderer had taken two lives. As Katherine laid her hand over Susanna's slightly rounded belly, she vowed that it would not be three.

CHAPTER SIXTEEN

L yle yawned, slouching in his seat over the cup of tea Lorna had fixed for him. He looked as though he hadn't slept a wink, despite it being near ten of the morning now.

"I must beg your forgiveness for the way I parted with you yesterday." *Except for you,* Katherine thought in Wayland's direction. He stood by the window again, more interested in the street than in the information being imparted in the room. How early did she have to call a meeting in order to ensure that he did not attend? Did he *live* with Annandale now?

Pru squeezed into the chair next to her fiancé, leaving the last free for Katherine, though she continued to stand. Annandale's valet, as always, stood by his elbow, far more interested in this investigation than she would have expected.

"I recognized the earring at once and went to chase down its owner and learn the truth of the matter."

Pru's mouth dropped open. She squeezed her eyebrows together as she asked in a small voice, "Why wouldn't you tell me?"

Lyle sat straighter. "Yes, why? We're your friends. You can trust us."

Katherine gave Wayland a lingering look, which he ignored. She glanced only briefly at McTavish and Annandale, newcomers to their circle. Although Pru trusted them with the details of the investigation, when it came to Katherine's own family, she preferred to handle the matter herself. If it had only been her, Pru, and Lyle... She might not have said a word in any case. She still felt overwhelmed by the turn of the investigation.

With Susanna's explanation, she was confident that her stepmother hadn't committed the crime. She would be able to corroborate it with Lord Bath, but also Susanna would not risk harm to the baby that a struggle in pushing someone off a balcony would certainly entail.

However, that brought her no closer to solving the murder unless she was able to find Lady Rochford's lover. That, as it had nothing to do with her step-mother, she vowed to do with her friends in tow. After all, they were something of a team, now.

"I am confident that the owner of the earring did not murder Lady Rochford. I have promised to hold her confidences, and therefore I must keep her identity to myself. However, she did impart some other pieces of information that might prove helpful."

Wayland turned away from the window for a moment. He raised one eyebrow askance. "You're withholding information?" His voice dripped with disapproval.

Katherine straightened her spine. "What do you care? You aren't a part of this investigation. Unless, of course, you've changed your mind on that subject?" It wasn't an invitation, precisely. Her words were more of a challenge.

He didn't rise to the bait. He shrugged. "Hardly. I'm only here because I have nothing better to do."

He was *infuriating*. Their investigation would be better off if he would only stop hanging about and *do* something.

Gritting her teeth, she turned back to the others and attempted to ignore him. "I've learned that Lord Bath did not know Lady Rochford prior to Lady Dalhousie's ice ball. He has been selling vials of healing waters to pregnant women, and that is why he was seen following our victim."

Lyle shifted in his seat, his expression one of bald interest as he set down his cup and saucer. He looked as though he might have guessed who the owner of the earring was, but he kept the information to himself. Let the others puzzle out the truth if they could.

Katherine continued, "Lady Rochford was seen on Charles Street near the corner where it meets St. James's Square near Norfolk House. From her suspicious demeanor and disheveled appearance, we can assume that her lover lives somewhere nearby."

"St. James's Square is nae far from here," Lord Annandale volunteered. "The day's a mite cold, but I reckon we'll warm up before long if we take the walk."

"And do what?" Pru asked with a laugh. "Knock on every door on Charles Street until a handsome man answers?"

"I think not," Annandale answered darkly.

Katherine bit back a laugh. "We can ask if anyone has seen Lady Rochford. It might be better than doing nothing."

"Try Lord Conyers's residence," Wayland advised from the window in a bored voice.

Lyle rolled his shoulders as he stood. "Lord Conyers? I didn't know he lived in St. James's Square."

Katherine gave Lyle a curious look. Did he presume to know where all the peers in London lived? Perhaps it was part of his job to know, as they likely didn't care to have Bow Street Runners near their residences, for all that men of Lyle's caliber made the streets of London far safer.

Wayland answered, "He purchased a house on Charles Street some months back to conduct his trysts. You ought to know that being an engaged man wouldn't stop someone of Conyers's reputation."

"That's deplorable," Pru exclaimed. She looked at Lord Annandale as if for confirmation.

"I have eyes only for you, love," he answered her softly.

Katherine tucked away a smile.

Wayland shrugged as if he didn't notice the brief heartfelt exchange. "If you ask me, Conyers is your best bet in that area. But if you don't know it, perhaps I'd better come along to point out the house."

Katherine crossed her arms. "How do you know where Lord Conyers's trysting house is? Has he invited you?"

Wayland smirked. "He does throw parties there from time to time, but no. My interest in his doings extends no farther than eavesdropping. He's particularly loud about his exploits while in the club." He paused. "I expect that's why I don't foresee him remaining engaged for much longer. Last I heard, his future father-in-law caught wind of his doings and challenged him to a duel if he didn't give them up. More gossip, of course."

Apparently, the men in London gossiped as much in their clubs as the women did at afternoon tea.

"Very well," Katherine said reluctantly. "Where does Lord Conyers keep his trysting house?

FIFTEEN MINUTES LATER, Katherine strolled behind Wayland's tall form, whose shadow fell over her and chilled her further as he led them to Lord Conyers's house on Charles Street. Lord Annandale strode beside him reluctantly, given the looks he shot over his shoulder at Pru. Katherine tightened her hold on Pru's arm, unwilling to give up her walking companion. She lowered her voice so only she and Lyle, on her other side, could hear her.

"He might have told us the address rather than leading us all the way here."

Pru smiled slyly as she studied Katherine's expression. "If you're so adamant to be in the lead, you could have accepted Wayland's offer of escort."

"I'd rather walk with you."

"And admire his form?"

Katherine choked on her tongue. "*No.*"

Lyle pretended not to hear the exchange, but the color flushing his cheeks gave him away. He walked with his head down, the brim of his hat pulled low, and his hands thrust into the pockets of his greatcoat.

Pru, satisfied, shrugged. "If you say so. I know I'm admiring the view."

Katherine looked anywhere other than at Wayland. Even without directly looking at him, she was far too aware of the way his greatcoat stretched across his broad shoulders and fell to brush the backs of his calves. He moved with a lethal grace that must have been learned while in the military.

"I never knew you so admired Captain Wayland," she teased.

A mistake. Pru's happy mood, it seemed, could not be shaken. "Then you admit he's worthy of admiration," her friend countered, her eyes dancing with delight.

Katherine certainly did not. Fortunately, she was saved from having to answer when a carriage hurried past. Wayland waited for it to depart before he gestured at the house opposite them.

"There it is, Conyers's house of debauchery."

"Is that what he called it?" Lyle drawled.

Wayland took a step back alongside them and grinned. "Likely not, but it seemed as good a name as any."

Katherine gaped at the huge house on the corner of Charles Street and St. James's Square. Why, it could rival Dorchester House. "If he's hoping to be discreet, I believe he fell short of the mark."

With a laugh, Wayland pointed out the far smaller house, which was at least half the size, if not more, that shared a wall with the one on the corner. "His is Number 2 Charles Street. The livery is just behind us, if you've ever a need to stable your horses."

Did he know that Katherine was searching for a house near here? She didn't answer him. In fact, she avoided looking at him altogether. Number 2 Charles Street was a modest dwelling for a lord, a mere four stories in height. The carved wooden door, unpainted, though it was thoroughly polished, was flanked by two evenly spaced windows.

More windows continued all the the way to the roof of the house, where the windows of the servants' quarters were squat little things half the height of the others. A chimney poked up one side of the house, where a remarkably narrow path presumably led down to a servants' entrance or the backyard. The entire edifice had been painted a cheery yellow, recently enough that Katherine didn't notice any signs of weathering from the unseasonable cold this autumn. The shutters were dark black, most pulled shut save for two on the upper levels. In short, it was a rather charming house. Not what she would have pictured for an adulterer.

"Let's see if he's in," Katherine said.

Wayland squared his shoulders. "Why don't I? It would be rather peculiar for a pair of women to call upon a man they don't know."

Katherine rounded on him, arms akimbo. "Whatever do you mean by that? Don't presume to tell me what I can and cannot do in the name of an investigation. I am every bit the detective that you are."

Eyes widening, Wayland held up his hands in surrender. He looked past her, likely at Lyle, as he sought an ally. He would certainly not find one in Pru.

"I've always been open in my admiration of your detective skills, Lady Katherine. But didn't you say that it is imperative no one become suspicious of the investigation? Two women calling upon Lord Conyers would be cause for suspicion."

Sard it, but he had a point! Katherine bit back an expletive and motioned with her hand. "Very well.

Knock on the door, but take Lyle with you. He knows every detail of the investigation."

The side of Wayland's mouth lifted in a smirk. "Have you been keeping something from me?"

"I thought you weren't interested in this investigation. If that's the case, you must not have been listening as well as Lyle." She turned to her friend. "Lyle, would you mind?"

"Of course not," he said, suddenly alert now that he had more to do than follow along. She shot him a grateful smile. Perhaps she ought to have used Lyle more for the investigation so far, but he had duties of his own to attend to, and she hadn't wanted to overwhelm him.

The two men strode across the street, both tall and lean, although Lyle's shock of ginger hair drew attention to him as much as Wayland's pronounced height —inches taller than even Lyle, who topped Katherine. Satisfied that they would accomplish their task if Lord Conyers was in residence, Katherine turned to her friend.

She stopped short as she found Pru in the circle of Lord Annandale's embrace. She must have gravitated toward him the moment Katherine released her arm. Katherine buried a pang at the sight, a reminder that she might very well lose her newfound friend.

Although she and Pru had only grown close since August, these past few months had found them to be friends and allies. Pru had the same zeal for investigation that Katherine had, albeit she hadn't grown up at the heels of a renowned detective.

Katherine turned away as she suggested, "Perhaps we can try another door. One of the neighbors might have seen something that can help."

"Let's try Number 3. A woman inside has been alternately staring at us and swishing the curtains closed for the past five minutes."

Katherine smiled at Pru's suggestion. "That sounds like an excellent place to start."

Trailed by Pru on Annandale's arm, Katherine led the way across the street to Number 3 Charles Street. Built much the same as its neighbors, it shared a wall with Number 4 and stood no taller or wider than Number 2. A quaint little edifice for a well-to-do man or woman who couldn't afford to live in the heart of Mayfair.

Straightening her shoulders, Katherine knocked on the door. To her left, she heard Wayland swear and try the knocker again. Presumably no one had answered him. *Excellent.* It would give her time to learn what she could from the neighbor without his interruption.

At first, no one answered. Katherine feared that

perhaps Pru had been mistaken and no one was at home. However, after a prolonged minute during which Katherine stamped her feet and rubbed her gloves together to keep warm, the door creaked open by a bare inch or two to reveal the woman behind.

Her placket-front dress, a light beige in color, attested that she was likely home alone or could not afford servants. The delicate wool seemed of too great a quality for her to be the hired help. Her hair was shielded behind a colorful scarf, and in the shadowed doorway, Katherine couldn't precisely tell her age. Older than she, by an estimate.

"Do I know you?"

Katherine clasped her hands in front of her and met the woman's wary eyes. "I'm afraid not, but I'm hoping to have a moment of your time. You see, I'm looking to retrace my friend's steps, and I believe she's come to this address several times over the past few weeks."

A lie, but perhaps it would loosen the woman's tongue.

"Who is your friend?"

Because Katherine saw no use in lying, she informed, "Celia Rochford. You might know her by the seal on her carriage, a blue crest with a—"

"Horse rampant," the woman completed. Clearly,

she was schooled in the heraldry of high society, not entirely surprising given where she lived. If she lived in the house alone, she had access to some form of income, and that likely meant a connection with one or more lords at some point in her family tree.

The woman reached behind her, rustling as she pulled a shawl around her shoulders. As she stepped out into the cold, clad in plain house slippers without any mittens or muff, she pulled the door shut behind her.

She lifted her chin. "I won't stand here with the door open. But I don't see fit to invite potentially unsavory characters into my home."

Katherine nearly laughed at the look she gave Lord Annandale.

Pru gasped. "Don't you recognize a marquess when you see one?"

The woman narrowed her eyes in suspicion. Although she gave him a curtsey and a polite incline of her head, she summarily dismissed him and looked at Katherine. "And you, madam?"

"Forgive me. I am Katherine Irvine, and this is my friend, Prudence Burwick, on Lord Annandale's arm. And your name?"

"Vera Ramsey."

"Mrs. Ramsey, I know it's cold, and I beg your

forgiveness for intruding, but we noticed you watching us just now, and we thought perhaps a woman as astute as yourself might have seen our friend, Lady Rochford."

"I've seen the carriage a few times," the woman said slowly. In the light of day, she was prettier than Katherine would have expected from the spinster cut of her clothing, high necked and long sleeved, not to mention plain in color. She looked no older than ten or fifteen years Katherine's senior, if that.

"When did you last see the carriage?" Katherine asked. With luck, she would be able to place Lady Rochford in the vicinity of Lord Conyers's trysting house shortly before her death.

The busybody drew her shawl closer around her shoulders and shivered. "Last week, but she isn't the only woman to visit. Lord Conyers, next door, has quite the array of female companionship at his beck and call. I've even seen them peering in the windows, they are so anxious to get in."

Her eyes, a light blue like the summer sky, twinkled with mischief. She leaned forward, as if waiting for Katherine to ask precisely whom she had seen here other than Lady Rochford. Although Katherine was mildly curious, she didn't have long before Wayland quit his efforts to bring someone to the door of the neighboring house and looked in on them.

Katherine asked, "Would that have been Monday or Tuesday of last week?" It would have been a mere day before Lady Rochford was killed. If she had delivered the news of her forthcoming child to her lover, possibly the father, she might have sparked a murderous intent in Lord Conyers then.

Mrs. Ramsey thought a moment. A furrow formed between her eyebrows, one of disappointment. After a moment, she said, "Perhaps Monday, but I certainly saw it on Wednesday or Thursday. I go out to do my charity work on those days, you see, helping out young women in need."

That couldn't possibly be true.

"Are you certain?" Katherine asked. "The exact date would be helpful." When Mrs. Ramsey turned a shrewd eye on Katherine, she hastily added, "You see, Lady Rochford was due to take tea with me, and she didn't show up. I wondered if it might have been something illicit."

To Katherine, it was a shabby excuse, but a gossip like Mrs. Ramsey seemed to accept the explanation readily enough. "It was certainly Wednesday or Thursday when I saw the carriage last. As I said, I go out on those days, and I saw it when I returned. If I had to say which day for certain, I might think... Thursday. Yes, Thursday. But it is possible that she also was here on Monday. Given the frequency with which I've seen that carriage the past few months, she and Lord Conyers were very familiar with each other, if you understand me."

Katherine couldn't possibly mistake her. But given that they were searching for Lady Rochford's lover, she had expected such speculation. It seemed they had the right address.

Even if they couldn't be certain of the date. Mrs. Ramsey seemed to be confused or perhaps fabricating a good story. Katherine tried to keep her opinion from her expression as she thanked the woman for her information and bade her adieu.

There was no possible way that Lady Rochford could have been on Charles Street last Thursday. She had died on Tuesday. Which begged the question—was Mrs. Ramsey's information unreliable, or was there something going on that Katherine had not yet considered?

CHAPTER SEVENTEEN

K atherine only half-expected Lord Conyers to
attend the musicale at Lady Edgerton's that
evening, even if he was engaged to her niece. He
seemed the type to prefer more titillating entertainments than a few young women barely out of the
schoolroom as they demonstrated their musical
prowess.

Fortunately, Katherine had another aim in
attending the musicale tonight. Now that she knew
that Lord Bath hadn't been responsible for Lady
Rochford's death, she could match him with Elizabeth
Verne with a clear conscience. *If* Elizabeth heeded her
note and attended tonight. Katherine's note had been
rather hasty, and she had only the vain hope that Mrs.
Fairchild could arrange an invitation to attend

tonight's event. Katherine didn't know the hostess well enough to wrangle one for Elizabeth herself.

As another pair of women entered through the door, Katherine sighed in relief. She recognized Mrs. Fairchild's brown hair and round figure instantly next to Elizabeth. Of course, she had expected for Elizabeth to bring her matchmaker to the event, but it added a layer of difficulty to the arrangement. Fortunately, if Elizabeth had attended, then she had decided to give Katherine's idea a try.

A try was all she needed. Lord Bath could be over-protective of the women in his life—or so Grandma Bath continually complained—but he had a good heart, deep pockets, and a title that dated back to the Norman invasion. In the world of lords and ladies, it was an aberration that a man such as him wasn't yet married. A testament to his stubbornness, if his grand-mother was to be believed.

Raising her glass of lemonade slightly, Katherine caught Elizabeth's eye. She was rewarded with the briefest of nods, an acknowledgment that Elizabeth would deign to be introduced to Lord Bath. With that assurance in place, Katherine waited for her to slip her chaperone and venture nearer.

With luck, that wouldn't be too long. The three young women, each between the ages of sixteen and twenty, were sitting at their instruments and awaiting their mother to quiet the gathering so they might perform. Grandma Bath had already been led to her seat, though Lord Bath must have departed to fetch her another glass of lemonade or champagne, for Katherine didn't espy him with her. She joined the old woman instead, bracing herself for what was to come.

Laughingly, Pru had abandoned her on the pretense of searching for Lord Conyers the moment they had arrived at the party. Katherine had no one to distract from Grandma Bath's insistence that *she* marry Lord Bath.

Battling for serenity, Katherine slipped into the seat next to Grandma Bath. Although she cringed at the question, she had to ask, "Where is your grandson?" After all, if Lord Bath were not present, Katherine couldn't introduce him to his future wife.

Grandma Bath turned an assessing eye on Katherine. "Missing his company, are you, Lady Katherine?" The old woman waved her hand through the air. A jewel on her ring finger winked in the light shed by candles around the room. "Ernest has gone to fetch me a bit of champagne to wet my throat. I hoped he might meet you along the way."

"Why? Did he have something important to tell

me?" Perhaps Lord Bath had been overwhelmed with guilt for lying to her and wished to confess the truth.

"No, no. I just hoped he might find the company of a young woman more scintillating than an old biddy like me." She winked.

Katherine bit the inside of her cheek to hide her frustration. "I'm afraid he'll have to find some other young woman instead."

"You *are* supposed to arrange that, aren't you? Where are your candidates? I'd like to meet them."

"In due time," Katherine answered, distracting from the fact that she had but one candidate and that particular woman was not convinced. "For now, why don't we enjoy the evening?"

Movement caught her eye, a flash of periwinkle skirts and burnished gold hair as Elizabeth wove through the throng of what must be near fifty guests all crammed into Lady Edgerton's large drawing room. Chairs faced the corner pianoforte, where the girls had arranged their instruments, in rows, leaving only a narrow path along the perimeter for the woman to navigate.

As Grandma Bath harrumphed, Katherine added, "I hope you don't mind, but I've asked a friend to sit with us tonight."

"That Burwick girl?" the old woman asked with

genuine interest. She must approve of Pru. "She has a sensible head on her shoulders."

Now Katherine wished that she had asked Pru to accompany her after all. "No, this is a friend you haven't met. Her name is Miss Elizabeth Verne, and I assure you she has as sensible a head on her shoulders as either Pru or I."

Grandma Bath narrowed her eyes. For a moment, Katherine thought she would ask the golden question of whether this woman was a candidate for marriage. However, instead, Grandma Bath merely nodded and said, "Very well."

Those two words rendered Katherine speechless for a moment. However, when the back of her neck prickled from the nearness of a body, she realized why Grandma Bath had cut the inquiry short.

"Here you are, Grandmama," Lord Bath said. He leaned forward to hand a flute of champagne to his grandmother. "Katherine, I hadn't realized you would be sitting with us as well tonight, or I would have brought you one too. I can fetch you a glass, if you're thirsty."

Katherine hefted her lemonade as she turned in her seat to view Lord Bath. Tonight, he wore those wide, ridiculous sleeves, as always. However, the cut of the rest of his clothes was fashionable, the color a dark maroon that suited him well. His smile, as always, was genuine.

"How is your father?" he asked. "He's been too busy for me to pin down since I've arrived in town."

"Papa is well. I'll remember him to you," Katherine answered politely.

Behind him, Elizabeth slipped between two people to stand at the edge of the chairs. She looked a bit frazzled but took a moment to pat herself down. As Katherine stood, the smile on her new friend's face was as serene as if she hadn't just escaped her chaperone by the skin of her teeth.

Katherine held out her hand to Elizabeth, gesturing her forward. "Lord Bath, may I present my friend Miss Elizabeth Verne. You might have crossed paths with her at Lady Dalhousie's ice ball."

At the mention of the murderous event, the marquess stiffened. He recovered marginally, smiling, but the expression did not meet his eyes. He'd scarcely inclined his head and murmured his polite delight upon meeting one of Katherine's friends when the hostess rang a spoon against her glass to call the room into order. As the clear peals of sound faded, everyone hurried to find their seats.

Somehow, in the mad scramble, Katherine found herself wedged between Lord Bath and his grandmother. Elizabeth was on Grandma Bath's far side. How had that happened? The pair would never fall in love if they weren't allowed to sit with one another.

As the girls in the corner of the room were introduced and each took a bow, their cheeks rosy with the admiration, the violinist pronouncedly shaky in her hands as she picked up her violin, Lord Bath leaned closer. "Katherine, my dear, I hope this is not an extension of your queries into my unmarried state. Your friend is lovely, but I haven't the time to devote to a wife."

Thankfully, his voice didn't carry. Katherine kept her expression even. "Of course not," she lied through her teeth. Thus far, her schemes to match two people together had always worked better once they decided for themselves that marriage was what they wanted. Forcing either party wouldn't make for a happy marriage.

The performers began their musicale to eddied whispers in the crowd gathered. The fact that they didn't seem to have the full attention of the guests seemed to frazzle the violinist even more. She continually darted her gaze toward the pianist. When it was her turn to join in, her first draw of the bow across the strings was jolting and discordant. She cringed, her face filling with color as she froze upon making the mistake. Her mother jumped to her feet. "Felicia. *Play*. I know you know how. We pay enough for lessons."

The cheeks of the other two girls turned pink with sympathy at their sister's embarrassment. They bowed over their instruments, prepared to start again.

Two chairs down, Elizabeth tsked under her breath. "That isn't how you handle a child's mistake. You have to nurture talent, not command it."

"Oh?" asked Grandma Bath in a loud whisper. "How would you have handled it?"

"Better to encourage her to continue and carry on as if the mistake had never been made. Everyone makes mistakes, and she seems particularly skittish of performing. After this, I doubt she ever will again."

Katherine smiled to herself at the conversation. Elizabeth would be able to handle Grandma Bath with aplomb, and perhaps she'd bring up the possibility of a school in Bath while she was at it. Now, Katherine had only to seat Lord Bath a touch closer so he, too, could hear.

She leaned closer to him. "Would you mind switching chairs? It's stifling in the middle."

"Certainly," he answered without question.

After they had made the move, the girls were ready to play again, and they began the song anew, from the beginning. Although the violinist was almost in tears and played so softly that Katherine barely even heard the instrument, when she joined in, she made no mistakes. The onset of their musical performance limited Elizabeth's conversation as she gave them her rapt attention. Hopefully, Grandma Bath would engage her in conversation again, and Lord Bath would have the opportunity to admire her intelligence and gracious conversational skills.

Katherine turned in her seat, searching the crowd for Lord Conyers. As expected, she didn't find him, but Pru and Annandale were seated near the back next to Wayland. Katherine stifled a sigh. Apparently, he went everywhere with Annandale, so she was going to have to get used to having him around.

Avoiding Wayland's gaze, she attempted to put him from her mind and continue her attempt to find Lady Rochford's lover. Presumably all the guests were now in the drawing room, no one at a card table set up elsewhere. If Lord Conyers wasn't in this room, he hadn't attended the event. Unfortunate but far from surprising.

The violin's notes became shaky as her stage fright overwhelmed the violinist. When her mother stood to chide her again, this time the poor girl turned her back and rushed from the room, likely to lose her lunch. Katherine winced in sympathy.

As did Elizabeth. "If she doesn't like to play, her mother shouldn't force her to. It's cruel. I'm sure the girl has other talents."

Grandma Bath harrumphed. "How do you expect her to find a husband if she's too shy to show her talents?"

Elizabeth scoffed. "We women are good for more than finding a husband, as you ought to know. She could teach or compose or find any number of other ways to pass her time."

Katherine opened her mouth to contribute to the conversation, but in the disorder of the room, she lost her voice. At the back of the room, Mrs. Fairchild had finally located her charge, if the glower on her face was any indication. And she certainly thought Katherine was poaching Miss Verne.

Hastily, Katherine muttered her excuses to Lord Bath and got to her feet. She had to have a word with the fellow matchmaker before Mrs. Fairchild ruined what had the potential to be a great match. She sidestepped a couple rising from their chairs to circle the perimeter as the hostess hastened to create order among her daughters before the night was proclaimed a disaster. It was likely too late, especially in the eyes of the poor violinist.

The moment they met halfway down the line,

Mrs. Fairchild glared daggers at Katherine. "You have no honor," she spat. "Stealing my client—"

Katherine held up her hands. "I am not stealing your client. Lord Bath is *my* client. If you'll only listen to me a moment, you'll see—"

"Lady Katherine!"

Tarnation! Why couldn't everyone leave her alone?

Lady Dalhousie, dressed in a peacock-bright gown that shimmered in the light with silver embroidery, laid her hand on her prized necklace as she stepped between the pair of matchmakers and their respective clients. The gossip smiled coyly. "Was that the Marquess of Bath I saw you sitting with?"

"Along with his grandmother and Miss Verne, yes." The last thing she wanted circulating were rumors that would feed Grandma Bath's delusion that Katherine should marry her grandson.

"How brave of you," Lady Dalhousie said, drawing out the statement. She stepped closer to them as others jostled their way to the perimeter of the room to mingle while the hostess called order.

Katherine felt a headache begin in her right temple, but she asked nonetheless, "Why is it brave of me to sit with a friend of my father's?"

"Why, because of the theft, of course!"

Theft?

Mrs. Fairchild asked, "What theft?"

"Haven't you heard?" Lady Dalhousie's eyes gleamed with perverse pleasure as she leaned in to share the latest *on-dit*. "Lady Rochford was missing a ring—a family heirloom—when her body was found. Do you think the theft had something to do with her death?"

Katherine's mind reeled with the news of the allegedly missing ring. Images of Lady Rochford's scraped finger and bloody knuckle surfaced. The killer had taken the ring. But why?

However, before she could puzzle that out, she urgently needed to stop Lady Dalhousie from spreading rumors about the Burglar of Bath or that Lady Rochford's death was not an accident. If the killer learned there was an investigation, they might take more care to cover their tracks.

She gazed into the crowd, searching for an ally. Pru and Annandale's backs were turned, but at that moment, Wayland, standing with them, glanced sideways. Their gazes locked. Katherine pressed her lips together, silently pleading for his help. He had come to her aid in Bath, after all.

Despite the desperation sure to be in her gaze, he turned away.

"How do you know the ring was missing?" Mrs.

Fairchild asked.

"I heard Lord Rochford demanded his wife's belongings from the police. He claims she always wore the ring, but it was missing. I'm not sure why they were holding her belongings." Lady Dalhousie leaned in and lowered her voice. "Perhaps they had suspicions about the circumstances around her death."

"I thought Lady Rochford's death was ruled a terrible accident."

"Exactly so," Katherine said, reinforcing Mrs. Fairchild's words even if they were wrong. At all costs, she had to find a way to stop Lady Dalhousie from repeating her fanciful tales before she created a panic and caused the murderer to flee. Especially since—

"Do you think it might be the Burglar of Bath?" Lady Dalhousie asked, her voice not quite pitched at as low a whisper as Katherine would have preferred.

She swallowed a groan.

Lady Dalhousie, unfortunately, took the matter one step further and glanced toward the chairs. Thankfully, she lowered her voice further before she added, "You know, the name of the burglar was never announced. You don't think it might be Lord Bath, do you? He was in both places, and I saw him following Lady Rochford upstairs mere minutes before she—"

"Och now, Lady Dalhousie," boomed a Scottish

burr. Lord Annandale insinuated himself into the conversation with more confidence than tact. He gave both Lady Dalhousie and Mrs. Fairchild a dazzling grin.

Katherine had thought he hadn't seen her plight from his position, but he must have been wrong. Her knees weakened. At least Pru had chosen her future husband well. He knew when to come to a lady's rescue, for instance.

Loudly, Lord Annandale proclaimed, "What's that story yer telling? Might it be how ye found those pretty wee gems around yer throat, back in Bath?"

Lady Dalhousie flushed with color. She clasped her hand to her throat, as if to cover the necklace she never let out of her sight. "I— no, I was merely discussing the evening's entertainments."

Lord Annandale scoffed. Judging by the crinkle in the corners of his eyes, a sign of mirth, he didn't believe her. "Och now, there's little to talk about. I hear there's a fine tale about the origin of that wee pendant. Something about the war?"

Although hot color continued to drench Lady Dalhousie's cheeks, she welcomed the topic and offered a tentative smile. "Why yes, my lord. Haven't you heard? This necklace once belonged to Josephine when she was empress..."

Relieved to find Lady Dalhousie so occupied, even if she couldn't stand to hear the embellished and ever-changing tale even one more time, Katherine mouthed her gratitude at Lord Annandale. He nodded once, indicating his acceptance, and pretended to pay rapt attention to Lady Dalhousie, even though he must have heard the story as many times as she. In Bath a couple months ago, the old biddy hadn't been shy about letting everyone know the highly unlikely tale of her distinctive necklace.

Taking the opportunity to break away from the group, Katherine checked over her shoulder to ensure that Elizabeth was still well situated with Lord Bath and his grandmother. Sometime soon, she would have to find a private moment with Mrs. Fairchild in order to explain her motives, but for now, she satisfied herself in the conversation that appeared from this distance to be flowing freely.

Then, walking along the perimeter of the room in search of Pru, Katherine mulled over Lady Dalhousie's latest fixation. She thought Lord Bath was the murderer, a possibility that Katherine had already disproven upon discovering the reason why Lord Bath had been absent from the ballroom preceding Lady Rochford's murder.

Katherine figured he must have lied to protect his

clients. It was likely that Susanna had begged him not to tell anyone lest Katherine's father learn of the healing waters and become worried about the pregnancy. Probably Lady Rochford felt the same way.

Now that Katherine had a moment to think, she wondered about this new development with Lady Rochford's ring. If, indeed, that detail wasn't a concoction of Lady Dalhousie's penchant for dramatics, it might be another clue.

"You look worried. Has something happened?"

At Pru's voice, Katherine glanced up. She was less than ten feet from Lord Annandale's continued conversation, having stopped in her tracks while she thought. She had to get better control over herself, lest all her thoughts show on her face.

Fortunately, Pru was her ally, and she felt free enough to whisper, "Lady Dalhousie mentioned that Lady Rochford had been wearing a ring, but it was absent from her finger when she fell."

"A ring?" Pru glanced around the room, studying those around them before she stepped closer and lowered her voice. She fiddled with the sleeves of her delicate muslin gown. It looked pretty on her. "Did she say what the ring looked like? Perhaps if we find it…"

Katherine pressed her lips together grimly as she completed the sentence in her head. If they located the ring, they might locate Lady Rochford's killer. "It was a family ring that she always wore. Should be easy to get a description of. Perhaps, if I find a moment, I'll ask her in private."

Although if Katherine did that, she would only encourage the old biddy to continue spreading her gossip.

Pru frowned, tapping her chin. "Could it have been lost during the struggle?"

"We didn't find it."

"But we weren't looking for a ring." Pru jabbed her finger at Katherine. "Maybe Rayner picked up more than an earring that night."

"Do you think the killer stole the ring as some sort of keepsake?"

Katherine nibbled on her lower lip as she thought. "If it were her jilted lover, he might have taken it to remember her by."

Pru nodded. "If Lord Rochford were the killer, he would have no cause to rip it off her finger, as he would get the ring in her belongings anyway, so it seems we're back to her lover once more."

"Until we find and question Lord Conyers to learn where he was during the time of the murder, I don't see how we can move past him to another suspect."

At the front of the room, the hostess once more

called for order as her daughters—minus the violinist—prepared to continue the performance. Katherine parted from her friend to return to her seat, but she couldn't help but scan the room one last time as she went.

If she wanted to solve this murder, she had to find Lord Conyers and the sooner, the better.

CHAPTER EIGHTEEN

Harriet squarely blocked the front doorway of Dorchester House, her arms splayed to reach from one side of the frame to the other. Upon seeing her determination, the butler muttered under his breath about finding Katherine a warmer pair of mittens and made himself scarce. The servants might be daunted by Harriet's behavior, but Katherine certainly was not.

"I need to return to Charles Street and question Lord Conyers. If you won't move and call for the carriage, I'll trounce through the snow myself and pay a call to the livery. Tarnation, I'll walk all the way to St. James's Square if I must!"

Positioned between Katherine and Harriet with some vain hope of being let outdoors, Emma whined.

The wrinkles on her face deepened as she glanced from one woman to the other. Katherine and Harriet weren't often at odds, not the least because Katherine employed the latter.

"You've gone mad. First I hear you nearly walk home at night, alone, in the freezing cold—"

"When have you been talking to Wayland?" No one else could possibly have given her that information. Come to think of it, why was Captain Wayland speaking with Katherine's servants? That couldn't bode well at all.

As if she hadn't heard the question, Harriet continued overtop, "And now you want to call upon a gentleman, *alone*, before half of London has yet arisen!"

Katherine stifled a sigh. "You're exaggerating. It's half seven in the morning. Anyone who works for a living will be awake."

"Not this lord you're bent on rousing from his bed."

Hopefully with his mistress, Katherine thought privately. If Lord Conyers so often brought women to his townhouse on Charles Street, it was likely that he slept there as well. Which meant if she rose and called on him early enough, she might be able to confront him before he could avoid her. Again.

Not that he could have known that she would attend a musicale organized by one of his soon-to-be relatives. But he hadn't been there, which, if Katherine had been affianced to him, she would have found highly irregular. She didn't have a hope of being let into a gentlemen's club, and the thought of asking Wayland to check left a sour taste in her mouth, so she had no other recourse. She would call upon him so early that he would have no option but to meet with her.

Then when she questioned him she would be able to progress this investigation, so if nothing else, her stepmother might be able to find some peace. When Katherine had returned home from the musicale last night, she had found her stepmother curled on the settee in her father's embrace as he rubbed her stomach. At this rate, Katherine, too, feared that her stepmother might lose the baby.

With a fierce look, Harriet added, "You'll be turned away at the doorstep and told that the lord you seek is not in residence."

Katherine laughed. "Lord Conyers, turn away a woman? Not judging from his reputation. He'll let me into the house, I wager." Not that she intended to step into the house. She would insist that the lord meet her at the door himself.

Given that no one had answered the door yesterday when they'd called, Katherine thought it likely that he didn't keep a full staff on at that particular residence. Perhaps he sent a maid over from his official residence to clean or brought a valet with him when he stayed overnight. Had there been more servants at hand, one would have answered the door.

Therefore, Katherine likely had only the valet to convince that she was one of his master's paramours seeking a moment alone with him. It shouldn't be too difficult, she hoped.

"No," Harriet answered vehemently. "I will not let you step out of this house if you're intent on seeking your grave. You'll have to turn me out before I'll let you through this door."

Emma whined again, lowering herself to the floor as if to make herself smaller.

"Be reasonable," Katherine chided.

"I am being reasonable. If you're so bent on speaking with this lord, you should bring someone with you. For protection."

Katherine crossed her arms. "Are you volunteering?"

Harriet's complexion paled. "Certainly not! I'm not entering the home of a murderer, and you shouldn't either!"

"So he's jumped from being a suspect to a murderer, in your estimation?"

"If the possibility exists, then you must consider the worst. Or have you forgotten the Pink Ribbon Murderer?"

Katherine's stomach lurched. That investigation had resulted in a close brush with death for Katherine. But she'd survived. She could undoubtedly survive another.

The touch of a furry head rubbing against her skirts returned her to the present. Emma craned her neck back, her ears inquisitive as she whined again.

"I haven't forgotten."

"By staying home," Harriet said firmly. "Or at the very least, sending a note to one of your friends to accompany you. Why not Captain Wayland? He's seen war. He could protect you."

"I can protect myself," Katherine reminded her. Between her father and Lyle, she had learned enough tricks of her fists and elbows to deter an opponent, even a stronger or larger one. Her fear was getting the better of her again, and she couldn't let it do that.

Given the way Wayland had been acting, Katherine was not about to ask him for help. He'd all but ignored her. Not that she cared, did she?

A strong rap sounded at the door behind her, three

sharp taps of the knocker followed by silence. Emma looked from one to the other before she faced the door and barked with enthusiasm, tail wagging. Harriet remained still, blocking the path.

"Don't you intend to answer the door?" Katherine asked.

"Who could be calling this early in the morning? It's likely a footman here to leave his mistress's card."

Katherine raised an eyebrow as Emma's barking almost overwhelmed Harriet's disgruntled mutter. "You won't know until you open the door."

With a sigh, Harriet turned and bent to scoop up Emma. She thrust the pug into Katherine's arms wordlessly. Fearing that Emma might barge into the street if she let her down, Katherine hoisted her pet onto her hip.

Harriet opened the door to reveal a weary-looking Lyle. "Thank goodness," Harriet exclaimed with feeling. "You're here."

Lyle stood mutely, blinking at her as if he couldn't comprehend her words. Harriet caught him by the hand and towed him into the house. Color rose in his cheeks as he stumbled through the door.

"You can talk some sense into Lady Katherine. She's bent on finding herself the murderer's next victim, and she won't listen to me."

Lyle blinked several more times, a whirl of snowflakes following him into the house along with a gust of wind. He stared down at his glove, which Harriet still held. "Oh. That's why you're relieved to see me."

She dropped his hand and shoved the door closed, shutting out the frigid air. It had still intruded enough upon the house for her to hug her arms and rub them to warm herself. "Of course it is. You're one of the few people who can talk sense into her. I'm not letting her go out alone to pay a call on a potential killer!"

"No," Lyle said slowly, turning his gaze to Katherine as if seeing her there for the first time. "That would be unwise. Why are you planning on interviewing a suspect alone? You always have Miss Burwick with you now."

Yes, and Katherine had best learn not to rely on having her friend near at hand. Once Pru married, she would be off to Scotland, only in town during the winter months, if then. No, Katherine had to find a way to conduct her investigations without relying on Pru's canny insight or Wayland's unpredictable aid.

Calmly, Katherine informed them, "I hoped to interview Lord Conyers at his townhouse. If I catch him early enough, he might yet be with a... lady friend and less likely to balk when I confront him."

"Ah." Lyle's cheeks flushed again. He removed his hat and gloves to camouflage the reaction.

"Tell her not to go," Harriet insisted. She stepped forward, briskly retrieved Emma, and fiddled with the bow around her neck. Harriet must not think Katherine in danger of walking out the door if Lyle was inside, never mind that she had already dressed to go out.

"Why do you believe he will be there? No one answered yesterday when Wayland and I knocked. The house is likely empty." Lyle tucked his gloves into his pocket then rolled the brim of his hat between his palms. "Oh, that reminds me. I'd hoped to hear what the neighbor had to say. I saw you speaking with her, but you refused to say a word when we rejoined you." He darted his gaze to the drawing room. "Perhaps we can sit someplace warm?"

He looked as though a strong wind might bowl him over. Katherine wrinkled her nose. "Did you work through the night again?"

He nodded. "I've been handed another investigation. I've only just ended my shift, and I'd dearly love to sit down."

After depositing Emma on the ground, Harriet helped Lyle with his coat. "I'll see if there's some tea ready so you don't fall asleep while she's convincing you to let her out of the house. I trust you won't let her run off." Harriet pierced him with a stern look, making the color rise in his cheeks again.

He stumbled over his tongue, which she took for an answer and turned to shut away his greatcoat and hat in the closet. Katherine ushered him into the nearest sitting room.

"What's gotten into her?" he mumbled as he all but fell into a spindly, uncomfortable chair. He didn't appear to notice its hardness.

Katherine shrugged. "She's convinced that Lord Conyers is the murderer, I suspect. She won't hear of me speaking to him."

"How will you know if he is to blame without speaking to him?"

With a triumphant smile, Katherine dropped into the chair opposite. "Exactly!" The click of Emma's claws was muffled against the carpet as she trotted toward Katherine, who obliged her by picking her up and placing the dog in her lap.

"What makes her think Lord Conyers is the murderer?" Lyle asked as he rubbed his forehead, fatigued. "We can't even say for certain that he is Lady Rochford's lover."

"Actually, we can," Katherine corrected sheepishly. "His neighbor, Mrs. Ramsey, confirmed that she had seen the Rochford carriage several times on that street over the past week."

"Several times?" Lyle raised his eyebrows, dubious.

Katherine's cheeks flushed with heat. "Yes, well, the woman seemed to like gossip and might have been confused. She has seen the carriage multiple times, but she seemed certain that the last time was on Thursday, when Lady Rochford was already dead. She clearly has her days mixed."

"Can we be certain that she wasn't concocting the entire tale?"

Katherine scratched beneath Emma's ribbon. The pug made a contented sound and leaned her chin against Katherine's leg. "Mrs. Ramsey was able to recollect the Rochford crest in detail. How else would she have been able to do so if not by having seen the carriage often enough to recognize it?"

"Debrett's?" Lyle asked, naming a popular genealogy record for titled families.

Katherine had to concede the point to him, even if she added, "Why would she bother to say it was the Rochford crest if she was not sure? I'm inclined to believe her, at least until I can confront Lord Conyers and ask him myself how intimately he knew Lady Rochford."

"You don't need to call upon him at his trysting house in order to do so—"

Whatever Lyle was about to suggest, he was interrupted by Harriet as she carried a silver tray in through the doorway, struggling to angle it so that she didn't nip her fingers as she walked through. As the tray tipped, laden with teacups, a teapot, plates and saucers, and a slab of seedcake, Lyle jumped to his feet and hurried to help her steady it.

"I have it," she said, sounding a bit out of breath from her run to the kitchen. "You should sit before you fall down."

He didn't protest. As he returned to his seat, Harriet crossed to the nearest table and set down her tray. She poured out a cup of tea, fixed it the way Lyle liked it, and added a thick slice of seedcake to the dish before handing him both. She made no move to offer the same to Katherine.

"Thank you," Lyle said, his gratitude tentative as he eyed the space between the two women.

Harriet straightened but didn't look at Katherine. Primly, she said, "I only serve people who are not dressed to go out."

Katherine was still wearing her pelisse and hat. With a sigh, she tugged the latter off and shifted Emma to the floor in order to unbutton the thick garment ending at her calves. "Very well. Consider this your victory—for now. I still intend to speak with Lord Conyers. If he happens to have Lady Rochford's ring..."

"Ahhh, the ring. That is what Lord Rochford said was missing." Lyle returned his teacup to its saucer with a clink.

Katherine supplied, "Lady Dalhousie was blathering on about how Lady Rochford had been robbed before she had been killed. I think the scrape on her finger and blood on her knuckles is because the killer ripped the ring off her finger."

"See?" Harriet said, shaking her head. She arranged the seedcake on Katherine's plate. "The killer is dangerous. Lady Katherine has more ambition than sense this morning."

"If you ask me, Lord Rochford is protesting too much about the ring. He was at the ball that night with his wife." Lyle ate a piece of seedcake.

Katherine paused with the teacup halfway to her lips. "Are you saying Lord Rockford took the ring and then pushed his wife over the balcony? Why? He would get the ring back with her things."

"Maybe he was angry. It was his family ring, and if he discovered her affair, it would be an insult to his family." Lyle pressed his lips together. "Or maybe he had a more nefarious reason. He might have been intending to use the ring to frame the lover for her death."

Katherine frowned as she slowly sipped at her tea. It could have used a minute longer in the pot, but she didn't say as much aloud, as she had more important things on her mind. "I recall when I paid a visit to Lord Rochford on Thursday, his housekeeper was lamenting that the day before, he had been too deep in his cups to tell his daughter the terrible news. If that is true, then he would have been in no shape to plant a ring anywhere. No matter what, it seems we must speak with Lord Conyers."

Lyle nodded slowly. He picked at his seedcake, tearing it into smaller and smaller pieces. "If you're set on talking to Lord Conyers, then there is one location we'll be sure to find him today."

"Yes," Katherine answered, stalwart. "At his townhouse."

Harriet made a noise of dismay and took Katherine's half-finished teacup. She bustled, arranging everything on the tray. Her movements were jerky and tight with disapproval.

"As luck would have it, you're better off waiting and trying to find him at Hyde Park later today."

Katherine frowned. "Hyde Park?" It was the

middle of winter; hardly anyone went for a ride or walk in knee- or hip-deep snow if they could avoid it. "Why would I find him there?"

Smirking, Lyle shook his head. "How is it that I manage to hear of social events before you do? There's to be a miniature Frost Fair like the one on the Thames two years ago."

"It was colder then. I can't imagine that the Thames has frozen solid enough to walk an elephant across." Katherine had barely been able to see the beast, the crowds flocking to the Thames had been so thick.

"It isn't to be held on the Thames. Some vendors have decided to set up their stalls on the Serpentine in Hyde Park, since it has been frozen solid for the past two days at least." Lyle shrugged. "I'm sure you'll recall the last Frost Fair. Even if this one will cater only to residents of Mayfair, Bow Street expects it to be every bit as rowdy as the first and has asked for volunteers to patrol Hyde Park and keep the peace."

Katherine raised her eyebrows. "Are you calling the demure sea of debutantes and chaperones rowdy?"

"Not precisely," he answered with a shrug of one shoulder. "But their presence begs the presence of male escorts, which breeds more vendors, more money at hand, and let's face it — pickpockets. You know how lords and ladies behave if they believe they've been robbed."

"Are you one of those who will be patrolling the park?"

"I am," he confirmed. He rose, stretching as he offered his plate and teacup to Harriet with a smile. "Thank you for the tea and cake, but I fear I must get some sleep before I take patrol. I'll keep my eye out for Lord Conyers and let you know if I see him," Lyle promised Katherine.

She nodded. "Very well. Your way might be best after all, but if I don't find him, I'm going to call on him tomorrow morning at Charles Street."

Harriet sighed as she escorted Lyle out of the room to fetch his greatcoat. She didn't quite lower her voice enough not to carry as she murmured, "Thank you for trying. At least you postponed the inevitable."

"If we don't find Conyers at the Frost Fair, I'll make certain I accompany her to the townhouse."

"I'd rest easier," Harriet answered in relief, her voice fading as they stepped out of earshot.

Katherine leaned forward and plucked her teacup from the tray, finishing it in two sips. "I'm not help-less," she muttered under her breath. "And I'm not reliant on my friends."

Stating the matter aloud didn't help her to gain

confidence in the subject. She feared that she had become altogether too reliant on solving her investigations with help. Lyle was overworked, and Pru was shortly to depart. Oh well, Katherine was perfectly capable of doing her detective work on her own.

CHAPTER NINETEEN

Katherine should have gone to Charles Street. For one thing, it would have taken less time even though St. James's Square was farther from Dorchester House than Hyde Park. She'd sent a footman with a note to Pru with the idea the moment Lyle left. Of course, Pru had insisted upon waiting for Lord Annandale. While in London, it seemed that Lord Annandale was attached to Wayland. Or perhaps the latter was attached to the marquess. Either way, the pair were inseparable, and by the time the soon-to-be-married couple called upon Katherine, Wayland was in tow.

On her doorstep. In plain daylight! Katherine's heart jumped into her throat. She accepted her winter wear hastily, not even noting which pelisse, hat, and gloves the butler handed to her before she stepped out and shut the door behind her. Had he recognized Captain Wayland? With his height and broad shoulders, Wayland wasn't easy to mistake. If word carried to Papa's ear that she was keeping company with him, it would not be good.

Katherine scurried down the stairs and attached herself to his elbow without complaint. "What are you doing here?" She hissed the question under her breath as she tried to stuff her hair beneath her hat using only one hand.

Wayland, a gentleman even if he was also a scoundrel, paused to help her with the task. His expression was even, giving away no satisfaction or unease or any other emotion Katherine might ascribe to him.

"Annandale invited me to the Hyde Park Frost Fair. It sounds like it will make for a diverting afternoon."

"You plan on skating and drinking hot chocolate and eating gingerbread, do you?"

He shrugged. "If I'm in good company, why not?"

"You haven't brought any skates."

"Neither have you."

Katherine didn't plan on skating if she could help herself. She had a reputation for clumsiness after the past two investigations—unearned, she might add. However, if anyone ever witnessed her on skates, she would be confirmed as the clumsiest woman in all England. Since she spent nearly all her time in London, she rarely had the opportunity to practice.

With an air of friendliness and an easy lope, Lord Annandale strode abreast of them with Pru on his arm. Her cheeks were pink, perhaps from the exertion of keeping up with his stride. Clearly eavesdropping, he interrupted. "I've McTavish waiting near the park with blades. I was nae sure if ye Londoners had skates, so he brought ye some extra."

Tarnation! Somehow, she would have to find an excuse not to use them.

"I'm not attending to socialize. We must find Lord Conyers at once."

"Aye, and I'll keep watch, ne'er ye fear."

Did Lord Annandale even know what Lord Conyers looked like? Katherine opened her mouth to ask, but Wayland spoke overtop her.

"As will I."

She narrowed her eyes. "I thought you weren't helping this investigation."

He shrugged, his muscles bunching beneath her hand on his sleeve. "I'm not. I'm helping a friend.

Annandale doesn't remember meeting Conyers, so I'll point him out."

That answered that question. Wayland was helping Lord Annandale, *not* Katherine. If it benefitted her, did she have the right to complain?

Perhaps he, too, was only content in conducting his own investigations.

But did that explain his change in behavior toward her? Since he'd returned, he hadn't complimented her, hadn't cajoled information from her or gone out of his way to find himself alone with her. He certainly hadn't stood as close to her as he had in the alley in Bath, when they had been evading the city watch and pressed up behind a set of crates to shield themselves...

She didn't want him to stand so close to her or pay her so much attention. She needed no man in her life to do those things, him above all. But a small part of her seemed stuck in the past, in Bath, when she must have imagined the amorous look in his eye now absent.

"Katherine?"

She blinked hard as she returned to the present. They'd reached the grand gates of Hyde Park, open for all to venture inside. She turned her head to meet her friend's inquisitive gaze. "Yes, Pru? I'm sorry, did you say something?"

A sly smile passed across Pru's face. "Nothing of

import. Where do you propose we search for Lord Conyers? Perhaps we should split up, to better cover more ground."

"The vendors and skating are all set up on the Serpentine. It would be counterintuitive to look elsewhere."

"If you insist," Pru answered, adjusting her hood. "I thought you might want a bit more time alone... with your thoughts."

How long had Katherine been brooding? Heat flushed her cheeks, and she snatched her hand from Wayland's arm in order to adjust her hat. "I'm here to find Lord Conyers and question him regarding Lady Rochford's murder. The sooner we do that, the better."

"There's no reason you can't mix business and pleasure. We are attending the Hyde Park Frost Fair." Although Wayland didn't look at her while he made the suggestion, his words were clearly aimed at her.

"Said by a man who has no business to attend to at present." And who likely was steady on his feet on the ice. Where did Wayland's family keep their country estate? He might have grown up skating around frozen ponds in the north, for all Katherine knew.

Softly, he countered, "Simply because I choose not to involve you in my business doesn't mean I have none." He offered his arm, stiff. "Shall we?"

She'd offended him. He, like her, was a detective. Unlike her, the son of a viscount and a decorated war hero attained far more respect in the profession. To her knowledge, he'd even been asked to consult by Bow Street, much like her father. Katherine, on the other hand, had to sneak about in order to conduct her investigations so she wasn't given the cut direct by high society. Eccentric earls' daughters or not, gently bred young women did not conduct investigations. At least, not in the eyes of polite society.

Her views on the matter were very different, hence why she had taken Pru under her wing so readily.

"It looks as though we aren't the first to arrive."

Her thoughts had consumed her once again. When she glanced up, they had rounded the bend in front of the Serpentine. Here, the ground gently rolled toward the bank of the manmade lake in the middle of the park. Now iced over, the scene was precisely as Lyle had described: vendors had set up their stalls in a long row down the middle of the ice. They hawked their wares, steam rising from vats of coffee and chocolate to drink, roasted chestnuts, steamed oysters, and more. Young girls skated with trays hanging from their necks, laden with pies and warm gingerbread. On the banks, officers of Bow Street stood guard, keeping a watch on the festivities. Music lilted into the air from bagpipes more suited to the north and flutes deftly played. These street musicians had hats upturned at their feet for coin.

In between, everyone still in London appeared to have turned up to skate and mingle. Katherine recognized debutantes gliding on the gallant arms of their suitors, their chaperones waiting on the banks or skating slowly behind them. Families had brought out young children, hoisting them between adults so they wouldn't fall on unsteady legs. Young girls not yet out in society skated in figure eights while casting eyes at men who pretended not to take notice. Their skirts were held up with sashes to avoid their tripping over them with the skates, displaying their stocking-clad ankles.

In the whirl of bodies, Katherine couldn't pick out those she knew from those she had only been introduced to once or twice or even guests from the country who didn't typically winter in Town. Faces blurred into one another, gentlemen with hawkers, ladies with pie girls. People skated along the narrow Serpentine, and more still strolled along the banks, the snow having been stamped down to make for even footing.

"Do you see him?" Katherine whispered as she clutched Wayland's arm.

"Not yet."

With a sigh, she slipped free. Lord Annandale raised his arm to hail the distinctive ginger head of his valet, standing head and shoulders above most of the crowd. Beaming, McTavish winked at the young woman offering him chestnuts along the shore and navigated the crowd, nodding in deference as he passed peers. He wasn't the only manservant or lady's maid in the throng today.

Katherine followed Pru and Annandale to meet the valet midway, in an open patch of snow. He held up four long blades to be attached to their boots. "There ye are, milord. I've yer blades sharpened and ready."

With a shudder, Katherine stepped back, hoping to be excluded from the procession. McTavish was already fawning over Pru and coaxing her to the side of the Serpentine, where it would be easier to access the ice. Perhaps splitting up wasn't the worst idea if they hoped to search the crowd.

Wayland, unfortunately, attached himself to her side. "Where are you going?"

"Pru had the right of it. There are so many people here that we can't hope to catch sight of Lord Conyers if we don't take separate paths. I'll walk along the shore and see if I can find him."

"There are only servants, chaperones, and watchmen along the shores that I can see."

Katherine took another wary step or two backward. "He might have hidden himself among them. In plain view, so to speak."

"Why would he?" Wayland raised his eyebrows. "If he's attended the fair, it's to woo a ladylove or perhaps curry favor with his rich fiancée."

"I thought you said her father had rescinded the engagement."

Wayland shrugged. "I would if I were him, but I haven't heard definitive news on the subject. It might be that Conyers has decided to wait out the gossip before he returns to polite society."

With a scoff, Katherine shook her head. "Why would he care? He already has a reputation for being a rake."

"Perhaps... but his future father-in-law is a very rich man, if not from an old family. Half the peerage is in debt up to their eyeballs. They need business arrangements with such men if they're to keep their ancestral estates in one piece."

Katherine pursed her lips. "Are you speaking from experience?"

Scowling, Wayland snapped, "Hardly. I work for a living. A cardinal sin in the eyes of my father, so I'll thank you to keep that information to yourself before I'm disowned."

"You take money for your services?" Katherine made a face as the words slipped out of her mouth. "Directly, I mean. I employ a solicitor to collect the fees. It keeps my name from getting tarnished from my matchmaking endeavors." She laughed. "I doubt I'd ever be invited into another elite event without a client if I took the money directly."

His disapproving expression eased, the corners of his mouth tipping up slightly. "I think you underestimate yourself. But no, I don't see the reason to waste money on such a ridiculous expenditure. My family speaks for itself. I would only think less of myself if I laid about all day and exploited my tenants."

From the amount of paperwork Papa had to look after regarding his estates—employees, tenants, upkeep, and keeping the peace when squabbles arose—Katherine knew there was far more to managing an estate or even a household. However, she couldn't disagree with his opinion of high society in general. It was fashionable not to lift a finger to work, not even to brush one's hair. Katherine liked to think she was more sensible than to be coddled all the time.

In an attempt to maintain civility, Katherine murmured, "I doubt a man like you would take well to sitting back while others did all the work. What would you do with your time? Read the latest novels?"

"Or write them," he said with a wink.

She laughed. "You ought to meet Lady Brackley. She always has an idea for a novel on the go, if not several. She was at the latest Society meeting."

"I'm sorry to have missed it," Wayland said, his eyes crinkling in the corners with mirth. "Our friends are getting away from us. Shall we?"

Katherine, pained, looked out over the shore once more. Perhaps she could use Lyle as an excuse to avoid those wretched blades.

"You know how to skate, don't you?"

"Of course," she said hastily. "I attended the last Frost Fair." Even if it had been the first time she'd ever set foot—or blade—upon the ice.

"Good. It won't take long for you to adjust, then. All it takes is a moment to catch your balance."

Or fall flat on her face.

Unfortunately, she couldn't deny his enthusiasm. For all that she would have preferred to remain on solid ground, he was right. The only people waiting on the shoreline were those of the working class or older matrons who watched their charges from afar. If she wanted to find Lord Conyers, it appeared as though she would have to meet him on the ice.

She swore under her breath, but Wayland seemed not to hear.

McTavish waited with a grin to hand them their blades. As he bent to tie Katherine's to the bottoms of her boots, she leaned heavily on Wayland for balance. Even once McTavish stood, she couldn't seem to find her balance—and she hadn't yet stepped onto the ice!

"Easy, now," Wayland whispered in her ear. "If you can't manage to walk, I can carry you to the ice. Mind the bumps near the edge. That's where the ice is thinnest and liable to crack."

Katherine swallowed the urge to renege on her decision to skate. However, between the two men, she soon found herself deposited on the ice. McTavish retracted his arm first.

"Are you ready?" Wayland asked. "I have to put on my skates. If you stand on your own for a moment, I'll return shortly to help."

"I'm perfectly able to stand on my own," she lied.

The moment he stepped away, she regretted the decision. Even hoisted up, her skirts seemed to get in the way. Her skates slid in opposite directions, and she flung out her arms in a desperate bid to keep herself upright. She bit her lower lip hard as she careened backward despite her efforts.

She impacted Wayland's firm body with enough

force to lose her breath. He grunted as he took an involuntary step backward, one foot on the ice and one on solid ground. She held tight to both his arms around her middle, her back to his chest, as she tried to angle the skates beneath her again. They had a mind of their own, intent on leaving her bereft of footing.

"You should have admitted you couldn't skate."

"I can," she insisted, feeling embarrassed at their awkward position, which somehow didn't *feel* so awkward. "If you'll only tip me upright again instead of hauling me back, I'll make do."

"Liar," he said, though he adjusted his position so she stood straighter.

Around them, people had stopped to gawk and giggle behind their hands. Her face flushed hot. "Release me," she commanded, breathless.

"You'll fall."

"You don't know that for certain."

"Stubbornness alone will not keep you upright."

Katherine gritted her teeth. "Neither will you. You haven't even donned your skates."

"You didn't give me time," he said, his voice thick with good humor. "Let's get you back onto solid ground again. McTavish?"

"I don't need your help."

At that, he was silent. He released her into

McTavish's grip as he stepped back to don his skates. At the moment, with everyone staring, all she wanted was to remove hers and blend with the crowd on the banks. Surely Lyle was nearby.

"Lady Katherine! Come, give an old woman your arm."

Katherine stared, agog, as Grandma Bath gracefully skated down the Serpentine and came to an elegant stop in front of her. She skated as if she had been born with blades on her feet! Weakly, Katherine answered, "I fear I'll pull you to the ground."

"Oh, nonsense. I'm sturdier than you make me out to be."

Before Katherine could protest further, she found herself propped on Grandma Bath's shoulder. As they started to move away from the bank, Katherine flung out her free arm and leaned more heavily than she intended on the elderly woman.

"It's in your posture, not the position of your arms. You can't skate as though you are walking down Bond Street. You have to position yourself over your skates. Keep your weight just behind the balls of your feet." As Katherine adjusted herself, tentatively retracting her arm, Grandma Bath pushed off with her skate again, propelling them further. "There, that isn't so bad, now is it?"

If it hadn't been for the old lady, Katherine would have fallen on her face by now. She managed a tentative smile.

"Now, if you'd care to go faster, push with your skate on a slant, not with your toe pointed forward."

"I don't think I'd care to go faster at all." Katherine's voice emerged thin and reedy.

Grandma Bath laughed. "If you don't push, you'll stop."

"That would be acceptable to me."

"How would you get back to the bank? I'm afraid Ernest isn't available to help you."

And the only other option was Wayland. Grimacing, Katherine pushed with her skate. She nearly toppled onto the ice, but she clung to Grandma Bath's stout form instead.

"Careful, now. You're quite a bit heavier than you look."

Precisely as Katherine had attempted to warn her. She eased her weight off, her knees shaking, and tried to use the old woman solely for balance.

"If you don't mind, I think I'd like to rejoin Miss Burwick. She might be more suited to holding me up." Even if she would undoubtedly tease Katherine about it later.

"Ah, I just passed her skating after some young

buck and calling for him to stop. You'd think one conquest ought to be enough for her."

Katherine stood straighter. The miniscule change in position sent her off balance again, and she fell backward onto the ice. She hit with a crack that jolted through her. Had she splintered the ice? Her ears rang as she shifted her bruised body to look. No, it was whole. Perhaps it was her bones that had cracked.

Grinning, Grandma Bath skated a circle around her and stopped in front of her. "You must get up and continue skating when you fall. Elsewise, you'll let your fear rule you and keep you from trying again."

"You're thinking of horseback riding." Katherine grimaced as she twisted, wondering how she was going to get her feet under her once more without reintroducing herself to the ice. The cold assaulted her through her dress and pelisse.

"It applies to skating as well," the old woman said cheerfully. "Come on, now. You're a sensible girl. Up you get."

Katherine braced her mittens against the ice, but the blades on her skates slipped out from under her when she tried to stand. As her bottom made contact with the cold ice again, someone slipped their hands beneath her arms and hoisted her to her feet as easily as if she were a kitten.

"I see Conyers," Wayland whispered in her ear.

"What was that?" Grandma Bath asked, overly loud. "You aren't keeping secrets, are you?"

As if she wasn't embarrassed enough to be on the ice or to be at the mercy of Wayland's goodwill, Katherine's cheeks flushed further. The snowflakes that impacted them all but sizzled from the force of her mortification.

"We're looking for a friend, Lord Conyers," Wayland answered. He released Katherine but hovered his hands near her shoulders, braced in case she fell again. Thanks to the trick that Grandma Bath had taught her, she did not.

Though she undoubtedly would if she tried to move.

"Ah, is that what Miss Burwick is off doing, making friends? He's the fellow I saw her chasing."

If Pru had found Conyers, there was no telling what questions she would ask. She didn't have Katherine's experience investigating—not to mention, she didn't seem to agree with the tactful way Katherine was conducting the investigation to avoid arousing suspicion.

"We shouldn't tarry. Where did you see her?"

"Over by that gingerbread stand, but he seemed adept at eluding her."

"Lend me your arm," Wayland instructed. "If you can keep your feet, I'll guide us through the crowd to reach them quickly."

"I'll do better than that," Grandma Bath announced. "With the two of us on either side, she won't fall."

Katherine opened her mouth, but the pair immediately took up positions, latching on to each of her arms. Without hesitation, they struck off against the ice, flying down the perimeter. Women yelped and stumbled aside. Men raised their voices. Katherine had no breath left to answer them. She squeezed her eyes shut, her body tensed as the wind of movement buffeted her. On her left, Grandma Bath cackled with glee.

Suddenly, Katherine was flying free, without anyone to steady her on either side. She opened her eyes just in time to register the couple in front of her breaking ranks and allowing her to glide unharmed between them. Beyond them, a trio—two men and a woman—spoke on the ice by the far bank. The taller man and a brown-haired woman cornered a lean, foppish young man with black hair.

"Now look, you've lowered my fiancée's opinion of me with your incessant attention. There she goes."

"Och, I'd say 'twas yer wandering eye and hands that did it."

That voice belonged to Lord Annandale, and if he didn't move, she was going to career into his backside. If he was there, the others must be Pru and Lord Conyers. She'd found them. Now she was about to bowl them over.

"Katherine, turn your feet! Stop!"

If she could have done that, she wouldn't have needed Wayland's help to begin with. His shout alerted the trio. The man and the woman slid apart, turning harmlessly away from Katherine's path. Lord Conyers, on the other hand, froze in place, his eyes widening a moment before she crashed into him.

They fell to the ground in a tangle of limbs. Katherine groaned. His elbow or knee had dug into her stomach, winding her.

"Get off," he grunted, breathless.

"Och now, lass. We would have come to ye. Hold still. Stop yer squirming."

Like she was a rag doll, Lord Annandale lifted her up and deposited her on her feet. As the blades slid against the ice once more, Katherine fumbled for Pru's arm.

Lord Annandale grinned. "Not too steady on yer

blades, are ye, lass? I did hear ye was a bit on the clumsy side, so maybe skating isn't for yer."

She made a face but didn't deign to answer him.

Fuming, Lord Conyers got to his feet under his own power. The fact that she'd thrown him half into the bank made the matter easier. He glared at her as he brushed away the snow and bent to retrieve his top hat. "I have never been so mistreated in my life. A great brute like him, I understand, but an earl's daughter?"

Now he chose to recall who she was, despite reintroducing himself on every other occasion? Katherine flushed from her crown to her toes, radiating heat. "It was an accident, Lord Conyers. I'll take care not to repeat it."

"See that you do." He jammed his hat onto his head. "Good day, ladies. Annandale."

As he moved to skate around them, Wayland appeared, blocking his path. The young lord huffed a sigh. "Is this the Spanish Inquisition? I have to attend to my fiancée."

"She can wait," Wayland answered, crossing his arms. "I believe the ladies have a few questions first."

Warily, Lord Conyers eyed Pru. When he spoke, it was to Katherine with a bright smile that didn't reach his eyes. It looked brittle enough for him to have practiced it in the mirror. "Anything for a beautiful woman, but I do ask that you make it quick. I'm on thin ice, so to speak."

"Because of your affair with Lady Rochford?" Katherine asked boldly.

Lord Conyers flinched. His dark hair dripped from beneath his hat and onto his forehead. "Of course not," he answered loudly. "I would never be unfaithful to my fiancée."

Katherine highly doubted that woman was listening—or that she would believe a known rake like him. Resolved not to show the least bit of softening toward a bounder like Lord Conyers, Katherine lifted her chin. "We aren't about to whisper poison in your fiancée's ear. I'm certain she knows your measure already. We only want to know the truth about Lady Rochford's personal life. Did you venture above to see her the night of her death? Is that why she was on the balcony?"

"No," he snapped, his charming demeanor flaking off like old paint. "I was there with my fiancée. You can ask her if you have any doubts. I never went upstairs with anyone. In fact, I never left her side. If you'll excuse me, I should be attending to her now."

Without another word, he shouldered between Wayland and Lord Annandale, who let him pass.

Katherine watched him, frowning. "He's hiding something. Why was he so agitated?"

"I'd say he's feeling some pressure to do right by his fiancée," Wayland mused.

Lord Annandale grunted. "Aye, and well he should."

"He's lying," Grandma Bath said bluntly, stealing everyone's attention. She took hold of Katherine's arm once more, the one not clutched around Pru's for balance.

"Yes, he is. I do believe we saw him by the ice swan, and his fiancée was nowhere in sight," Pru said.

Grandma Bath gave them a sly smile. "Not only that, but he's also lying about Lady Rochford. Maybe he didn't follow her above stairs, but I saw the look in his eye when she crossed the room. He looked at her like a man besotted—much the same way my grandson is looking at young Miss Verne over there."

With her free hand, Grandma Bath pointed to a skating couple. Lord Bath skated slowly with Elizabeth on his arm, taking dainty bites of a round of gingerbread. They appeared so deep in conversation that they didn't seem to notice the world around them.

Grandma Bath elbowed Katherine in the ribs. "You waited too long, my dear. It looks as though Ernest has fallen for another woman. Do try not to get in the way of their union. I want great-grandbabies before I die."

With a smirk, Wayland lifted his eyebrows and met Katherine's gaze, amused. She stifled a groan. "I'm very pleased for them," she assured Grandma Bath.

Unfortunately, the elderly woman didn't seem to believe her.

CHAPTER TWENTY

The erratic pounding at her door nearly gave Katherine an apoplexy. Clad in her dressing gown, with her hair only half combed and Harriet close on her heels, she raced down the stairs to the ground floor, where the butler cracked open the door. Pru spilled inside, her cheeks ruby and her eyes gleaming. She looked past him to the steps, where Katherine sagged against the wall, out of breath.

"I have it!"

She kicked off her pattens and raced toward the steps. The harried butler chased after her, holding out his hands to take her cloak.

"What do you have?" Katherine asked.

"The answer! I know how we can prove that Lord Conyers killed Lady Rochford."

Katherine caught her friend by the hands before she bowled them over. "How?"

"Emma."

Although Pru didn't yell the name, her voice carried, and the immediate excited scrabble of small claws heralded the pug's approach.

"I beg your pardon?" Katherine asked. "Contrary to popular opinion, my dog does not solve crimes."

Harriet chuckled as she turned to pick up the excited dog, who yipped and licked her chin, tail aflutter.

Pru smiled smugly. "No, but she does steal trinkets. Trinkets like errant rings. If we pay a call on Lord Conyers and 'accidentally' set her free, she might return with the ring! If she does, we'll have him. Only the murderer would have that ring, don't you think?"

Katherine frowned. As plans went, Pru's felt about as substantial as netted lace. "If we're able to find the ring, perhaps it will lead to the murderer's confession... but Emma doesn't steal on command. In fact, I try to do everything in my power to keep her from doing so. We have no guarantee this will work at all. We might only annoy Lord Conyers by calling on him."

Pru's excitement diminished. Her beaming smile faded into a frown, and her eyebrows pulled together. "It will work," she insisted, but her voice lacked conviction. "If you won't do it, I'll borrow Emma and see to the matter myself."

"I'll go," Katherine answered hastily, if only to keep Pru from putting herself in unnecessary danger. In order for Emma to filch the ring, she would need to be let into the house, and so would Pru. She couldn't do that alone. "However, we should wait before we bring Emma out. We need to make certain that Lord Conyers is at home, or this will all be a waste of time."

Once again, Pru puffed up, proud. "I've already seen to that. His carriage is at the livery across the street, and I've posted Annandale out front to make certain he doesn't leave. But we must hurry!"

"It can't be eight of the morning!"

"It's half nine, you layabout. Hurry and finish dressing. We haven't a moment to lose." Pru finally gave in and doffed her cloak and gloves, passing them behind her to the impatiently waiting butler as she herded Katherine upstairs. "And Harriet, see that she wears something comely, will you?"

Her voice thick with amusement, Harriet answered, "I will do my best."

As HER CARRIAGE pulled to a stop on the corner of

Charles Street and St. James's Square, Katherine pulled Emma onto her lap and waited for the driver to open the door. As the door opened to reveal a man's figure, the collar of his greatcoat turned up against the chill, Katherine hugged Emma tighter.

"What are you doing here?"

Wayland raised his eyebrows. "Am I barred from walking in London now?"

"And opening the doors of ladies' carriages, yes."

"The driver has gone to fetch the steps. I figured I'd save time and rescue my greatest female admirer."

Katherine's mouth dropped open. Certainly he couldn't mean her! Never had she encouraged his attention. In fact, several times she had gone so far as to tell him to leave her be. Although there had been that time in the alley in Bath...

Impervious to how he'd shocked her, Wayland leaned into the carriage toward her. Katherine remained frozen in her seat as she met his gaze. Did he mean to pluck her from the carriage? From what she'd seen of his physique—he had been one of those in Bath to use the public King's Bath wearing nothing more than his shirtsleeves—he was muscular enough to do it, even if it would be indecent of him.

Wayland slipped his large hands around Emma's middle, engulfing her in one and stealing the leash in the other. As he stepped back, he tipped her into his arms with her belly in the air and gave her a rub. Shameless, Emma wiggled in his arms in delight.

Oh, had he been referring to Emma? What had Katherine been thinking? Sard it, she needed to get ahold of herself.

As the driver laid down the steps, Katherine sat back and composed herself, finally following Pru out of the carriage. Wayland finished showering her dog with attention and bent to lay Emma's paws gently on the snow underfoot. When he straightened, he offered Katherine the leash.

"Your sleuthing companion, my lady."

Was he making fun of her? She said nothing as she gathered the leash.

Pru, her hand slipped into the crook of her fiancé's arm, tipped her head back and smiled, radiant. "I hope we didn't take too long. Is Lord Conyers still inside?"

"He is," Lord Annandale confirmed. "But it does nae sit easy with me to have ye and Katherine running into a trysting house with naught but a dog fer protection."

Didn't he intend to enter with them? Perhaps Pru had already asked him to stand guard on the street.

"Will ye nae consider letting me and Wayland approach Conyers first?"

"And bring a little dog?" Pru asked, cross. "You'd look fair ridiculous. And I don't want to be cut out of the excitement of finding the ring and the murderer."

Lord Annandale laid his free hand over hers on his arm. "Nae, we'll try to learn the truth a different way. Man to man, so to speak."

Pru bristled. "I beg your pardon?"

Katherine couldn't help but smile. There was a reason she loved Pru so dearly, and that was because her friend refused to let any man tell her that he could do something better than she.

Wayland stepped in to assuage Pru. "He means that Lord Conyers might tell things to a man that he would keep secret from a lady. It is no reflection on your ability."

Disgruntled, Pru twisted her mouth but didn't protest further. Neither did she seem convinced, and as she retracted her hand from her fiancé's arm in order to cross her arms, Lord Annandale seemed to notice her disapproval.

To Wayland's explanation, he added, "When ye asked him yesterday, he gave ye a fat lie. Could be if I approach him as a soon-tae-be-married man asking for advice on how tae keep a mistress secret from my new wife..."

Pru's posture stiffened. Katherine bit her lip hard

to squelch the urge to laugh. Lord Annandale, it seemed, was not the most experienced at appeasing women. Even Wayland seemed amused by that answer.

"Your mistress?" Pru asked, biting off the word.

"I do nae have one," Lord Annandale said hastily, raising his hands in surrender. He looked at Wayland, seeming a bit like a cornered sheep as he silently begged for help.

Wayland stepped back to stand next to Katherine, no help at all. Emma seemed happy for the change and stood on her hind legs to plant her feet just below Wayland's knee.

Meanwhile, Annandale added, "And I will nae take one after we're married. Ye ken how I love you, Prudence."

Although Katherine expected that proclamation to appease her, she still seemed irritated. "So you say now..."

"Och, I would nae be marrying ye if I didn't think I'd love you till my dying day." He ran his hand over his beard, looking suitably chastened. "'Tis a ruse to learn if he has intimate knowledge of Lady Rochford, no more."

Pru grunted. Without bothering to relinquish her hand to him again, she turned and strolled the short distance to Lord Conyers's trysting house. "Try if you must, but if you can't find the truth, I'm going to enact *my* plan." With her tone alone, she made it abundantly clear whose plan she thought would work.

Looking a bit helpless, Annandale raised his gaze and said, "Wayland?"

Wayland shrugged. "I only came along for the walk. We might as well." He bent to pat Emma on the head before he strolled away.

She jogged to the end of her leash and whined when it prevented her from joining him. Katherine held firm.

Glowering, Pru joined Katherine in the shadow of the livery building. From here, the stench of horses wafted out into the abysmally cold air. "She seems to adore him."

"She also adores rolling in the mud. I wouldn't trust her tastes."

"I don't know," Pru said with a laugh, her expression lightening. "I've heard that mud does wonders to soften the skin. She might have better taste than you'd think."

Katherine made a face.

The two men knocked on the door. It took only a moment for a man, though not Lord Conyers, to open it and admit them. He seemed reluctant but couldn't very well deny a marquess. As the door shut behind the pair, Pru turned to Katherine. "Shall we get closer? The gap in the shutters there might allow us to peek inside."

"I'm certain your betrothed will be thrilled to see you're spying on him."

Pru made a face. "If he was so concerned, he should have let me inside with him."

Katherine laughed. "Wouldn't that be a sight?" She held out her hand theatrically. "Lord Conyers, please tell me your every secret to hiding your lovers from your fiancée! Who's this? Well, yes, I suppose that would be the woman I am trying to hide my lovers from."

Pru snorted. "It's no better a prospect than taking Captain Wayland with him. What man talks openly about his mistress in front of his friends?"

"It seems you chose well." Katherine winked. "Your marquess doesn't appear to have the least idea of how to carry on a discreet affair."

"I'd rather he not carry on any affair at all. Are you coming to see inside or not?"

Katherine checked the street—deserted. The house next door didn't appear to be occupied at the moment. When last Katherine had spoken with the occupant, Mrs. Ramsey, she'd said that she usually went out to conduct her charity work on Wednesdays, but since it wasn't yet half ten of the morning, the chance of her being out of the house seemed slim. However, Katherine noticed no movement in the shutters, which were closed tight against the winter air.

"Very well, but let's be cautious."

Pru led the way across the deserted street to Lord Conyers's house. His house, along with every other on this street, was neatly groomed in front. With no room for a garden out front, large, elegant planters with necks in the shape of neoclassical pillars flanked the steps to the door and framed the corners of the house. At this time of year, snow covered the dirt and dormant plant life. Pru didn't hesitate but tromped into the calf-deep snow next to the house in order to peek through the shutters.

Although the snow soared over her head, Emma happily leaped in Pru's wake, following her footsteps and hopping from one to another like a rabbit. On the other end of the leash, Katherine balked. Her boots only rose to mid-calf, and her skirts were sure to be mired in snow even with the pattens she wore to elevate herself from the street. Grimacing, she followed, trying to step only in Pru's footsteps.

"Pru! Peeking in the windows isn't ladylike." Katherine wasn't above peeking in windows herself, but the snow slipping down the necks of her boots was chilling.

"You know I care nothing about what society thinks." Pru gave her a sly look over her shoulder. "Perhaps Mrs. Ramsey will think we are just more of Lord Conyers's many female visitors."

Emma lunged for the planter, trying to get closer to Pru. The unexpected movement pulled Katherine a step forward. She gasped as more snow made its way into her boot.

Pru beckoned to her. "Hurry. I think I see them. They're talking."

"With Lord Conyers?" Katherine asked, stepping closer.

"No, with each other."

Katherine fought back a sigh. "They do that all day. It isn't worth remarking upon."

Turning from her perch, Pru glared. "I meant only to illustrate that I could see them. They're in a parlor. It doesn't look well decorated to me. Does anyone live here?"

"No. It's designed to be used only for romantic trysts. I doubt Lord Conyers cares much if his parlor would set the gossips' tongues wagging, so long as there is a bed."

Color stained Pru's cheeks as she hastily turned

toward the window once more. "Still," she mumbled under her breath almost inaudibly. "He ought to purchase some furniture for his parlor."

Katherine opted not to answer. As Emma started digging in the planter, Katherine shooed her away. "Stop that. You'll get your claws muddy, and Harriet will never let me hear the end of it."

Emma resolutely ignored her.

"Oh, there he is!" Pru exclaimed. She leaned closer, tilting her head as if she might hear if only she canted her head in the proper direction. "Lord Conyers, I mean," she added in an absent tone.

"At least he didn't send them away. We know he's inside."

"Yes. Hush! I think I might be able to hear if you'd only be quiet."

Through the windowpane? Katherine thought not.

She hoisted Emma around the middle and hefted her out of the thigh-high planter. "No, you don't. The earth is too hard for you to dig."

As Katherine lifted the pug away, Emma waved her legs like pennants and gave a hearty yip.

"Hush," Pru snapped.

Katherine dropped her pet into the vacant planter once more. With luck, it had frozen solid and Emma wouldn't be able to find any purchase to dig. Tail wagging, the dog buried her face in the snow up to her ears. Katherine shook her head. What peculiarities dogs had.

Pru turned her head again, her face wrinkled in concentration as she attempted to decipher whatever garbled sounds happened to meet her ears. When Emma yipped again, she scowled. "Will you be quiet?"

Emma emerged from the snow with something in her mouth. Katherine heard the loud noise of teeth on something hard as Emma attempted to chew. "What have you got now?" Katherine grumbled. She caught Emma by the back of the head and applied pressure to the hinge of her jaw in order to convince her to spit out her prize. Likely a stone or something else best left uneaten.

It was not a stone. Katherine gaped as a gold ring toppled from the pug's mouth and fell to the edge of the planter.

Frowning, Pru pulled away from the edge of the shutters. "Is that...?"

Katherine plucked up the ring to examine it. The delicate band and oval signet medallion with the scrolls letter "R" stamped on it certainly belonged to a woman. "It's a ring."

As her smile spread, Pru's eyes began to gleam. "Lady Rochford's ring."

They couldn't know that, but given that a planter was no place for a ring at all, Katherine could only hope that she was correct. Who else would have put it there if not Lord Conyers attempting to hide it should someone come to look? Perhaps he wanted to keep it as a remembrance but was afraid someone would investigate and search the house.

Katherine shook her head. "I cannot believe that your idea worked."

Emma danced on her hind legs, trying to wrap her front paws around Katherine's wrist so she could reclaim the ring.

"Certainly not," Katherine informed her. She palmed the ring and pulled away, thinking to tuck it into her reticule if her dog would only release her.

"We must confront Lord Conyers at once."

As Pru's ideas went, that wasn't the worst. "You might be correct. Better catch him off his guard while he's speaking with Lord Annandale. Come, let me take the lead."

Although Pru didn't seem happy to have her idea usurped, Katherine had the ring, and Lord Conyers hadn't much responded to Pru's haranguing yesterday at the Hyde Park Frost Fair. They had one chance to shock the truth out of him. Katherine was determined to make the most of it.

Although polite young ladies would knock at the door or send a footman to announce their arrival, Katherine wanted the element of surprise. With Emma bounding happily around her feet and Pru a mere step behind, Katherine tried the doorknob of the house and found it open. She stepped inside without hesitation.

Lord Conyers looked as though he'd woken in the most ridiculous of dreams. He stared at Lord Annandale, who stood beyond the threshold to the other room, out of sight, with no small measure of incredulity. Over his head, Wayland leaned against the wall and appeared to be struggling not to laugh.

Katherine straightened her shoulders. "Lord Conyers. I've found out your secret, and I demand to know the extent of it at once."

Even with his profile to her, Katherine noticed his wince. "I beg your par—" He turned, his face contorting in outrage. "Shut the door!"

Pru did so with alacrity.

Emma barked merrily, straining against her leash as she tried to join the gentlemen. They stood so near that she nearly touched Lord Conyers's boots. With a wary look, he stepped back, into the corridor and away from Emma's enthusiastic greeting.

"Have you come in to attack me?"

Wayland snorted. He lowered his face, but his grin was unmistakable.

"She's harmless, Lord Conyers. Why, are you afraid of dogs?"

"No," Conyers answered, a touch too quickly. He took another wary step back. "But I am wary of ones who look as though they'd like to sharpen their teeth on me."

Emma sat on her rump and cocked her head, confused. As was Katherine. A more friendly and gentle dog, she didn't know. Barring her predilection for theft, of course. Nevertheless, she used his fear against him without qualms.

"If you answer my questions plainly, she won't do you any harm." Katherine left out that Emma was unlikely to do him harm even if he chose not to answer.

He held up his hands in surrender. "Very well. I *was* having an affair with Lady Rochford, but I couldn't very well admit to that in front of my fiancée. Her father is a sneeze away from dissolving the arrangement as it is."

"Fer good reason," Lord Annandale said blackly.

Lord Conyers gaped like a fish. "You just ... you asked..." His gaze flitted to Pru, and understanding dawned on his face.

It seemed Lord Annandale had been convincing in his desire to keep a mistress from his future wife.

Katherine raised her hand, opening it to reveal the ring sitting in her palm. "Did you take this from Lady Rochford before you killed her?"

"*Killed* her—no! I've never seen that ring before in my life."

Pru scoffed. "An unlikely tale. It was found in your planter just outside."

"It isn't mine—*or* Celia's, that I know of. She never wore her rings..." Emma danced as she spotted the spoils of her digging, yipping with excitement. Lord Conyers paled. "I *swear* I didn't kill her. In fact, she ended our arrangement weeks before the ice ball!"

Emma cocked her head and whined.

"That sounds as though it gives you motive," Katherine answered, keeping her expression carefully neutral. She didn't want Lord Conyers to call his valet to eject them from the house. Even if Wayland and Annandale would likely protest vociferously.

"She found herself in the family way," he snapped, looking into each of their faces in turn. In between, his gaze fell to the dog, innocent though she was.

"And you didn't want the complications of your bastard?" Pru's voice dripped with disdain.

"Not so." Lord Conyers's mouth turned down in a

surly pout. "It wasn't mine. The child was conceived while I was on a tour of the country, visiting with my colleagues."

In other words, performing a yearly circuit of house parties and carousing with his male friends.

"She ended our association because she didn't want her husband to suspect the child belonged to another. She didn't love him, you know. She couldn't." He added that last sentence almost to himself, his head bowed. He looked the picture of misery. Softly, he admitted, "We all have to marry for our own gain, but it's rare that we find a true companion in anyone. Celia was my companion and I hers."

He almost sounded as though he was in love, as preposterous as it sounded.

Raising his head, he met her gaze resolutely. "I didn't kill her. I'm as shocked and devastated as anyone, though I'm the only person not permitted to show it."

Katherine turned the ring over in her hand, thinking. "And this?"

"I've never seen it before. That's the truth."

For now, Katherine could not think of any further questions. "Thank you for your time, Lord Conyers. Good day."

As she turned on her heel, Pru looked after her, mouth agape. "But Katherine—"

Katherine sensed that the young lord wasn't about to give them any other answer. She braced herself for the cold and opened the door. "Come, Emma. Outside."

Head held high, the pug happily followed her out the door. Her companions followed, Pru first among them.

Fortunately, Lord Annandale restrained her the moment they shut the door behind them. "I thought ye meant to let me have a go at him."

"You took too long, and I found the ring."

Katherine led the way back to her waiting carriage, the men on her heels and Pru on Annandale's arm.

"Och, ye could have waited a moment longer. I almost had it out of him."

Wayland laughed but didn't contradict him.

"Katherine, please don't say you believe in his innocence. We found the ring in his house!"

Turning, Katherine found herself nearly bowled over by Pru in her enthusiasm. She had released her fiancé's arm, much to his apparent chagrin. Katherine stepped to the side just in time to avoid being trampled. Emma yelped as she did the same.

Pru winced. "Sorry, Emma. I didn't see you there."

Katherine took advantage of the moment to put the ring in her bag. "First of all, we have no one to confirm that this was Lady Rochford's ring. If we can find someone to confirm it, we might be able to coerce a confession from him then."

"But you didn't find it inside his house, did you?" Wayland asked.

He knew the truth, of course, but Katherine nodded. "You're right. It was outside. Anyone could have had access."

"Not without being seen by Mrs. Ramsey. We should ask her," Pru insisted.

Katherine again glanced toward the neighbor's house. "She doesn't appear to be at home."

"Och now, did she nae mention seeing the Rochford carriage after the lady was dead? I'd say we ought to speak with Lord Rochford again."

"You're right. What if Conyers is telling the truth? Someone put that ring there, and if the carriage was seen here, it might have been Lord Rochford," Pru said.

Wayland raised his eyebrows, unabashedly curious. "I wonder if he knows his late wife was having an affair."

CHAPTER TWENTY-ONE

A s the carriage trundled through the wintery scene of Mayfair, Katherine found herself pressed from shoulder to hip against Wayland. Although she had originally tried to sit next to Pru, Emma had been far too frantic to show herself Wayland's biggest admirer. As a result, Katherine had had to sit backward, facing Pru and her fiancé. They both seemed pleased with the arrangement and held hands throughout the journey and subsequent conversation.

"I don't know that we can go in," Katherine admitted ruefully.

Pru's expression darkened, but before she could get a word in edgewise, Katherine carried on.

"We've already used my stepmother's condolences as an excuse once. It won't be accepted again."

"Aye, but I have nae offered condolences of my own. If Lord Rockford is three sheets tae the wind like ye say, then he will nae notice two bonny lasses so long as ye keep mum."

Wayland leaned forward, adjusting his hold on the pug. Emma squirmed, demanding his attention, to no avail. "After your performance with Conyers, why don't you let me steer the conversation?"

Lord Annandale bristled. "Och, now. Just because ye have more experience with interrogations does nae mean I cannae do as good a job."

Actually, Katherine was fairly certain that it did.

With a gleam in his eye easily discernible in the thin light peeking between the shutters of the carriage, the marquess added, "Besides, this investigating goes to the head like whiskey. I understand now why my lass is so enamored with it." He winked at Pru, who blushed, seeming pleased.

Did that mean he might consider staying in London more often? She hoped so, because that meant Pru would be around more often after they were married.

"Humor me," Wayland said, his voice dry. "You

can observe and put those observations into practice next time."

"Och, verra well." Lord Annandale didn't sound happy at the prospect, but he was still good-natured.

The carriage pulled to a stop just in time. With a debonair flourish, Wayland returned Emma to Katherine's lap. The pug whined softly at the change.

"Hush, you," Katherine whispered under her breath. "You've never taken issue with me before. So what if Wayland has stronger fingers?"

Despite her efforts to keep her voice low, as Lord Annandale and Pru stepped out of the carriage, Wayland made a stifled sound of amusement. Katherine turned her face away as it heated, rubbing Emma's collar.

Fortunately, Wayland didn't comment on her conversation with her dog. When he leaned forward, she felt the heat of his body acutely against her shoulder. He whispered, "Annandale has more enthusiasm than sense or experience. What would you say if I took him under my wing and mentored him the way you're doing with Miss Burwick?"

Katherine shrugged. "I'd say he's your friend. What you do with him is entirely your business."

"It would be to your benefit if he continues to join his fiancée in your investigations."

To that, Katherine didn't say a word and not only because Wayland was correct. By inviting Lord Annandale, she would essentially be inviting Wayland to help her solve crimes as well. Yet as long as she wanted Pru's help, it seemed she would have to accept them both.

Maybe it wouldn't be so terrible with four of them working on cases; they would solve them much faster. But what was Wayland's angle? Was he trying to horn in so he could take credit? Katherine had been under the impression that Wayland only took on cases for money or the credit in solving them, but the last few cases he'd received no payment. One of the cases Katherine had solved, but she could not take credit lest she be shunned. Wayland *could* have taken credit, but he had given it to Lyle instead. Could Papa be wrong about Wayland?

"Think about it," Wayland suggested as he climbed out of the carriage.

Katherine slid to the edge of the seat and accepted Lord Annandale's hand as she disembarked from the carriage. The driver stashed the stairs in the boot and drove off to the livery to await them.

Shortly after they knocked, the door was opened by a man who said, "May I help you?" in a tone of voice that indicated, to Katherine, that he would rather turn them away.

"Lord Annandale and Captain Wayland, here to give our condolences to Lord Rochford. We're hoping to catch him before he makes his way to the club."

"One moment. I'll see if Lord Rochford is in."

He'd best be! Katherine stamped her feet, shivering as they were left out in the cold. Pru leaned closer to whisper, "I wonder if the housekeeper was ejected from the house after all. She was far too rude, if you ask me."

"Lord Rochford might simply have hired a new butler."

Pru made a noise that was midway between dubiousness and agreement.

The door opened again, and they were quickly ushered inside, where a trim man no older than thirty divested them of their winter clothes. "I'm afraid the dog will have to remain here as well. Lord Rochford isn't fond of them."

Emma whined at the notion of being left behind, but Katherine had little choice. She offered the leash to the butler and told him, "My driver is waiting at the livery. He'll be more familiar to her. You might want to watch that she doesn't find something small to chew on while she's indoors."

Looking alarmed, the butler directed them down the corridor to the same parlor where Katherine and Pru had met with Lord Rochford the last time. The room didn't smell nearly as ripe now. She took that as a good omen.

Lord Rochford sat in the same armchair, a touch less disheveled with a glass of port in his hand rather than whiskey. He looked up from a letter as they entered and stuffed it into his waistcoat pocket.

"Good day, Lord Rochford," Wayland said, his manner friendly as he shook the man's hand.

Lord Rochford scrambled to his feet to greet him and Lord Annandale. As they exchanged pleasantries, Katherine curtsied for good measure and led Pru to the settee with her head down. They both sat, acting demure. Pru fretted with the drape of her skirts, not one to enjoy being left out of the conversation. Neither did Katherine, but the more like sheep they acted, the more Lord Rochford would be wont to ignore them. Perhaps, given his grief-stricken and intoxicated state when they last arrived, he wouldn't even recall their presence.

"Can I offer you something to drink? I'll ring for the housekeeper."

So she did still have a job. Considering that the baron hadn't yet imbibed himself into the grave next to his wife, she must have managed somehow to get through to him. That, or it had all been an elaborate act.

"Thank you, no. I'm afraid I'm not here only for pleasantries," Wayland admitted on cue. He and Lord Annandale took the remaining seats, with Wayland closest to him.

Lord Rochford drained his glass and set it on the neat table next to him. The only betrayal that this might not have been his first glass was the stain of a red rim on the wood. "What might this be about, then, Captain?"

After rummaging in his pocket, Wayland drew out the ring. On the drive over, Katherine had reluctantly relinquished it to him for safekeeping. After all, she wasn't to draw attention to herself. Still, it rankled.

"Do you recognize this ring?"

His hand trembling a bit, Lord Rochford reached over to take it. Sweat beaded along his brow, and the grooves of age deepened in his face. "This is Celia's," he whispered, almost too low for Katherine to hear. When he lifted his head, a sheen of tears gave his eyes a glazed cast. "It's a family ring I gave her for our third anniversary. Where did you get this?"

"Outside Number 2 Charles Street. Do you think you might have lost it there?"

"Me? No. I said this was Celia's ring, my wife's. I thought she was wearing it the night..." He folded his hand over it and clutched it to his chest. "It was not returned with her belongings, but she didn't lose it. She would have said as much."

"Does she have any business at Number 2 Charles? A friend, perhaps."

"I..." Lord Rochford's jowls trembled as he looked down at his clenched hand. "I'm not familiar with where all of her friends were located. Celia was very gifted at making friends."

"I ask," Wayland added slowly, "because that particular house happens to belong to Lord Conyers. He claims never to have seen the ring, but I have to wonder if he might be lying."

Lord Rochford shut his eyes as if in pain. "I can see you're working your way toward a question, Captain. Ask it and show yourself out."

Katherine and Pru exchanged a glance at such a blunt response. Didn't Lord Rochford care at all that he was entertaining a marquess? Perhaps hoping to intimidate with his looming height, Wayland unfolded himself and stood over Lord Rochford. "Did you suspect your wife was keeping company with Lord Conyers?"

The old baron deflated, and his hand moved

toward his glass as if he wished for a drink. It was empty, of course. After a shuddering exhalation, he admitted, "I didn't suspect. I knew. Celia confessed the affair to me."

"When?" Lord Annandale barked as if he couldn't hold in the inquiry.

Lord Rochford gave him a single withering glare then craned his neck back. "Oh, do sit down. I'll get a crick in my neck."

Wayland sat.

On the other hand, Lord Rochford rose. "I need a drink. Are you certain you won't have anything?"

The men declined. Katherine and Pru shook their heads. Unfortunately, Lord Rochford was a good deal soberer now than he had been before. He narrowed his eyes at them. "You were here before." He made a disgusted sound and stormed over to the mantel and the decanter of brandy that awaited him there. Apparently his housekeeper hadn't managed to remove it entirely. "You think the same as they all do. That I killed my wife."

Katherine sat straighter, suddenly alert. "But my lord, wasn't your wife's death deemed an accident?"

"So I've been told, but it doesn't stop the gossips from chittering in corners over how I orchestrated the entire thing. Drove my wife off the balcony or worse, to suicide. And the intrusive questions from Bow Street seem to indicate they suspect it was no accident." His shoulders bowed, he shuddered over his glass before he turned back to them. When he did, his eyes glistened. He returned to his chair and stared into his glass but didn't drink. "I didn't push her. I was in the ballroom when it... when she..." His voice cracked. In the deafening hush that followed, he cleared his throat. He gulped from the tumbler in his hand before he added, "As to the other... If I drove her to suicide, I don't know if I could live with myself."

Softly, she confessed, "Your wife did not jump. If she had, she would have landed in a different place."

He lifted his head, eyes narrowed. "How do you know this?" His voice was thick with emotion.

"Science." Since that wasn't answer enough, she added, "I have a friend adept at this sort of thing. He's certain on the matter."

Lord Rochford peered at Wayland and Lord Annandale, as if wondering if one of them were responsible for this conclusion. Katherine didn't elaborate.

Tentatively, Pru asked, "You were going to tell us of your wife's affair?"

His face crumpled with anguish, and he gulped from the glass once more. Only a shimmer of amber liquid remained in the bottom. His grief appeared genuine, but that didn't mean he wasn't the killer. He could truly be grieving the fact that he had killed her in a fit of anger. But what about the ring?

Katherine's gaze drifted to the table where Lord Rochford had placed it. Was it possible the murder was premeditated? That he took the ring as an insurance policy to frame Conyers later on should the police start to ask questions? Framing Conyers would be sweet revenge. Conyers had said Celia never wore her rings with him, but Lord Rochford might not know that. Katherine cautioned herself against jumping to conclusions. Conyers was also a known liar and cheat.

Lord Rochford paused as if trying to find the right words. No one interrupted him.

After he swallowed the last mouthful of brandy and set the tumbler on the table, he continued. He looked past them all, as if he spoke to himself more than to his audience. "I put so much pressure on her to conceive. After she couldn't, month after month, she began to wonder if I might be too old to sire an heir. Not that we had complications, but..." He rubbed his forehead. "She was afraid that I would be angry with her for being unable to conceive, think less of her. I... For a time, I made her life unbearable. I have no excuse."

Yes, but what of the affair? Katherine bit her lip to keep from speaking the impatient thought. She clasped her hands tight on her lap. Next to her, Pru picked at her skirts again as she waited.

"She told me that she'd hoped to conceive with someone else, someone younger. As long as she was pregnant, no one had to know the true father. So she took up with Conyers." Lord Rochford spat the name, disgusted. Though given the empty way he stared into the air, Katherine couldn't be certain if he was more disgusted with Lord Conyers or with himself. "But months passed, and she still couldn't conceive. When I found her at the chamber pot in tears, she confessed to me that she was certain the problem lay not in me but in herself. She thought she was barren."

Barren. The word echoed through the silence as everyone collected their thoughts. Pru stopped her fidgeting, but from the way she clasped her hand in her skirts, she was not as unaffected as she would like to seem. Finding oneself barren was the fear of every new wife.

After all, the marriage mart for lords and ladies existed for the sole purpose of finding a woman of good standing and breeding to bear a man an heir, although Katherine would like to think that Lord Annandale was more sensible than to lay the responsibility for conceiving or not at Pru's feet.

Well, she doubted that Lady Rochford had thought she would become the object of her husband's enmity when she married. She had been young, after all, perhaps even younger than Pru—there had been no reason for her to think that she might not be able to conceive.

"I gave up all hopes of an heir then and there. I hadn't realized how miserable I had made her, nor how I'd driven her into another man's arms simply to avoid disappointing me in other ways. I told Celia that we would no longer try so hard to conceive. If it happened, I would of course be happy, but I wouldn't expect it of her."

Katherine nodded slowly. "And then she conceived."

Lord Rochford released a shuddering breath. "She did. She told me that without needing to bear an heir, she had cut all association with Conyers. I believe her. We intended to start anew. New baby, new life. We had hope." His shoulders bowed inward, shaking with repressed grief. "She had no reason to wish herself dead, not now. We had the entire world in front of us. It didn't even matter if she carried the baby to term. I'd already started making other arrangements."

"Other arrangements?" Wayland asked, shifting his position. "What do you mean?"

"For the inheritance of my title if I do not produce a male heir," Lord Rochford explained, lifting his head. "I've petitioned the Crown to leave my estate and title to my grandson, should my daughter bear one, with she and her husband to act as regents in the interim. So everything might stay in the family."

"Have you heard back whether or not the Crown will accept? It is highly unusual."

"It is," Lord Rochford agreed, "but it is sometimes done. I imagine it will be some time before the Crown makes their decision. Now that Celia is dead..." He shook his head. "I don't even want to contemplate it. What do I have left?"

Lord Rochford's distress seemed genuine, but Katherine had to wonder if he'd truly forgiven Celia and accepted her reason for the affair so easily.

CHAPTER TWENTY-TWO

———————————

The pall that fell over the group as they departed from Lord Rochford's residence was nothing short of gloomy. So preoccupied was she in reviewing what they'd learned at Lord Rochford's house that Katherine didn't even notice when she took Wayland's hand to climb the carriage stairs, nor when he settled Emma in her lap. She noticed that he was near only when he seated himself beside her and Emma's claws dug through her clothes on her way to beg attention from him. Wayland gave that attention without comment as the carriage lurched into motion.

They passed several streets in silence before Pru broke it. "I don't think he killed his wife. He seems to have forgiven her for the affair and, indeed, blames himself. He has no motive."

Lord Annandale reached over to thread his fingers through hers and lend his support. Pru sounded a bit lost.

"I agree," Wayland answered, his voice a rumble in the near darkness of the carriage.

"Katherine?"

"It *seems* that way, but wouldn't he try to make us think that if he were the killer?" Why was everyone so ready to accept Rochford's story? Katherine knew that killers always lied. "With Celia dead, there is no one to dispute his claim that they were going to try anew. And you heard him say he suspected the police were not satisfied with ruling her death an accident. He would know that he is a suspect. He might have tried to plant the ring to move the suspicion away from him and onto Conyers. That would explain why Mrs. Ramsey spotted their carriage the day after Lady Rochford fell."

"But the housekeeper said he was too deep in his cups to leave the house even to tell his own daughter. When would he have planted it?" Pru asked. "You saw him yourself. He was in no condition."

"Perhaps that was all an act. Remember the house-keeper's highly irregular and insubordinate behavior? She is still employed. Perhaps she behaved that way on instruction from Lord Rochford to make him appear distraught and allow him to deny leaving the ring."

"Good point. I think we need to talk to Conyers again, given what we just learned. He was closest to Lady Rochford. He might know something we can use to prove it was Lord Rochford," Wayland said.

"Or to prove that *he* is the killer," Pru said.

"Yes, we can't rule him out. The ring was in his planter, but anyone could have put it there, including him. We must find something else to tie either Conyers or Rochford to the crime," Katherine said.

"Lady Rochford ended their affair," Pru argued.

"Months ago, if she and her husband had then reconciled."

"Not so," Pru said, shaking her head. "He was in the country during the summer. He might only have returned to London recently. And what of her carriage, spotted there multiple times the week she was killed? She might have been telling him it was over for good. If he had just found that out, he may have still been angry enough to kill her when he ran into her at the ball. Perhaps he made advances and she spurned them."

"I find Conyers's tale curious," Wayland said as he rubbed Emma's belly. The dog looked to be in heaven.

"How so?" Katherine asked. While he was in the carriage, she might as well avail herself of his expertise.

"He claimed that he and the victim had a special bond, something beyond the physical. He didn't call it love, but it seemed similar, as though he thought her the perfect partner. If so, wouldn't it make more sense for him to kill her husband in the hopes that she would then fall into his arms?"

Katherine cocked her head to the side as she considered it. Lord Conyers had seemed particularly aggrieved, but something didn't sit right with her. "You have a point. Or perhaps he was lying to us about it in an attempt to appear like the wronged party. She couldn't have felt as deeply about him, or she wouldn't have reconciled so readily with her husband. Lord Rochford knew everything, and the tale of her seeking out another bed partner in order to get with child isn't unlikely. In fact, it fits with what my stepmother has said of her."

"Why would he be so adamant they were two kindred souls if she did not return his feelings?"

Katherine shrugged, half turning to look at Wayland. "It happens often enough, especially among the young bucks and debutantes. Simply because he pines for Lady Rochford doesn't mean that she returned the sentiment at all. She might have chosen him only for his age and virility."

"Is a matchmaker claiming she doesn't believe in love?" Pru teased.

Wayland stiffened as Emma playfully nibbled on his finger. Maybe she'd bitten him too hard, though she was usually gentle.

Keeping one eye on him in case he took it upon himself to discipline her dog, Katherine answered, "Not at all. I know very well that love can exist and flourish even in a marriage mart such as our own. But not all matches are love matches, and not all affairs are of the heart."

Wayland wiggled his finger back and forth in Emma's mouth, carrying her head along a few inches. She seemed to be enjoying the attention, and he didn't seem terribly alarmed at his predicament, so Katherine let them be.

"Well, I suppose there is truth in that. After all, I never expected to fall in love. I wanted to become a dour old spinster, like Katherine."

"I'm twenty-five," Katherine reminded them as she pulled Emma onto her lap and scratched her behind the ears. The rascal seemed sad to leave Wayland's embrace.

"And you dress as though you're seventy-five," Pru teased.

When neither of the men jumped to her defense, Katherine sighed. "Can we return to the topic at hand? We must be able to find a better tie to Lord Conyers than a ring left on his doorstep. Or another suspect."

Pru slumped in her seat as she thought. "He was at the ice ball. I wonder where he went after his flirtation with the swan. He lied to us earlier about never leaving his fiancée's side."

"I think that was his friend's flirtation, but it might be worth asking around to see. Someone ought to have seen him or at the very least remarked upon his friend, so deep in his cups as to court inanimate objects."

Wayland chuckled. "You could ask the hostess."

"Lady Dalhousie? She does notice everything that goes on. I wouldn't be surprised if she knew the exact location of her entire guest list the whole night. But she has a penchant for exaggeration, so I'm not sure how much we can believe," Katherine said.

"It's worth a try." Pru leaned over to pet Emma. "Lady Carleton is holding a ball tonight. She was one of the Burglar of Bath's victims, if you recall. Lady Dalhousie will never be able to stay away, not wanting Lady Carleton to outstrip her and become the center of attention once more."

Katherine buried her hands in Emma's fur and murmured to herself, "I suppose I'd better dig out my invitation, in that case."

KATHERINE STOOD to one side of the ballroom and watched the swirl of dancers on the floor. There was nothing particularly memorable about Lady Carleton's ball at all. She hired the same musicians as everyone else, served the same food and drink, decorated in the same way, and invited the same guests. Unfortunately, Katherine did not see Lord Conyers among them, though the ball was overly crowded, making it difficult to see exactly who was there.

Pru sighed. "Perhaps we will have better luck if we split up."

Disappointment welled in Katherine's chest as she glanced at her friend. First Pru had included Annandale in the investigation, and now she wanted to look for suspects without Katherine. Oh well, Katherine had no problems investigating on her own… though she did have to admit she had grown quite fond of Pru's assistance. "Very well. You go toward the refreshment table, and I will go toward the garden.

They parted ways, each choosing a different route

around the perimeter of the ballroom. Katherine scanned the ballroom. But Lord Conyers still wasn't among the dancers or those around the refreshment table or even near the cluster of debutantes in the corner.

Preoccupied with her search, Katherine nearly stepped into Mrs. Fairchild as she squeezed between two gaily chatting groups just beyond the high vase. The set had ended, the men and women dispersing to find new partners for the next dance. As Katherine met her rival's gaze, a throb started in her temples. She didn't have the time or energy for a fight at the moment.

"It was all a lie on Lady Dalhousie's part. Lord Bath being the burglar, I mean. I misjudged him," the woman said quickly. As she nibbled her lower lip, she had never looked so young. Katherine recalled that for all her stature and experience in matchmaking, she couldn't be more than ten years older than Katherine.

"He's a good man." Katherine scanned the crowd over her shoulder. Where was Conyers?

"Do you really think he'd make Miss Verne a good match?"

Katherine's gaze pivoted back to Mrs. Fairchild.

"I do," she said softly, her words nearly drowned

by the crowd. "I wouldn't have mentioned it to her if I hadn't. But there is one problem."

"Which is?" Mrs. Fairchild regained her superciliousness as she raised one dark eyebrow.

"He's stubborn."

"Aren't all men?" she said with a laugh. "Are you having trouble bringing him up to snuff?"

"I'm having trouble getting him to admit that he needs or wants a wife. His grandmother, the Dowager Marchioness of Bath, approves of the match even if he has yet to make any commitment." Katherine wanted Mrs. Fairchild's cooperation, but her eyes kept straying to the crowd in search of Lord Conyers.

Mrs. Fairchild frowned. "He doesn't want a wife? But... isn't he your client?"

"Yes. I was never trying to steal your client, only to match her with mine. Though it wasn't he who sought me out but his grandmother who hired me to find him a match. He knows little to nothing of the arrangement."

"Then how can you be so set on Miss Verne marrying him if he wants nothing of marriage?"

"Lord Bath is a good friend of the family. If anyone can convince him to marry, it is me. Trust me, I can bring him up to snuff, and I will. So long as he has managed to acquaint himself with Elizabeth enough to see her many merits."

Mrs. Fairchild nodded tentatively. "She is a young woman of many merits."

Katherine had to wonder if Mrs. Fairchild was older than Elizabeth. When they had previously encountered each other, the rival matchmaker had put on such airs that she seemed five or even ten years older than she did now, infinitely more experienced and determined.

"Do you oppose the match?" Katherine asked boldly, hoping that the woman would not answer in the affirmative.

Mrs. Fairchild glanced into the crowd, no doubt seeking out her client. "Marchioness is a title that would make any woman jealous. He *is* a bit eccentric..."

"But not unkind," Katherine assured her. "He dotes upon his grandmother and tries to do right by his tenants. If you spend any length of time in his company, you'll see—"

The woman tucked a strand of auburn hair behind her ear and gave a slim smile. "What man with a title isn't a little eccentric? I never did listen to any of the drivel Lady Dalhousie had to say, anyway." She drew herself up. "I think Miss Verne would be very happy with him."

Thank goodness. Katherine released a pent-up breath. She held out her hand. "Shall we call a truce, then?"

Mrs. Fairchild clasped it, squeezing her hand only briefly before releasing it. "Only this once."

The two women parted ways, and Katherine focused again on her search until...

"Lady Katherine, what a surprise. I expected to find you with Lord Bath. Isn't that where you're most often to be found of late?" Lady Dalhousie's expression took on a hawkish quality as the gossip raised her brows. Katherine almost cursed out loud. She had an important task at hand, but she couldn't be rude and ignore Lady Dalhousie.

"He's faring quite well on Miss Verne's arm, thank you."

"Is he?" The old woman's smile spread. "How odd. I thought for certain I espied him dancing with someone else."

Tarnation!

Katherine's eyes darted to the dance floor as she prayed that the woman was mistaken. She didn't have the time to hunt down an obstinate marquess and force him to dance with a woman he was destined to become enamored with.

"Do tell, Lady Katherine. Have you given some thought to my suggestion that the Burglar of Bath has now returned?" Lady Dalhousie pointedly jerked her chin toward the dancers.

Katherine didn't give her the satisfaction of looking where she pointed, most likely at Lord Bath.

"The Burglar of Bath was apprehended in September," Katherine answered, desperately wondering how she could get away from Lady Dalhousie.

"Yes, I know. That was dreadful, and now we have the Lady Rochford scandal."

Katherine's eyes snapped back to Lady Dalhousie. "Scandal? I thought it was an accident." Was the gossip being her usual overly dramatic self, or did she know something of interest?

Lady Dalhousie leaned toward Katherine and lowered her voice. "I've heard it was no accident. And while servants these days are frightfully tight-lipped, one does overhear things..." Katherine had no doubt that Lady Dalhousie eavesdropped on her servants, and maybe that habit would come in handy for Katherine. The woman had her full attention now.

"What kinds of things?"

"I heard Lady Rochford was not alone on that balcony."

"Yes, you mentioned before you saw Lord Bath—"

"Not Lord Bath. I overheard one maid telling another that the man was small of stature." Lady Dalhousie made a sour face. "But when I asked for further information, the maids denied seeing any man near the balcony."

Darn! Harriett's contacts hadn't mentioned that. Was Lady Dalhousie making it up to spread gossip? Maybe Katherine should have Harriet visit the Dalhousie servants again. She might not have talked to the right ones.

"Did they mention any specifics as to who it could have been?" Lord Conyers wasn't exactly small of stature. Lord Rochford was shorter than Conyers.

"I'm afraid not—"

"Katherine!"

Turning, Katherine spotted Pru elbowing her way through the crowd. What had her so frantic?

"Katherine, come here." Pru tugged Katherine's elbow, but Katherine held firm. Whatever Pru wanted surely couldn't be as interesting as what she'd just heard from Lady Dalhousie.

"I was just talking to Lady Dalhousie. She had some interesting information on the accident at the ice ball. Lady Dalhousie, would you tell Pru what you just told me?" Katherine turned back to Lady Dalhousie only to find she'd drifted off and was talking to an older couple. Drat! Katherine wanted to know more about the man who had been seen with Lady Rochford!

"That can wait." Pru almost pulled Katherine's arm from its socket as she towed her across the room to a quiet corner far from the orchestra. "I believe I just spotted Mrs. Dillinger."

Katherine frowned. "Lord Rochford's daughter? What is she doing here? The family should be in deep mourning, not out at balls." Though the sour woman had never seemed fond of her stepmother, Katherine wouldn't put it past her to claim that since they weren't related by blood, she need not observe any period of mourning.

"I don't know why she's here. I thought it just as odd. That's why I left to find you immediately." Pru stood on her tiptoes to scan the crowd. "What did Lady Dalhousie tell you that was so interesting?"

Apparently when it came to performing detective work, Pru still wanted to do it together. Katherine couldn't agree more. Her heart warmed. "One of her servants saw someone with Lady Rochford that night, but she couldn't get a description. We may need to get Harriet to question them again." Katherine followed

Pru's gaze. "Where did you see Mrs. Dillinger? Let's speak with her and discover why she's come out of mourning for tonight."

"Was she ever in mourning?" Pru mumbled under her breath.

Mrs. Dillinger hadn't worn black when they'd met with her on Bow Street. In fact, her cloak had been scarlet. That didn't bespeak a woman in mourning.

"I saw her in that side corridor. I thought she would have divested herself of her cloak and be out in the main room by now."

Katherine eagerly followed Pru's footsteps as she led her across the room. At the mouth to the corridor, Pru stopped with a scowl. "Tarnation! Where did she go?"

"Keep your voice down if you're apt to use foul language," Katherine teased.

Pru's mouth twisted with distaste. She peered down the first of two nearby corridors. This one, wider, was the corridor that led to the front door. It was empty.

On a hunch, Katherine crossed several feet toward the second, narrower corridor through which the servants entered and exited. A large vase had been placed near the door, almost as if to obscure it and make the servants even more invisible.

Down the corridor were two figures. A woman, dressed in a dark-blue cloak, was standing close to a man. They looked to be in a heated discussion. The woman's face was turned away, but as the man turned to walk away, Katherine caught his profile.

"Lord Conyers!"

She hadn't meant the name to slip out, but the instant it did, he started. The woman fled down the corridor, and Katherine caught a glimpse of her pinched face. Mrs. Dillinger! Were they lovers?

Katherine would have given chase, but talking to Lord Conyers was more important.

As Pru stepped up alongside her, Katherine straightened her shoulders and strode down the corridor toward Lord Conyers. "I'd like to speak with you a moment, if you aren't set on running off after your lover."

"Her?" He glanced over his shoulder, his expression souring. "She isn't my lover. That's disgusting."

"Indeed. I think there are some things you haven't told us. For one, I'd like to know where you went after I saw you near the ice swan at Lady Dalhousie's ball."

His expression darkened. "This again? Why do you insist on bothering me about this? I had nothing to do with Celia's death. It was an accident."

"Are you still claiming that? How do you explain the ring?"

Lord Conyers frowned and glanced back in the direction Mrs. Dillinger had fled. "Why is everyone going on about the ring? Even Celia's stepdaughter. I have no idea how it got in my planter or what you people did with it after you took it. I tried to tell her that, but she wouldn't believe me. She even said that if I confess right away and claim it was an accident, she'd see to it that I don't hang. I suppose her family has the money to make good on that, but I won't confess because I am innocent." Lord Conyers sighed. "What does it matter anyway? None of it will bring my Celia back."

"So that *was* Mrs. Dillinger?" Pru said.

"Yes, and she was rather nasty too. Kept going on about that ring as if I stole it." Lord Conyers straightened his jacket and leveled Katherine with a look. "Now if you ladies will excuse me, my fiancée is waiting."

Lord Conyers brushed past Katherine and strode down the hall.

"Katherine, he's getting away!" Pru whispered.

"I know. But we have no reason to detain him."

"Why not? He had the ring, and he is the jilted lover."

"No. Something isn't right. And we aren't sure he ever had the ring. Why would he put it in the planter? It doesn't make any sense." Katherine watched Lord Conyers disappear down the hall then turned to Pru. "And if he was the killer, why would he be so perplexed about Lord Rochford's daughter asking about the ring?"

Pru nibbled her bottom lip. "You have a point. But why was Mrs. Dillinger here, and why run away when she saw us? Why would she seek him out and try to persuade him to confess? It didn't seem she cared enough for her stepmother to want to seek justice."

"No, but she cares enough for her father," Katherine said. "When we talked to her at Bow Street, she was very defensive about him. Maybe she suspects her father is the real killer and was trying to coerce Conyers to confess to ensure her father is the one that does not hang."

CHAPTER TWENTY-THREE

Katherine thought she might have made a mistake in sending Harriet to Lady Dalhousie's house again so soon. Gertie, the cook, had been suspicious enough upon the first visit and practically threw Harriet out when she found her there asking questions again.

If only Lady Dalhousie had not left the ball early the night before. After Katherine and Pru had talked to Conyers, she had searched high and low for the gossip, only to discover that she had gone home early. Luckily there was another ball this evening, so Katherine would be able to question her further then.

The other person Katherine wanted to talk to was Mrs. Dillinger. She assumed the woman was trying to cover for her father. Whether that was because she had knowledge that he'd killed Lady Rochford or not, Katherine didn't know, but talking with her would certainly reveal more. Both Lord Rochford and Lord Conyers had motive, and each denied killing her, but Katherine was sure it had to be one of them.

As Katherine was trying to figure out how she could finagle a way to talk to Mrs. Dillinger, she spotted Lord Bath's coach pulling up to Dorchester House. Tarnation! She hadn't the time to cajole him to take a wife, not when she was so close to solving a murder! But now that Mrs. Fairchild had agreed to work with her rather than against her, perhaps Katherine needn't worry about that any longer.

She put her notes aside, placing them in the book-case before venturing downstairs.

"Lady Bath awaits you in the parlor," the butler informed her as soon as her foot hit the foyer floor.

"Is Lord Bath here as well?"

"No. Only the lady, and she has refused a tea service. I believe she means to depart shortly."

Katherine winced. That couldn't bode well, could it? If she was here with happy news, she would have wanted to eat.

The moment she entered the room, Grandma Bath

got to her feet with difficulty. "Lady Katherine, it is a calamity!"

Katherine paused on the threshold, taken aback. "A calamity?"

"Miss Verne," the old woman exclaimed, her face contorted with agony. "Ernest is going to lose her! You must do something."

What had happened between last night and this morning? Had Mrs. Fairchild only pretended to work with her so she might instead work against her? Although Katherine would like to think that the union of Miss Verne and Lord Bath would be a cause for all parties to celebrate, she couldn't help but wonder if Mrs. Fairchild was that vindictive.

And that good an actress.

"Why would Lord Bath be in danger of losing Miss Verne? If he is worried, perhaps he ought to make his admiration plain."

"You know he won't do that!" Grandma Bath paced around the chair she had occupied, using it for balance. Katherine had never before seen her so unsteady on her feet. She must be near panic to exhibit such a weakness.

"I cannot force him to propose," Katherine answered calmly, though she stepped no nearer. Better to make a hasty escape if need be. "I'd hoped that once

I found him a suitable bride, he would develop some affection for her."

"He has," the old woman exclaimed, sounding as though she gnashed her teeth. "I'm certain of it. He gives no woman so much attention save for you, Katherine."

Oh dear. The very last thing Katherine wanted was for Grandma Bath to fixate upon *her* once more as a marital candidate. Desperate, she offered, "Perhaps I can speak with your grandson and bring him to see reason."

"You'd do better to ask that beau of yours to stop sniffing at Miss Verne's heels."

"Beau?"

"Captain Wayland," Grandma Bath said, her lip curling with distaste. "I thought he was partial to you, but he seemed particularly attentive to Miss Verne. You're not having very good luck with your suitors this month, are you? Can you not tempt him to offer for you so at the very least he can leave my grandson some sliver of happiness?"

Slowly, Katherine answered, "I don't believe Captain Wayland is courting Miss Verne. You must be mistaken."

"I am not! I saw them together at the ball last night. She was laughing—laughing!"

Katherine bit her tongue. She took an even breath before she said, "I'll speak with him. I promise. Miss Verne will be in no danger of being proposed to by Captain Wayland." *And he isn't my beau.* Given that Grandma Bath was certain Katherine had a preference for Lord Bath, she didn't put much stock in the old woman's observations. Still, if Wayland *was* interfering with the match...

Grandma Bath looked dejected. "I hope that is the case! I cannot reason with Ernest myself, or he'll defy me on principle. Stubborn man doesn't know what's good for him." The last statement was muttered lower, as if Grandma Bath meant it only to reach her ears. Unfortunately, she was a bit hard of hearing. With a beseeching look, she added, "If Ernest believes he's lost Miss Verne, he won't even try. I know him, and he's been crossed in love before."

He has? Why hadn't either of them told her of such a thing? Katherine fought the urge to step backward as she promised, "Never fear, Grandma Bath. You've employed me to see that your grandson is married, and I'm not about to let anyone, least of all Wayland, get in the way of that goal."

KATHERINE DID NOT HAVE time for this. She was so close to solving the case she could taste it. She wanted to question Mrs. Ramsey to see if the person in the Rochford carriage could have been Lord Rochford instead of Lady Rochford. She wanted to talk to Lady Dalhousie to find out if she'd discovered more from her servants about the person seen with Lady Rochford. Finally, she wanted to seek out Mrs. Dillinger again, as clearly she must have suspicions of her father, though Katherine had no idea how she would get them out of her. But she couldn't let Lord Bath lose Elizabeth. She knew they were perfect for each other.

Katherine had little time to chase down Wayland and convince him to stay away from Elizabeth, so she applied to Mrs. Fairchild to do the matchmaking work instead. Since she didn't think she would be welcomed if she showed up on her rival's doorstep unannounced, she sent a letter to her. To her surprise, she received a response within the hour, as she was getting ready to go out.

Mrs. Fairchild also offered some advice. She seemed genuine about their truce, at the very least. Katherine had to admit it brought her some relief.

Here's what we'll do: speak with Captain Wayland and see if he won't pay even more attention to Miss Verne—knowing, of course, that she isn't destined for him! Don't forget to mention that. It will rankle with Lord Bath to see another man courting the woman he's come to admire. Perhaps that will even be enough to spur him to propose.

Katherine had to admit that the idea held merit. In Bath, when Lord Annandale had thought that Katherine was considering Wayland's pursuit of Pru, he had found a private moment to make it known in no uncertain terms that he meant to be the victor of her hand. Fortunately, that particular rumor hadn't held the least kernel of truth.

If Katherine were able to convince Wayland to lend her such a favor again... She returned her attention to the page, satisfied, though Mrs. Fairchild had written more.

In case that isn't enough, let's use this recent death to our advantage, shall we? If we each, separately, whisper into his ear to remind him of how short life can be and how one must hold onto the people and things one cherishes, that ought to be enough to drive him to his knees with a ring in his hand. For good measure, have his grandmother lend a good word too.

Mrs. Fairchild then went on to describe how Katherine might subtly bring up such a topic. Katherine skimmed the last two pages, shaking her head. It seemed her rival couldn't waste an opportunity to be condescending.

At least she was able to ensure that Mrs. Fairchild would be helping even if it meant Katherine had to ask a favor of Wayland.

CHAPTER TWENTY-FOUR

Katherine did not have time to visit Mrs. Ramsey or Mrs. Dillinger that afternoon. Getting ready for the ball that evening took precedence, since she'd be able to accomplish two tasks in one evening—convince Wayland to feign interest in Elizabeth and corner Lady Dalhousie to see if she'd gleaned more gossip.

She found Wayland on the edge of the ballroom, swathed in the shadows of a neoclassical pillar that was more decorative than practical. The balcony above was wide enough only to hold the myriad pots the hostess had set up to provide some greenery to the room. Squaring her shoulders, Katherine took a deep breath as the orchestra set their bows to their instruments in a long, ravenous note meant to beckon dance partners to the floor.

"Are you free for this set?" Katherine asked.

Wayland's jaw dropped, and he looked caught somewhere between amusement and disbelief. "Are you asking me to dance?"

"I am." It would be less conspicuous if they conducted this distasteful conversation on the dance floor.

"I believe that's *my* job."

"Then ask, if you're so offended."

He crossed his arms, stalwart. "You hate dancing."

"I don't hate it." Katherine grimaced. "I simply... have better things to do. But at the moment, it is the best place for a somewhat private conversation, unless you'd prefer to find a quiet spot along the corridor?"

He raised his eyebrows. "Apparently you've forgotten what happened the last time you dragged me into a secluded corridor. No."

Katherine let out an exasperated breath. "Those rumors abated soon enough once I let everyone know it was business we were after."

"And I nearly lost my closest friend because he thought I was courting his future wife!"

Stepping closer, she lowered her voice. "Actually, I

believe it was that falsehood that spurred Lord Annandale to propose, and I need you to do it again."

"You want me to flirt with Miss Burwick?"

"What? No. Don't be absurd."

Wayland pierced her with a look that told her he thought *her* the absurd one. Perhaps she wasn't being clear.

"I'm trying to match Miss Verne with Lord Bath, but he's been dragging his heels. All I need you to do is to be as attentive to Miss Verne tonight as you were last night, and I'll have them matched by the end of the week. If he thinks someone else is interested in Miss Verne, he might propose sooner so he doesn't lose her."

Wayland stared at her, far too quiet for comfort.

"What is it?" she asked. She turned, looking behind her, but no one seemed to be paying them any mind.

He still seemed unusually solemn. "Are you certain you want me to flirt with Miss Verne and make a good show of courting her?"

"Yes, of course. I told you, Lord Bath—" The look on his face stilled her tongue. "You aren't interested in her for yourself, are you?" She hadn't thought of that.

He didn't answer.

Katherine cleared her throat. In a falsely light tone, she added, "I suppose it doesn't matter one way or another. At least Miss Verne will be well settled as she deserves. Either you or Lord Bath propose to her."

"I thought he was your client, not her." Wayland's voice was stiff.

"She isn't, but she's become a friend. I want the best for her."

"And the best is for me to get down on bended knee?"

"No." Katherine choked on the word. As Wayland's expression grew smug, she added, "The best is for Lord Bath to offer first. He *is* my client, as you've said."

"Is that the only reason?"

Katherine dropped her gaze from his intense hazel eyes to his knotted cravat. She couldn't answer that question. For some reason, the thought of Wayland getting down on bended knee for anyone rankled. And it had nothing to do with what had happened in Bath, she told herself resolutely. She swallowed against the lump in her throat.

"Just do it, and we'll see who comes out the triumphant man."

Wayland made no answer, but his jaw tightened. He nodded tersely in what she hoped was an agreement, and they parted ways. As Katherine stalked across the ballroom in search of Lady Dalhousie, her stomach knotted.

Wayland wouldn't offer for Elizabeth first. Her plan was sound. The moment he started flirting with her in earnest, he would drive her into Lord Bath's arms.

But... Wayland was an attractive man, even if he didn't have a title. And he was closer to Elizabeth's age too. But tarnation, she and Lord Bath were so well matched! The thought of losing the match because Wayland had formed some kind of tendre for Elizabeth after keeping her company for one night burned the back of her throat.

Perhaps she ought to do as Mrs. Fairchild suggested and whisper to Lord Bath of the frailty of life and how he ought to hold onto the love he'd found.

Oh, with her luck, Lord Bath would propose to *her* if she tried! She was stretched too thin, her head throbbing with vigor, as she stopped along the wall and dropped into a vacant seat. Most of the debutantes in attendance were dancing.

"Lady Katherine, are you feeling quite the thing?"

Her luck was turning! It was Lady Dalhousie, and to Katherine's surprise, she sounded genuinely concerned. When she sat next to Katherine, Katherine smiled wanly at her. "Lady Dalhousie, you're just the person I wanted to see. I was hoping we could continue our conversation from last night about the person seen with Lady Rochford."

Lady Dalhousie laughed, a throaty chuckle. "You're as hungry for gossip as I am! But I'm afraid I have to disappoint you. I don't have any further information other than a shadowy figure."

"Could it have been Lord Rochford? Perhaps he wanted to speak to his wife alone."

Lady Dalhousie pressed her lips together. "Are you implying he might have killed his own wife?"

Katherine tried to look aghast. That was exactly what she was implying, but she didn't want Lady Dalhousie to know that. "Of course not! I simply meant that perhaps they stepped aside at some point for a moment alone, and that is what your servant saw. Before she fell over. Perhaps they had words and she went out for a breath of fresh air. I believe the common thinking is that it was an accident."

Lady Dalhousie pressed her lips together. "Perhaps. I don't recall where Lord Rochford was at the time she fell." She leaned toward Katherine. "Of course, I wasn't in the ballroom at the time, either. I had to help Lord Conyers with his friend who had had too much champagne. Poor chap is visiting from Italy, I believe. And here I thought they could hold their liquor."

Katherine turned to gape at the old biddy. "You were with *Lord Conyers* when Lady Rochford fell?"

"Yes, that's what I said. Helping his friend. The rascal was in no fit state to walk, so Lord Conyers, Mr. Erikson, and I piled him into his carriage. Lord Conyers wasn't in much better shape, but at least he was walking upright."

Although Katherine hadn't answered, the gossip added, "Lord Conyers and I had just returned inside when a shout rang out, and there she was, in the garden."

Lord Conyers was not the murderer. Katherine's ears rang. Lord Conyers hadn't been lying. Someone must have planted the ring in his planter. Mrs. Ramsey had seen the Rockford coach there the day after Lady Rochford died. That left only one suspect.

She had to tell Pru about this break in the case! She extracted herself from Lady Dalhousie and went in search of her friend.

As she made her way around a large pillar, she spotted Lord Bath's flapping cuffs as he led Elizabeth into the shadow cast by two of the pillars. With the ball in full swing, no one appeared to notice that he'd taken her aside. Katherine, also shaded beneath that overhang, paused in her step, not daring to breathe lest she interrupt an important moment.

Lord Bath pressed Elizabeth's hand to his heart and sank down onto one knee.

He was proposing already! Katherine stifled a gasp and hastily stepped back, hiding herself behind the pillar to give them a private moment.

Mrs. Fairchild found her there. "See? Child's play. It only took Captain Wayland asking to fill her dance card later this evening and a whisper in his ear about the seriousness of the captain's suit."

So Wayland had done as she asked.

"You're right. This match couldn't have been made without you."

Mrs. Fairchild smiled and inclined her head at the compliment. "Nor without you."

At Katherine's startled look, she continued. "And I do say your matches end in love. Like Miss Burwick and Annandale." She inclined her head toward the dance floor, where Pru and Annandale were whirling around, joyous smiles on their faces, apparently oblivious to everyone else.

Katherine's thoughts turned to the case. She was bursting to tell Pru that Lord Conyers had been occupied at the time of Lady Rochford's death. They needed to make a new plan. Perhaps Harriett could talk to one of Lord Rochford's staff and see if he really was indisposed the next day or if he could have gone to Conyers's townhouse and planted the ring. If only the dance would end so she could discuss this with Pru and Annandale.

Miss Fairchild's words interrupted her thoughts. "...though Miss Burwick is a bit eccentric. The two seem to fit. I daresay they will make a handsome wedding couple. I hear she has engaged the most expensive seamstress money can buy."

"Mrs. Burwick will hear of nothing but the best for her daughter," Katherine said with one eye on the dance floor. When would Mrs. Fairchild stop blathering on so she could catch Pru's attention?

Mrs. Fairchild nodded. "It's true, that seamstress is in high demand. There is a waiting list for her concoctions. I'm surprised Miss Burwick could get in."

"Perhaps she took advantage of a cancellation," Katherine answered absently. However, the moment the words left her lips, she recalled her visit to the shop the day after Lady Rochford's murder, when the lady and her stepdaughter had missed the appointment in the morning.

Zeus! She did not have just one suspect left. She had two... and if her suspicions were correct, one of them might be unhinged enough to do something drastic. They *had* to talk to Mrs. Dillinger right away.

Glancing back at the crowd, she saw Pru swept up in Lord Annandale's embrace, oblivious to the world.

Zounds! They were so wrapped up in each other that she didn't have the heart to interrupt, not that Pru would notice even if she jumped up and down to catch her attention. Who else could she enlist? Lyle was at Bow Street. Wayland, perhaps? He'd done as she asked before, so maybe they could work together just this once.

She bade Mrs. Fairchild adieu and made a quick circuit of the ballroom. Wayland was nowhere to be found. Very well, she would follow the lead herself. After all, she needed to learn how to handle her investigations on her own, and there was no time like the present.

Still, as she paused on the threshold of the street, she left instructions for the butler to tell Pru where she had gone should she ask. For now, she was on her own.

CHAPTER TWENTY-FIVE

L ight seeped from the drawing room of Mrs. Dillinger's house, alerting Katherine to the fact that someone was at home. Perhaps, as Mr. Dillinger had said, his wife was in mourning, if only to keep up appearances. With as small a presumed stipend as had been given to her husband—evidenced by the townhouse that shared its walls with both its neighbors in a long, squashed row—the Dillingers couldn't afford a carriage of their own, nor possibly a male servant. Katherine hadn't seen a livery nearby as she'd made her way, so she didn't know where they would stable the horses if they had any. At Katherine's guess, Mrs. Dillinger used her father's carriage. In fact, her suspicions hinged upon it. Therefore, she didn't bother checking to see if the carriage was in.

Instead, leaving her own carriage to wait outside, Katherine climbed the steps and used the worn brass knocker. It shuddered a sound through the house.

Mrs. Dillinger answered, her eyes narrowing when she recognized her visitor. "Lady Katherine? What brings you here at this time of night?"

"Just a few questions." Katherine mustered all her bravery and pushed in through the open door. She intended to get answers.

"If this is about my husband, he's not home."

"It's not about your husband. It's about your stepmother."

Something flashed in Mrs. Dillinger's eyes. Guilt? Fear? Anger? Katherine's resolve wavered. "Wait in the sitting room. I'll get some tea."

Katherine shut the door softly. Apparently Mrs. Dillinger did not follow formalities. To her right, Katherine saw the small sitting room. It was sparsely furnished with a worn sofa and two chairs. A small fire burned in the hearth. A hound dog lay nearby. He opened one bored eye to assess Katherine then, apparently finding her of no interest, went back to sleep.

Should she leave her cloak on? She glanced around and spied a coat rack down the narrow hallway to the left. She'd just have to hang it up herself.

There were two cloaks already on the rack. The

scarlet cloak matched the one Mrs. Dillinger had worn to Bow Street. Next to it was another, dark in color. Katherine's heart stilled.

She pulled it off the hook to peer at the color. It was dark blue.

Everything clicked into place.

The lack of remorse Mrs. Dillinger had shown, the lack of mourning attire at Bow Street.

Her father's carriage outside Charles Street *after* Lady Rochford's death.

Lord Rochford's housekeeper griping over how she'd had to rouse Lord Rochford *in the afternoon* so he could break the terrible news to his own daughter.

The missed seamstress appointment that morning.

Mr. Dillinger being arrested for attending the pugilist match the night of the ice ball.

Mrs. Dillinger couldn't possibly have known of her stepmother's demise the morning after she was dead, not if she hadn't attended the ice ball as she claimed, because her father didn't tell her until the afternoon. So why had she missed the appointment with the seamstress? There was only one reason: she knew her stepmother would not be showing up. And how would she know that? If she already knew the woman was dead.

Mrs. Dillinger had claimed she was at home the

night of the ice ball, but with her husband in jail, there would be no one to verify that.

Her heartbeat ratcheted higher, roaring in her ears as she spotted a distinct white stain on the blue cloak, a stain precisely like the one Katherine had seen on her stepmother's cloak in the closet. Katherine had found a telltale clue. Lady Rochford had a vial of the waters from Bath, too, and it must have broken during the struggle! This proved that Mrs. Dillinger had been at the ice ball.

The maid and cook had not been unreliable—there had been *two* cloaked women running out of the house that night. That explained the conflicting descriptions of the path the woman had taken. Mrs. Dillinger didn't have her own carriage, so she would have needed to hail one on the main street, whereas Susanna had parked hers on the side street so as not to be noticed.

"What are you doing?"

Katherine whirled around. "I was, err... hanging up my coat."

Mrs. Dillinger stood blocking most of the light in the narrow hallway. Even with such little light, Katherine could see that her face was pinched in anger. She held something behind her back, and Katherine didn't think it was tea.

"Tell me, do you know Lord Bath or his grandmother?" There was a slight chance that Mrs. Dillinger had spilled some of her own waters of Bath on the cloak. Katherine had to make sure before she accused her.

"No. You ask too many questions. An earl's daughter should stay at home or attend balls at night, not wander about, knocking on people's doors."

Katherine swallowed the bitter taste in her mouth. "Then tell me. How do you explain this?" Bending, she grabbed the bottom of the cloak and displayed the stain. "I know what caused this stain: a liquid only Lady Rochford could have had on her person." If Lord Bath hadn't been acquainted with Lady Rochford prior to Susanna's introduction, he certainly wouldn't have known her stepdaughter. "And she retrieved it the night she was killed. You were there, at the ice ball."

Mrs. Dillinger whipped her hand out from behind her back. A pistol!

In as small a house as this, Katherine stood no farther than three feet away from Mrs. Dillinger, a distance the murderous woman would not squander. She would not miss, nor would Katherine be able to run away, as Mrs. Dillinger stood between her and the hallway that led to the door.

Perhaps she should not have come alone after all.

The only hope she had was that Pru would decide to leave the ball early, receive the message from the butler, and knock on the door to this townhouse before Katherine was shot. She needed to buy herself time.

"You killed your stepmother, and you're going to kill me too."

"You don't need to be a detective to figure that out." Mrs. Dillinger's voice dripped with disdain.

"Will you at least tell me why? Your father is nearly in his grave over the loss of his wife. He loved her dearly. Why didn't you?"

"That grasping, conniving harpy?"

If nothing else, Mrs. Dillinger had a good vocabulary.

"She only married my father for the prestige of being baroness. She never loved him. She cavorted openly with Lord Conyers and God only knows who else!"

"So you decided to plant her ring in Lord Conyers's planter?"

"How do you know about that?" Mrs. Dillinger asked, sounding startled. "That ring should have been mine by rights, you know. But Papa gave it to *her*. I got it in the end, ripped it right off her finger as she went over the railing. I found it again at Papa's house. I assumed Lord Conyers found it in the planter and was trying to use it against my father somehow."

"How could Lord Conyers use the ring against your father?"

She shrugged. "To frame him, of course."

"Why would he need to do that? Everyone thought your stepmother's death was an accident."

Mrs. Dillinger frowned, her grip on the gun tightening visibly. "They did at first. But I heard talk at the police station when I was there with my husband. And then there were too many questions, too many whispers that Papa had killed Celia. I didn't want him accused, so I thought it better to send the rumors in Lord Conyers's direction with a few well-placed slips of the tongue and some rumors about her ring."

So that was why Mrs. Dillinger had been so open about the affair at the police station. She was trying to start the rumor so people would look to Lord Conyers if it came out that Lady Rochford did not fall by accident.

"Is that why you confronted him at Lady Carleton's ball?" Katherine asked.

"I wanted to warn him off of trying to frame Papa. To buy more time for me to produce evidence against him. He was rude and uncooperative. Insisted Father must have done it. I might have been able to work something out with more time, but you came along and ruined my chances."

"I must say, dropping the ring into the planter wasn't the best move. Anyone could have put it there, so it's hardly damning evidence against Conyers."

"I was actually trying to get it inside his house. Some nosey neighbor caught me trying to pry open a window. I intended to drop it in, but since that old biddy was watching, I had to resort to the planter." Mrs. Dillinger raised her arm, the gun now pointing at Katherine's head.

Katherine swallowed hard around the lump in her throat. "Then satisfy my curiosity. What did Lady Rochford do to anger you so? It couldn't be only her affair."

"Why not?" the murderer sneered. "She brought this on herself. And when she gleefully told me that she was with child—"

Mrs. Dillinger cut off, the poison in her voice so potent it thickened the air. Katherine didn't dare move, not even to breathe. Her heartbeat grew louder in her ears, but Mrs. Dillinger didn't pull the trigger.

If she had stood a touch closer, Katherine might have tried to thrust the arm with the pistol aside. However, lunging at Mrs. Dillinger held its own perils.

She had to keep the woman talking and wait for help to arrive.

If, indeed, help was on its way. Katherine had no idea whether or not Pru had received her message.

Mrs. Dillinger composed herself and spat, "Lord Conyers's child has no business inheriting Papa's estate. Even if, by some miracle, the child *was* my half brother, he didn't deserve to be baron. *I* am Papa's daughter. *I* deserve his estate when he cocks up his toes. Besides, she was older than I. If anyone should have been able to conceive..." She dropped one hand to her belly.

Money and jealousy. Powerful motives.

"Does that satisfy your curiosity?" Mrs. Dillinger hefted the gun, smug. "It turns out it is a lucky thing I purchased this pistol. I thought I'd need it when I killed Celia, but happenstance provided a better opportunity, one that looked like an accident."

"Aren't you afraid your neighbors will hear the gunshot? You'll be swept off to Bow Street before you can sneeze."

Mrs. Dillinger sounded grim as she answered, "As long as you're dead, the only tale to spread will be the one I tell. And you broke into my home. I have a bad habit of leaving the door unlocked, you know. Perhaps you even attacked me." She cocked her head, considering the notion. "I'll have to find a knife from the kitchen, of course, but it wouldn't take me long to fit it into your cold, dead hand. Enough chatter. I have to kill you before my husband comes home and—"

A shadow moved behind Mrs. Dillinger, followed by a tremendous ringing thunk, like the peal of a padded bell. She gasped as she fell, hitting the floor and remaining there, still. The person responsible stepped into the light leaking through the street-side window. Katherine sagged against the wall as she recognized Pru.

Her friend huffed. "I can't keep hitting murderers over the head for you." She adjusted her hold on the cast-iron pan, which she must have snatched from the kitchen. How had she done that so silently? "She *is* the murderer, isn't she?"

Katherine nodded. "She confessed to me in full."

"Hound's teeth, Katherine," Pru swore, prodding the unconscious woman with her toe. "Whatever possessed you to come here alone?"

"I need to learn to do my investigations on my own. When you marry Annandale, you'll go back to Scotland." Katherine stared down at Mrs. Dillinger. "Thanks for rescuing me. I do hope she is not dead."

"I'm not leaving." Pru's voice was resolute, determined. She held the pan to the side as she squatted next to the body and pressed a finger to her neck. "Not dead, and you're welcome."

"Lord Annandale doesn't live here. He barely comes to London. He'll want you in Scotland."

"I don't give a flying farthing what he thinks on the subject," Pru said. "I'm not leaving, not any time soon. We have our investigations. Moreover..." She paused. When she continued, her voice was small. "You're my friend, Katherine. I've already lost one friend lately. I don't intend for it to be two."

Katherine didn't trust herself to speak, but she squeezed Pru's hand tightly. She hadn't realized how much she'd enjoyed having Pru's assistance. And she did have a point: it was much safer to bring someone along when interrogating suspects.

"Do you think I hit her too hard?" Pru asked after a moment.

Katherine shrugged. She hadn't the faintest idea. Until they lit the candle, they wouldn't know the extent of Mrs. Dillinger's injury. "She's still alive. How did you get in, anyway?"

"I peeked in the window and thought I saw Mrs. Dillinger with a gun. The front door was unlocked. I knew you had come here, so I simply let myself in just in case. Good thing, too, or you might have ended up with a bullet in you." Pru reached forward to grasp the pistol and remove it from where it had fallen inches from Mrs. Dillinger's hand.

Katherine gasped, "No! Don't!"

Too late. As Pru lifted the weapon, it misfired, blowing a ragged hole through the wall. In the sitting room, the hound barked.

Katherine shouted over the ringing in her ears. "Pistols misfire if not handled carefully." Or sometimes, even if handled with care. That was why no one loaded a pistol before they intended to use it.

Pru dropped the weapon with alacrity. Not that it could do any harm now, with the lead ball already discharged.

Bang! The door burst open, startling them both. Pru hefted the pan, prepared to defend herself.

Wayland swept the hall with his gaze and sighed. "Again?" he asked wearily.

Katherine pressed her lips together to hold back a wave of hysterical laughter, but it was no use.

CHAPTER TWENTY-SIX

D espite the merriment of those skating along the Serpentine, Katherine remained firmly on the bank, shivering in the cold air and staring toward the smoke wafting from the roasting chestnuts on the far bank.

"Aren't you going to skate?"

Katherine jumped at the sound of Lyle's voice, even though she'd seen him approach earlier. They'd stood in companionable silence, letting the joy of the Hyde Park Frost Fair wash over them. Since Katherine had confronted Mrs. Dillinger, it was one of the few times she had been able to remain still and relax.

Despite the darkness in that woman's heart, happiness still existed in this world. It showed in her nephews as they flopped on the ice, held up only by their parents' hands. It showed in the careful way her father made sure Susanna stood on the sidelines away from any ice that could cause a fall, adjusting her hood when it fell back from her forehead. Her family was whole and happy, and even Susanna was able to smile today despite the loss of a friend.

"I don't skate," Katherine answered. "Would you?"

Lyle grunted. "I signed up to watch the crowd and keep the peace."

"Has the date for the trial been set?"

After Pru had hit her over the head, Mrs. Dillinger had been knocked unconscious, hurt but not killed. She had been remanded into a special room at Bow Street, one that her father had paid for privately.

"Lord Rochford tried again to negotiate the magistrate down to paying a fine rather than incarceration or death for the murder." Lyle's voice was tense. When Katherine glanced at him sideways, she found his jaw clenched with anger and his hands balled at his sides. "He might have succeeded, too, if not for Lord Conyers."

"Conyers stepped forward?" Katherine asked, surprised.

"Lady Rochford had no family to speak of, no one to avenge her if her husband did not. Lord Conyers is set to testify against Mrs. Dillinger, having proof that she tried to frame him for the crime."

"What proof?"

"His neighbor saw Mrs. Dillinger plant the ring. She is able to identify her and has also agreed to testify. Not to mention his own testimony that she tried to bribe him to confess to the murder."

An eye for an eye, a life for a life. Even if it would keep someone with as much hatred and desperation as Mrs. Dillinger from hurting anyone else, it still didn't sit easy with Katherine. Her heart ached for Lord Rochford. He'd lost a wife and two children.

"That's something, I suppose."

Lyle clapped her on the shoulder, jolting her nearly out of her skin. "The verdict is for the magistrate to decide. You did your part in catching her, Katherine."

"Thank you." She didn't feel appeased.

Pru skated into view and stopped neatly in front of them on the ice. Her eyes gleamed. "Katherine, you'll never believe what I've just heard!"

Katherine searched the throng for Lord Annandale. "Where is your fiancé?"

"Over there with Lord Bath and Elizabeth. He got cajoled into escorting Grandma Bath around as she tries to hand out samples of the Bath water."

"They must be frozen over," Katherine muttered under her breath with a shake of her head. Louder, she added, "You left him there alone?"

"He's with three other people," she said, amusement in her voice. When Katherine continued to look, she added, "If it's Wayland you're hoping to find, he isn't here today. A shame, since you're wearing something halfway decent."

Katherine ignored the taunt, too weary to complain. Wayland had come to their rescue at Mrs. Dillinger's, but they'd already had the killer well in hand. But how had he even known she was there? Had he followed her, despite pretending to be aloof? Pru had later told her that Wayland hadn't left with her. And he'd even complimented Katherine on her skills of deduction. She'd almost felt that they could be friends.

Likely Wayland did not feel the same, though she did find it curious that the day her father attended the Hyde Park Frost Fair, Wayland did not. Papa still refused to be any more specific as to why he disliked Wayland, but there must be a reason for them to avoid each other like that. Why, then, did Wayland seem to always seek her out?

Forcing a smile, she asked Pru, "What did you learn?"

Her face brightening, the other woman gushed, "I've been speaking with Lady Brackley about her next book."

At that, Katherine chuckled. "Lucy is always nattering on about her next book. Or about her past ones, if you ask."

"Her book was brilliant! I couldn't stop reading, so I'm more than willing to hear what she has next. But that isn't why I came to speak with you."

"No?" Katherine raised her eyebrow.

Pru reached out to clasp Katherine's hands even though it put her on precarious footing. "She wants to do some research about an old, unsolved murder here in London. Her next book will have something to do with the mystery, but she needs to solve it first, and she wants our help, Katherine!"

Returning to the present more fully than she had since Mrs. Dillinger's arrest, Katherine found her friend's enthusiasm infectious. "Finding us jobs, are you, Pru?"

Grinning, Pru winked. "Of course. I wouldn't want to be bored over the winter."

Lyle said, "You know I'm willing to lend a hand, too, in any way I can."

"What do you say, Katherine?"

Katherine couldn't say no to two sets of eager eyes.

She smiled. "Very well. Let's talk with Lady Brackley and see if this investigation isn't too old to be solved."

It would be more convenient if Katherine could invite her back to a townhouse of her own, where they wouldn't be overheard by prying ears. Now that this business of the murder investigation was over, she wondered if Lord Conyers might be persuaded to sell her his townhouse on Charles Street. In her line of work, having a neighbor as observant as Mrs. Ramsey could come in handy.

****

More books in the Lady Katherine Regency Mystery series:

An Invitation to Murder (Book 1)
The Baffling Burglaries of Bath (Book 2)

Sign up to join my email list to get all my latest release at the lowest possible price, plus as a benefit for signing up today, I will send you a copy of a Leighann Dobbs book that hasn't been published anywhere...yet!

http://www.leighanndobbs.com/newsletter

IF YOU ARE ON FACEBOOK, please join my VIP readers group and get exclusive content plus updates on all my books. It's a fun group where you can feel at home, ask questions and talk about your favorite reads:

https://www.facebook.com/groups/ldobbsreaders/

IF YOU WANT to receive a text message on your cell phone when I have a new release, text COZYMYS-TERY to 88202 (sorry, this only works for US cell phones!)

IF YOU LIKED THIS BOOK, you might also like my Hazel Martin Mystery series set in 1920s England:

Murder at Lowry House (book 1)
Murder by Misunderstanding (book 2)

Cozy Mysteries

Blackmoore Sisters
Cozy Mystery Series

* * *

Dead Wrong

Dead & Buried

Dead Tide

Buried Secrets

Deadly Intentions

A Grave Mistake

Spell Found

Fatal Fortune

Lexy Baker Cozy Mystery Series

* * *

Lexy Baker Cozy Mystery Series Boxed Set Vol 1 (Books 1-4)

Or buy the books separately:

Killer Cupcakes

Dying For Danish

Murder, Money and Marzipan

3 Bodies and a Biscotti

Brownies, Bodies & Bad Guys

Bake, Battle & Roll

Wedded Blintz

Scones, Skulls & Scams

Ice Cream Murder

Mummified Meringues

Brutal Brulee (Novella)

No Scone Unturned

Cream Puff Killer

Kate Diamond Mystery Adventures

***

Hidden Agemda (Book 1)

Ancient Hiss Story (Book 2)

Heist Society (Book 3)

Silver Hollow

Paranormal Cozy Mystery Series

***

A Spell of Trouble (Book 1)

Spell Disaster (Book 2)

Nothing to Croak About (Book 3)

Cry Wolf (Book 4)

Mooseamuck Island Cozy Mystery Series

* * *

A Zen For Murder

A Crabby Killer

A Treacherous Treasure

Mystic Notch

Cat Cozy Mystery Series

* * *

Ghostly Paws

A Spirited Tail

A Mew To A Kill

Paws and Effect

Probable Paws

Hazel Martin Historical Mystery Series

***

Murder at Lowry House (book 1)

Murder by Misunderstanding (book 2)

Lady Katherine Regency Mysteries

***

An Invitation to Murder (Book 1)

The Baffling Burglaries of Bath (Book 2)

Sam Mason Mysteries

(As L. A. Dobbs)

***

Telling Lies (Book 1)

Keeping Secrets (Book 2)

Exposing Truths (Book 3)

Betraying Trust (Book 4)

Romantic Comedy

***

Corporate Chaos Series

In Over Her Head (book 1)

Can't Stand the Heat (book 2)

What Goes Around Comes Around (book 3)

Careful What You Wish For (4)

Contemporary Romance

***

Reluctant Romance

Sweet Romance (Written As Annie Dobbs)

Firefly Inn Series

***

Another Chance (Book 1)

Another Wish (Book 2)

Hometown Hearts Series

***

No Getting Over You (Book 1)

A Change of Heart (Book 2)

***

Sweetrock Sweet and Spicy Cowboy Romance

Some Like It Hot

Too Close For Comfort

Regency Romance

* * *

Scandals and Spies Series:

Kissing The Enemy

Deceiving the Duke

Tempting the Rival

Charming the Spy

Pursuing the Traitor

Captivating the Captain

The Unexpected Series:

An Unexpected Proposal

An Unexpected Passion

Dobbs Fancytales:

Dobbs Fancytales Boxed Set Collection

Western Historical Romance

***

Goldwater Creek Mail Order Brides:

Faith

American Mail Order Brides Series:

Chevonne: Bride of Oklahoma

Magical Romance with a Touch of Mystery

***

Something Magical

Curiously Enchanted

ROMANTIC SUSPENSE

WRITING AS LEE ANNE JONES:

***

The Rockford Security Series:

Deadly Betrayal (Book 1)

Fatal Games (Book 2)

Treacherous Seduction (Book 3)

USA Today bestselling author, Leighann Dobbs, discovered her passion for writing after a twenty year career as a software engineer. She lives in New Hampshire with her husband Bruce, their trusty Chihuahua mix Mojo and beautiful rescue cat, Kitty. When she's not reading, gardening, making jewelry or selling antiques, she likes to write cozy mystery and historical romance books.

Her book "Dead Wrong" won the "Best Mystery Romance" award at the 2014 Indie Romance Convention.

Her book "Ghostly Paws" was the 2015 Chanticleer Mystery & Mayhem First Place category winner in the Animal Mystery category.

Find out about her latest books by signing up at:

http://www.leighanndobbs.com/newsletter

Connect with Leighann on Facebook

http://facebook.com/leighanndobbsbooks

Join her VIP readers group on Facebook:

https://www.facebook.com/groups/ldobbsreaders/

About Harmony Williams

If Harmony Williams had a time machine, she would live in the Regency era. The only thing she loves more than writing strong, funny women in polite society is immersing herself in the nuances of the past. When not writing or researching, she likes to binge-watch mystery shows and spend time with her one-hundred-pound lapdog in their rural Canadian home. For glimpses into the secrets and settings of future *Regency Matchmaker Mystery* books, sign up for her newsletter at http://www.harmonywilliams.com/newsletter.

Printed in Poland
by Amazon Fulfillment
Poland Sp. z o.o., Wrocław